Another Fox Bites the Dust

MARY FRAME

Book Cover by Qamber Designs

https://www.qamberdesignsmedia.com/

Content edits by Catherine Felnagle

Copy edits by Betsy Judkins at Maine Woods Editing

To my brother-in-law, Gabe Abel, a truly exceptional soul who loved great music and was taken too soon. You are missed every day.

Preface

Dear reader,

This book contains references to suicide and past deaths of a parent and young sibling by illness and accident. There are also characters struggling with past and current alcohol abuse/addiction.

Thematically, this entire series is a little more heart-wrenching than my other books, but there still is humor—because life is messy, but it's also funny.

I provide this warning so you can make an informed decision about whether or not to proceed. If you would rather read something more lighthearted, please check out the Imperfect series or The Dorky series if you haven't already!

Take care of yourself,

<3

Mary

Description

She's sworn off dating musicians. She wasn't expecting him to rock her world.

Mindy Fox is sick of drama. After being dumped by her rock-star boyfriend and losing her record label job in one scandalous swoop, the betrayed A&R talent seeker decides to strike out on her own. And when she hears an audio clip from a struggling songwriter, the former music mogul believes she's found her first artist in the handsome crooner.

Luke Fletcher hides his paralyzing anxiety behind a charming exterior. But guilt is a constant companion when he conceals his crippling stage fright from the gorgeous entrepreneur who's giving him a shot at making it big. And if that wasn't distraction enough, the easy-going guitar player quickly realizes he's got chart-topping chemistry with the dark-eyed beauty.

Pulled out of her workaholic world by an onslaught of intense family strife, Mindy struggles to stop a feud with her sister from poisoning the fledgling project. And while Luke comes clean about his hang-ups, he fears his attraction to the off-limits woman has become a forbidden refrain.

Can they recompose their future into a delightful duet?

Chapter One

Mindy

"Jeanette's pregnant." Blake's voice is a deep rumble, a timbre that's launched five platinum albums and over a dozen top-10 singles.

At first, the words don't register. Once they do, they sink into my skin, reverberating through my bones.

But the logic still doesn't quickly click.

"But you haven't been together in—"

My mouth snaps shut.

Of course they've been together.

I'm an idiot.

He winces, his eyes darting away from mine.

The sun is rising over Turtle Pond, spread out in front of us. The stillness of the water and the quiet tranquility of the park are a stark contrast to the storm taking place inside my mind.

The park bench is cold underneath me. Even though it's midsummer, the morning air is cool and damp. I take a slow breath, trying to calm my pounding heart.

My hands clench into fists in my lap, tightening so hard my nails dig sharp points into my palms.

"I wanted to tell you before it leaks to the press. I wanted you to hear it from me, because I care about you, Mindy. I am torn up about all of this." His soft hand covers mine where it's clenched in my lap.

His fingers are icy.

I wrench away. "Wow. Thanks." Sarcasm drips from the words.

"I would never do anything to hurt you."

"It's a little late for that, don't you think?"

He doesn't reply.

A sharp pain lances through my chest, but it's over in a second, the slender thread becoming encased in a much larger, thicker pipe of steely anger. I wrap my arms around my middle like the action might contain the fury burning a scorching path through my veins.

"How far along is she?" I angle my head to stare at his profile.

His head dips, his throat bobbing as he swallows.

Blake is not conventionally attractive.

His nose is slightly too large for his face, his dark hair flirts with his chin, his eyes are a touch too small, and his mouth a little too wide. None of it should fit together, and yet he commands attention. He's tall, over six feet, and as broad as a tank. On top of that, he plays the guitar like the instrument is part of his body. When he sings, he can bring a stadium full of people to their knees. He's the reason that his band, Vacation Mustache, is Rebel Records' largest client. My client.

I dismissed his flirting and ignored his flattery for years. Until I didn't. Then I fell. Hard. But I didn't fall alone . . . at least, I didn't think I did.

We've lived in our little bubble of sex and romance for nearly a month. It was like no one else existed. He overwhelmed me with his sheer presence. With his relentless persistence. With the way he would simply watch me like I was everything.

Maybe he looks at everyone that way. Maybe I saw what I wanted to see.

The past two weeks have been hell. I've barely slept. Giant gray bags have taken up residence under my eyes. Airlines would charge me extra to fly with these things. I've lost 5 pounds.

Blake looks fine. Great, even. He ran here, under the pretense of taking a jog, apparently, sporting a fashionable athletic tracksuit and the most expensive Nikes money can buy.

He's bright, alert, and well rested.

I look like I've been run over by ten dump trucks, set on fire, then left in a pile of molding sandwiches.

"Eight weeks," he finally answers.

We were together for three weeks. It's been two weeks since the press dropped the bomb on our fledgling relationship. When did Jeanette conceive? Before or after he told me he was devastated by me?

Devasted. That's the verb he used the last time we

were together. He was devastated by me, by what we had together.

"You don't want children."

He told me he didn't want kids. He also told me he and Jeanette weren't together and that they hadn't been a true couple for years.

One broad shoulder lifts in an approximation of a shrug. "It was a surprise."

Finding a twenty dollar bill on the side of the road is a surprise. Getting a curly fry mixed in with an order of regular fries is a surprise. A baby is a life-changing event.

They were about to separate publicly. Then, when a reasonable amount of time had passed, Blake and I could stop hiding our relationship. We had plans. I couldn't wait to share my joy with everyone, including my friends and my family, announce it to the world, and maybe even go on an actual date with Blake that went beyond my bedroom.

"You were never going to leave her." I don't bother making it a question. It's an unequivocal fact that I couldn't comprehend before now because I was too busy being dazzled by Blake and everything he is.

He was devasted. I was dazzled. Clearly a recipe for disaster.

He drapes an arm behind me on the bench. "I can't leave Jeanette now. Splitting from her when she's pregnant?" He shakes his head. "I can't do that. What would people say? We've both agreed that we have to do what's best for our careers. I know that you of all people can understand that."

I don't understand. It's true that I've been single-minded when it comes to work, which is the main reason I was able to resist him for so long, but this is . . . beyond even my greatest flaws and ambitions. He's talking about having a baby for his career and staying in a loveless marriage for show.

The real ass-kicker is that none of this is a surprise. I've always seen him clearly, and despite his obvious self-absorption, despite the anger churning in my gut, *even now* if he said he would give it all up to be with me, I . . . I don't think I could resist him.

I'm such a fool.

"I already have three songs written about what I've been going through. All of this press stuff," he waves a hand, "even though it's a little hard right now, think about how much interest it will generate in my music."

Blake keeps talking in soothing tones, low and intimate, but the words are lost over the roaring in my ears.

I doubt he'll notice I'm not listening and responding. He can't comprehend a world where people don't hang on his every syllable. I've never had blinders on when it came to Blake's flaws, but I loved him anyway. I'm not sure he could say the same about me. I'm not sure he loves anyone, really, except himself.

On the one hand, I miss him. On the other hand, he's being a total self-absorbed asshat and I hate him, and I hate myself for wanting him still.

"Maybe after the baby is born and things calm down, we can try again?"

The steely anger burns a path through my veins. "Are you kidding me?"

He frowns, a crease forming between his brow. "Is that a no?"

"It's a hell no."

His mouth pops open in surprise.

Before I have a chance to enjoy his astonishment at being rejected, my phone rings, the jarring, musical sound filling the space between us. I pull it from my pocket and stare at the number on the screen.

It's the executive VP of Rebel Records.

"Hey, Sonya." Mouth dry, I stand, taking a few steps away from the bench, putting my back to Blake and his words and this entire conversation.

"Hi, Mindy. Can you come in sometime today so we can chat?"

I've been on administrative leave, waiting to hear from them about the status of my position for weeks. "Absolutely. I can be there in twenty minutes."

This has to be good news. They can't fire me, not without firing Blake, too. They would never do that—he's worth too much.

So am I.

I turn back toward Blake. "I have to go." And then I walk away.

He doesn't stop me.

Twenty minutes and an Uber ride later, I walk through the glass doors of Rebel Records, offering a tight smile to Skip at the security desk. He nods and waves me through.

I make a beeline for Sonya's office, crossing paths with

a few employees along the way. One woman talking into a headset about a mechanical license stops the conversation midsentence and then rushes quickly past me, her voice continuing in hushed tones.

I keep moving.

At Sonya's office door, her receptionist stands to greet me.

"They're all waiting for you in the conference room," Arthur says, not quite meeting my eyes.

My career has been my whole life for the past decade. They have to recognize how valuable all my contributions have been. I can't have my whole life derailed over one poor decision.

I round the corner and stare at the conference room door. They can't get rid of me. They need me. Don't they?

I slip inside, shutting the door.

"Mindy." Sonya's smile is strained. "Thanks for coming in so quickly."

She's not alone. Peter from legal and Amy from HR flank her on the opposite side of the gleaming mahogany table that spans the length of the room.

I swallow. Today is the day for awful conversations, apparently. "I see they've sent in the triumvirate of terror."

Amy coughs a laugh into her palm.

"Please, sit." Sonya gestures to the chair opposite them.

I sit, folding my hands in my lap and keeping my head high. "Give it to me straight."

Sonya nods. "I'm afraid it's not the best news."

My teeth clench. I can't believe this.

"You're letting me go." It's not a question.

"We have to mitigate the damage. What happened, it wasn't good for the label's image of professionalism, not to mention our reputation in general."

What happened.

I have to press my lips together to avoid a snarky retort, definitely the opposite of professionalism. What happened was my fault, and I can't take it back. I slept with Blake. I agreed to a sexual relationship with him, gave in to his advances and entreaties despite my initial misgivings.

"I've made this label millions. I've dedicated my life to this job."

Sonya's eyes are pitying. "Mindy. He's married."

"Yes. *He* is. I, however, am single. Maybe this is a conversation to have with him."

"Unfortunately, that's not how it works and you know it. He was your client."

Was.

All the fight bleeds out of me.

Peter won't meet my eyes. Amy's face is nearly green with misery, like she might throw up at any moment.

Of course. He'll be fine. I'm the other woman. The slut, the homewrecker, the bad guy. It's not only because Blake is a man, although that's a big part of it.

His wife though . . . .

Jeanette Adams is one of those America's sweetheart–type actresses. Everyone loves her. She's charming in late-night interviews, witty, quirky, and self-deprecating.

She and Blake were, I mean, they *are*, a media-darling

couple. They've been able to use their relationship as fodder over the years to help fuel both of their careers.

He was going to leave her for me.

They were waiting until she wrapped up her next film, then they planned to publicly split, and she could have used the tabloid fodder when she had her press tour.

Terrible but true: There's no such thing as bad press.

Except now she's pregnant. Maybe they were never going to split. Maybe it was all a lie.

Blake and I are completely, unequivocally over.

And I'm being fired.

"Peter has some paperwork for you to sign. Skip will escort you to your office to grab your things."

"Right." I won't crumble. I won't let this be the end, be *my* end. I will find another job. Perhaps even a better job.

Brave thoughts, but my stomach is shredding and my heart, what's left of it, is shattering all over again.

I stand up, hold my head high, and walk out.

Skip is waiting for me right outside the door, holding an empty box. "Sorry about this, Miss Fox," he murmurs.

"Not your fault."

He hands me the box and waits outside my office.

I was so proud when I moved in here. The hard work and sacrifice over the years had finally paid off, or so I thought. I had *made* it. I had a corner office in Manhattan. I had walls lined with my accomplishments and awards. Now they are worth nothing.

When I'm done, I stand in the center of the room, taking in the space that used to be mine for the last time.

I pick up the small box of my things and follow Skip out.

I've lost my job and my boyfriend. At least things can't possibly get worse.

I'll find another job. I'll pick myself back up and move on to something even better. I built my career from nothing, and I will rise from the ashes like a phoenix.

Chapter Two

MINDY

"Although your qualifications are very impressive, we've already made a decision to proceed with another candidate who will be a better fit with our team. I'm so sorry I wasn't able to reach you before you made the trip here."

I choke back the sharp questions threatening their way up my throat. *Why am I not a good fit for your team? Because you think I'm going to sleep with all of them?*

Damn it, I'm never going to find a job.

"Thank you for letting me know," I tell Nina, the hiring manager at Last Resort Records. It's not her fault. She stares down at the floor like she wants it to open up and swallow her.

The irony of the label's name isn't lost on me. This job is, quite literally, my last resort.

Variations of this same rejection have played out again

and again. That is, when they even bother to inform me of anything.

Almost half of the companies I've applied to either ghost me or don't bother calling for even a token interview. I've received generic emails about how "we won't be moving forward with your application" and "we're moving in another direction" and one job offer for half my proposed salary—a number I had already reduced from what I was making previously. I said no, but now I'm almost considering calling them back to see if they'll take me. A third of my prior income is better than no income at all.

They had scheduled an interview this morning at Last Resort, but apparently Nina has been living under a rock and didn't realize that I've been blacklisted by the entire music industry.

Someone must've filled her in—probably right before I arrived.

I give her a tight smile and then walk back to the elevator with my head held high even though on the inside I'm a boiling mess of frustration and despair.

The elevator doors shut, and once I'm alone, all of the bravado holding me together dissipates. I deflate, my shoulders slump, a discouraged breath gusting out of me.

It's been four months. Four months since Blake and I imploded along with the rest of my life, and I'm still getting the looks. The side glances. The knowing smirks.

When will it end?

I should have listened when Finley offered refuge back home in Whitby. I could have rented my apartment temporarily and applied for jobs remotely to save money.

But I couldn't leave. I don't run away from problems. I face them head-on and find ways around them or through them. Leaving would have been admitting defeat.

Damn my pride.

I didn't think I would still be searching the never-ending mice maze for gainful employment with no end in sight.

My savings are almost depleted. I can't go on like this. I'll have to start dipping into my retirement if something doesn't shake loose. Living in New York, especially in a trendy apartment nestled in the West Village, isn't exactly cheap.

My search for a job in the city ends here. It has to. I've exhausted all efforts. I'll have to start looking at labels in Nashville and California. My heart sinks along with the dip of the elevator, coming to a smooth stop on the ground floor.

Out on the sidewalk, I join the morning rush of pedestrians. I'm meeting my sister Piper in Central Park in an hour and a half. She wanted to be there to either celebrate or commiserate with my latest attempt at finding work.

Commiseration it is.

Tugging my deep blue blazer closer, I squint up at the cloudy sky, keeping pace with the scurrying bodies around me.

My phone rings. Still walking, I pull it out of the side pocket of my briefcase.

I thumb the answer icon. "Hey, Finley. Is everything okay?"

My sister wouldn't be calling right now unless it was important.

"Mindy." Surprise laces her tone. "I didn't think you would answer. I had my mind set on venting on your voicemail. Don't you have an interview right now?"

I grimace. "Don't ask. I'm not ready to talk about it. What's going on with you?"

She sighs, and I could reach out and touch the stress weaved into the sound, even through the phone line. "I don't want to worry you. You have enough going on."

I hasten my steps to get around a group of slow-moving tourists. "Finley. We've talked about this. You don't need to carry all your burdens alone. Spill it before I drive over there and waterboard it out of you."

She releases a sound that's a half groan and a half laugh. "I almost wish you would." She pauses for a few seconds and then imparts the next words in a rush. "Jake fell off the wagon last night."

I stop at a busy intersection, waiting for the light to turn, my stomach a riot of distress. All my worries about money and my career diminish under the weight of concern for my little brother. "Oh, no. Is he okay?"

"He's fine. Hungover, but fine. I think he's mad at himself more than anything."

The light turns green and I move with the crowd into the crosswalk. "We knew this could happen. Sobriety is a tough journey and can be a twisted path with ups and downs and everything in between."

"I know. But this is Jake. The little guy who used to fall asleep between us on the couch every Friday night. The same kid who was afraid of the dark until he was fifteen and wouldn't answer to anything but Batman for a full month when he was four."

Our mom left when Finley was eight and I was seven. Jake and his twin sister, Aria, were babies. They don't remember her. I barely remember her anymore. The only mother Jake and Aria had was Finley, and me, but mostly Finley. She's always taken care of all of us.

"I want to punch him in the face, but also wrap him in bubble wrap and lock him in a room where he can't hurt himself anymore."

"I know." A pang of guilt slices through me. "I should have come out when you asked me last month."

She offered me a place to stay if I needed to get away. Maybe she needed me there for support more than I needed a break from the job search, and I couldn't see past my own problems. I'm a self-centered moron.

"It's fine, Mindy. You have a lot going on."

I swallow. "It's not your fault he slipped up, Finley. You're doing the best you can. We can't take away what he's gone through."

We can't take away what any of us went through after Aria died. Since Jake was with her, and they were twins, the loss was especially brutal. I didn't realize how bad his drinking had gotten until he crashed the truck earlier this year. I was too focused on my own life and my career to comprehend how much he was struggling, and how much Finley was shouldering.

He hadn't drunk for over nine months, but sobriety is like walking a razor's edge sometimes.

"So what happened exactly?"

"He went out with Frank." Finley says Frank's name

like someone might say phlegm or mucous or moist. "They've hung out periodically since Jake got out of rehab, but for whatever reason, this time he couldn't say no to a few drinks, which led to a few more drinks, which led to him calling us in the middle of the night, drunk and upset. Archer picked him up at Frank's house at three this morning."

I sigh in frustration, trying to find the silver lining. "At least he didn't drive."

Her responding chuckle is bleak.

"How's Archer dealing with it?" I ask.

"You know how he is. He's already making a list of activities to keep Jake occupied."

"That sounds like him."

"Taylor is coming home soon, so that will help distract Jake, I hope."

I press my lips together. Every time I think about Taylor, my stomach fills with a twisting dread that I can't shake. Of course she's coming home to visit—she doesn't have a job. She flits around the country from one music festival to the next, working odd jobs and living in her van.

"Mindy?"

"Yeah, I'm here." And I'm going to change the subject. She knows I don't want to talk about Taylor. I don't know why she's always trying to bring her up. "So, has Archer proposed yet?"

She huffs. "We haven't even known each other a year."

"Didn't stop you from moving in with him," I tease.

"Hey, that's not true." She pauses. "He moved in with me."

I can't help but smile. Even though my life is in shambles, at least I have Finley, and she has Archer. "Well, make room because I might move in with you, too, at least temporarily."

She gasps. "You know, I hate you're going through a rough time, but if it means you'll come home, even for a little while, I can't say I'm not gonna be excited. Do you want to talk about your interview yet?"

"No." I glance around, taking stock of where I'm walking and adjusting my course toward the 79th Street transverse through Central Park.

Finley sighs. "Fine, fine. Just let me know when you plan on coming out and we can make some plans. We have plenty of room. I know Jake would love to see you, too."

"I'll keep you updated." And I'm definitely not going home until Taylor's visit ends. "Thanks, Finley. Love you."

"Love you, too."

I shove my phone back in my briefcase and quicken my steps, like if I walk fast enough I can outpace my problems.

Coming across the stairway leading into the park, I jog up the steps.

Once I'm at the top, the view of Belvedere Castle freezes me in place. I'm a short distance from Turtle Pond.

A pang of distress resonates deep in my stomach. *No.*

I clench my jaw and shove the unwanted, unnecessary emotions to the side.

Central Park may have been where Blake chose to end our relationship, but there is no way in hell I'm going to let him ruin the park for me. He already destroyed my career.

"Asshole!"

An elderly couple shuffling nearby startles, the gentleman giving me a dirty look.

I wince. "Sorry."

I continue walking, burning off my aggression with each forceful stride down the curving path. I take a deep breath and focus on my next objective. I will face Turtle Pond. I will return to the scene where it all ended. I have plenty of time until I need to meet Piper.

With each step, my stomach twists tighter and tighter.

I haven't talked to Blake since the morning everything went to shit, but I haven't been able to avoid encountering all his social media updates and the press surrounding Jeanette's pregnancy. I need to keep on top of what's happening in the industry, and unfortunately, especially lately, updates on their "bundle of joy" are everywhere.

The pregnancy did do one thing: It took all the heat off Rebel Records. Fuckers.

The most recent picture that went viral was of the two of them picking out a crib. It was an obvious setup, completely fabricated, like they don't have assistants running around at their beck and call to do all their shopping and errands for them. Please.

From a purely PR perspective, it was a good shot. He was standing behind her, his chin on her shoulder while they both looked down at their potential purchase, his arms wrapped around her, one hand resting on her stomach.

It's like everything that happened between Blake and I was just a figment of my imagination or some kind of fever dream.

I come to an abrupt halt in the middle of the path. I don't think I can do this. I don't need to face this demon, not today.

I spin around suddenly and trip over a walking guitar and the ground rushes toward me.

Chapter Three

Mindy

"Are you all right?"

I open my eyes, staring up at a dreary gray sky offset by a swath of red maple leaves flickering in the breeze. A blurry head blocks the view, moving into my line of sight.

I blink a few times and the face comes into focus, right along with the events of the past thirty seconds.

Shit.

I ran over someone—someone's guitar—and then fell onto the sidewalk like a felled tree.

The man looming over me is . . . attractive. Maybe mid-to-late-twenties, with bright, concerned eyes, an average nose, and wide cheekbones that give him an almost a baby-faced look save for the golden stubble adorning his strong jaw.

He's vaguely familiar. I swear I've seen the same

shaggy light brown hair stuffed under that same cowboy hat somewhere before.

Do I know you?

"Are you all right?" he asks again. The vowels are slightly elongated, giving the words the hint of a Southern accent.

I nod and the motion scrapes the back of my head against the hard pavement.

Wincing, I push myself up onto my elbows and black spots crowd my vision. "Um." My mouth is dry, my tongue stuck to the roof of my mouth. I swallow and try again. "I'm okay. How did this happen?"

The man's mouth pulls into a wince. "You tripped over my headstock." His head tilts to one side, toward the tuning pegs of the guitar resting next to him.

"That part, I remember." I got tripped by a guitar. If that's not irony, I don't know what is considering I've been banging my head against the music industry's walls for months.

"I may have been following behind you a little too closely. You have a subcutaneous bruise here." His fingers hover over the side of my face.

As if his fingers are remotely connected to my skin, the side of my head gives an answering throb.

"I'm more worried about the back of your head where you hit the pavement." Concern furrows his brows. "You might have a slight concussion. Do you feel okay? Is there someone I can call?"

"No. I'm fine. I'm meeting my sister soon." I shift, propping myself up on my hands so I can push myself to standing.

He stands and offers his hand.

I take it, thankful for the warm, stable grip as he smoothly pulls me to my feet.

After a second, I let go and immediately waver on my heels.

"Whoa there." His hands clasp my shoulders, steadying me.

My face goes hot with embarrassment. I am not some damsel in distress. I grit my teeth and pull myself together, brushing dirt and leaves off my navy-blue slacks.

"Thank you for your help. You can release me now."

He does, immediately, but the worried divot between his brows deepens. "Do you have any nausea?"

"No."

"Blurry vision, ringing in your ears, or light-headedness?"

I eye him with curiosity. "Are you a doctor?"

"Used to be."

I squint at him. "You seem young to have retired from a career that requires over a decade of school and residency."

One corner of his mouth tips up, a faint dimple appearing in his cheek. "Now, why can't I tell if that's a compliment or an accusation?"

Unfamiliar heat stirs in the pit of my stomach.

What is that?

Attraction.

The same annoying sensation that got me into my current mess.

After a second, he rubs the back of his head, his gaze

darting away. "I skipped a few grades, and the emergency medicine program I was in only had a three-year residency." Pink tinges his cheeks, like he's embarrassed at the admission.

I'm still reeling that I'm somewhat attracted to this handsome stranger—is he a stranger? I could swear I've seen him somewhere before, the memory hovering at the edges of my mind.

I must be imagining things. Maybe I hit my head harder than I thought.

"Thanks for all your help. I have to go. My sister is waiting for me."

I move around him.

"Wait, Mindy," he calls out.

I turn around.

He opens his mouth as if to speak and then changes his mind and shakes his head. "Never mind. Just promise me you'll see a doctor if any symptoms crop up or worsen. Okay?"

"Yeah. I will."

Heading back the way I came, I attempt to shrug off the strangeness of the encounter.

It's not until fifteen minutes later, when I've almost reached Bethesda Terrace and I'm waiting by the fountain for Piper, that a realization strikes me, almost making me stumble.

How did he know my name?

~

"Come on. Tell me everything." Piper loops her arm in mine and drags me over to the edge of the fountain and sits, patting the hard concrete next to her.

I can't tell her *everything*. I'm definitely not mentioning how I ran face first into a guitar.

Maybe it's the head wound speaking, but I unleash a small measure of my frustration.

"I can't find a job." The gurgle and rush of the water behind us forces my voice higher than I would like. I take a sip of the latte Piper brought me and stare straight ahead. "I've applied everywhere. I've run out of options. I've ruined my own life. The whole world knows I slept with Blake Bonham. I might as well sew a giant A onto all my clothes."

Piper rests her shoulder against mine, a slight and comforting warmth. "They don't know the whole story. They don't know how he led you on and lied to you. You did the right thing. You told the truth." She shakes her head and blows out her breath, a small crease forming between her brows. "You told the truth to protect me. It's more my fault than yours."

Initially, the press dropped a story that Blake was having an affair with Piper. I had to come clean to protect her, and I was immediately put on administrative leave while they investigated and evaluated my situation at the label.

Of course I had to come clean. Piper has gone through enough. When she first came to stay with me last spring, she was a tired, thin wisp of herself.

Now she looks healthy, happy, and vibrant, even with

her hair pulled back in a messy bun and wearing old, faded jeans and a deep blue hoodie.

I frown at her. "It's not your fault, either. Let's blame Ben."

She grins and takes a sip out of the disposable coffee cup in her hand. "Perfect."

Ben is Piper's ex. He was a super psycho who's now doing hard time for stalking, attempted murder, and defamation, to name a few amid the litany of charges thrown at him.

I can't blame Ben for all of my problems, though, as satisfying as that would be. I chose to give in to Blake's advances. I can only blame myself and the loneliness that I let fester into desperation. I'd had short-lived relationships in college, and since graduating—almost ten years ago now —I'd eschewed all romantic entanglements in favor of focusing on my career except for periodic flings when I needed to blow off some steam. There was no time for a real relationship. I was too busy kicking ass in the music industry. And I was happy, with work, anyway. Rebel Records raked in millions from my efforts. I've signed dozens of acts and watched them all succeed. I've plucked future Grammy winners from the bowels of obscurity, for fuck's sake.

And then I fell in love and my whole life fell apart.

He made me believe I could have it all, and then it blew up in my face.

Never again.

Piper tilts her head, considering me. "You know, not all men are like Blake."

I resist the urge to roll my eyes. "Of course not. Some

of them are eccentric billionaires that are completely obsessed with their girlfriends."

She grins, covering the motion with her coffee cup. "They sure are," she says with relish before taking a small sip.

A smile tugs at the corner of my mouth. If anyone deserves happiness, it's Piper. Especially after the nightmare she went through with her ex. At first, I had my doubts about Oliver. He is kind of a prick. But there is no doubt in my mind that he would move the sun and Earth for her. It's the only reason I put up with him—because Piper deserves someone who treats her like a queen, and he treats her like a goddess.

I smack Piper on the knee. "Come on. I need to walk. It's too cold to sit here. Let's go toward the Mall."

She nods and we head in that direction.

"I love Central Park in fall." Piper tilts her head back, taking in the giant elm trees on either side of us, creating a lush golden canopy that blocks out the overcast sky.

"It's beautiful," I agree. "Did you finish your piece for the gallery?"

"Almost. I have another month to get it completed. It was a little more challenging than I thought it would be, but I can't wait for you to see it." Piper is a metalwork artist. She does commissioned and original work using metal and copper and bronze and the like. She's been creating pieces for a gallery in SoHo owned by Oliver.

"Did Finley call you about Jake?" she asks.

I nod. "Yes. I talked to her this morning."

We commiserate on the topic for a minute.

About halfway down the path, strains of soprano strings catch my attention.

"Do you hear that?" Piper tugs on my elbow, and we set a course toward a crowd of about six circling a middle-aged woman playing a violin.

It's a familiar song: "Sunday Bloody Sunday." There's something haunting about the notes being played with the solo string instrument. I take a deep breath of the cool fall air and try to immerse myself in the music.

"Remember when I would come and visit before I moved to LA and you would take me to listen to your favorite buskers?"

I nod. After Aria died, I made a point of spending time with my younger siblings whenever they asked, whenever they needed to get away from Whitby for a spell.

Piper considers me, her gaze thoughtful. "You were always so good at unearthing raw talent. Have you ever thought about starting your own record label?"

The question knocks me back on my heels. "No."

I wouldn't even know where to start. Is it an option? I never would have thought of it. Before I have a chance to ruminate on the idea, Piper's hand squeezes my arm, pulling me from my thoughts. "Look, it's that guy."

I follow her gaze across the crowd, and when my eyes lock on *that guy*, my entire body flushes with embarrassed heat.

It's the guy from earlier, the guitar-wrangling doctor. The one who somehow knew my name. Piper's words are another piece in the mysterious puzzle.

I tilt my head toward hers. "How do you know him?"

"You don't remember?"

I shrug. "Should I?"

"Well, yeah. He was at that release party we went to at Nowadays last summer."

I frown and check him out again, mind rifling through the events of that night, most of which involve Piper's ex. I had dragged her with me to the party, and Ben had snuck into the event. She left with Oliver, and I took Blake home for the first time that night. Two relationships that have had opposing trajectories since that momentous occasion. While she's ecstatically happy in paradise, my life is in shambles.

I shove the thoughts away and focus on Piper's words.

"He wanted you to sign him with Rebel Records. What was his name? Liam or Linus?" Her nose scrunches. "Larry?" She glances at me for confirmation.

I shrug. Until this morning I didn't know him from Larry.

Her look is skeptical. "He held up a boombox outside your building to get your attention. That doesn't seem like something you would forget easily." She snaps her fingers. "Luke! That's it. Luke . . . something or other."

Oh. *Wait.* The boombox does trigger something. I do remember him. I was annoyed at his efforts. It was before my life went to shit, back when I was a big deal and falling in love with an asshole and thought I was too good for such theatrics.

How the mighty have fallen. Now I'm the one who might be holding up boomboxes to get an interview.

"He was really nice to me. We should say hi." She takes a step in his direction, dragging me along with her.

"What? No." I dig in my heels, forcing her to stop.

"Why not?"

One, I don't want him to tell Piper about my head injury and make her worry. Two, I'm mortified. How did I not recognize him? Am I *still* so self-centered?

Before I can come up with any kind of adequate excuse, she's dragging me along again. "Oh, he's walking away. Come on, let's catch up."

I try to remove my arm from hers, but she's latched on like a python and marching even faster now.

"We shouldn't bother him."

We weave through the small crowd, moving farther away from the violinist, the music fading away behind me.

"He's got his guitar—maybe he's looking for somewhere to busk. I want to hear him play. Luke!" she calls.

Half the people walking along around us glance over at Piper, who's waving her free hand frantically while still dragging me behind her. "Hey, Luke!"

He turns.

Our eyes lock.

A smile quirks at his lips when he takes in Piper heaving me in his direction, a dimple appearing in his right cheek.

If I was into men right now, which I'm not, I might find him extremely attractive. But the attraction is overshadowed by the intense humiliation.

He must think I'm a complete moron, which is fine, right? I don't care what he thinks. Why would I? The last thing I need is a hot musician in my life.

And then he's in front of us and Piper is stretching

out her hand to him, and his eyes meet mine, full of knowing amusement.

My face goes scorching hot.

If this day gets any better, by noon I'll be rolling around in shards of glass.

Chapter Four

Luke

"Hi, Luke. It's so nice to see you again." Piper shakes my hand, smiling warmly.

Mindy stands behind her, hovering like a helicopter parent.

"Piper Fox. Always a pleasure." I release her hand and nod toward Mindy. "Hi there."

"Hey." Her cheeks are flushed. She forces a smile, crosses her arms over her chest, and looks away.

The first time I saw Mindy, almost a year ago, she was a vibrant force of energy.

Now—and I think it's a result of more than our little crash—she's paler and thinner. Lines of tension bracket her mouth and radiate from her eyes.

Concern pinches at me. Perhaps her frailty is at least partly because of our run-in this morning, although I'm sure the past few months have taken their toll. "How's the head? It bothering you?"

Piper frowns, her eyes flicking from me to Mindy. "What? What happened to your head?"

"Nothing. It's fine. I'm fine. Everything's fine." She clears her throat. "Are you busking somewhere nearby?"

I suppose this means she didn't tell Piper about our little run-in, considering the not-so-subtle subject change and nervous, repetitive statements.

I don't want to lie, so I settle on a half-truth. "Just scoping out the competition." I wave a hand at the violinist and offer an easy smile, but the thought of pulling out my guitar and playing right here on the main thoroughfare sends a swarm of nerves prickling up the back of my neck.

Piper squints at me. "Any progress since last summer?"

Mindy's mouth twitches. "Yeah, anyone else fall for the whole John Cusack *Say Anything* routine?"

Ah, so she does remember. "A couple of bites. Nothing solid yet." And the bites were more like nibbles since most of them had me escorted off their property.

I had to do it, though. I promised Kevin I would try everything, and I keep my promises. He loved that damn movie.

Piper cocks her head, studying me. "I would love to hear you play sometime."

Mindy watches the exchange, her bow-shaped mouth puckering slightly in thought.

Don't stare at her mouth.

I wrench my gaze back to Piper. "No gigs coming up.

I could email you some audio files, though, if you're really interested." Since that's the only way anyone will ever hear me play.

Piper brightens. "I would love that."

"Really?" I'm sure she's just being nice.

"Yes. Don't you agree Mindy?" She nudges her with an elbow.

Mindy glances at me and attempts a smile that's only halfway successful. "Yeah. Sure."

"Let me give you my email." Piper shoots Mindy a glare so quick I almost miss it. "In return, I'll send you an invite to my next showing. You have to come, if you're not too busy."

She gives me the address and I key it into my phone while dipping my head in acknowledgement. "I can't wait to see it. I heard your last piece sold well at auction."

Piper beams. "It did. I've been very lucky. We're also going to be showcasing some up-and-coming talent which I think is really exciting."

I glance back over at Mindy, who won't meet my eyes. "Well, I better get going. It was really nice to see you both again."

"You, too."

Mindy nods her goodbye.

"Good luck with everything. Don't forget to send me those files. I mean it," Piper calls over her shoulder as they're walking away.

I tip my hat to them. "I will."

~

"I brought you a sandwich," I tell Walter, walking into the common area of the hostel I've been staying at for nearly a year now.

His eyes gleam behind his thick-framed glasses. "Roast beef?"

I give him a pointed look. "Turkey."

He grunts but holds out his hand for the paper-wrapped hoagie.

I toss it over, shrugging the strap of my guitar off and laying it on the coffee table before taking a seat on the sagging old sofa next to him.

He probably hasn't eaten all day. Most people in the hostel are temporary visitors, but Walter has been here longer than me.

"How was it out there today?" His bushy gray eyebrows rise at me in inquiry.

"I ran into Mindy Fox." Literally.

He unwraps the sandwich. "Huh. Who is this Mindy Fox, and is she the one who put that smile on your face?"

I rub my jaw. "Sort of. She's a very well-known A&R director. Well, she was."

"A&R? What does that mean?" He takes a bite of his sandwich, chewing slowly.

"It stands for artists and repertoire. A&R people sign and develop musical talent, help in planning an artist's entire career, and supervise recording projects. They basically act as a liaison between the artist and the label." I shift on the lumpy sofa, trying to find a comfortable spot around a spring digging into my thigh. "It's kind of funny, actually. When I first came to the city, I was sort of fixated on signing with Rebel Records because of her."

"She's that good?"

"It's more than that," I tell Walter. "She thinks about music the same way I do."

It's a lame explanation, but if I tell him the full truth, he'll probably think I'm some kind of obsessive stalker. A few years ago, when I was still in residency, I read an interview with her in *Rolling Stone* and she quoted something about music and grief and how a simple song can heal thousands of souls. It was like she reached through the pages of the article and grabbed me by the heart and squeezed. Like with her words, she forged this bond between us, something almost tangible.

A completely moronic and fanciful notion but true all the same.

I give him a synopsis of both the first run-in with Mindy this morning and then the subsequent conversation with her and her sister.

"So you think this Mindy Fox could help you with your music?"

"I don't think she's working right now." I'm not sure what she's doing, but I haven't seen or heard anything about her since the story on her and Blake hit. I've seen plenty of news about Blake Bonham, though, and his wife's pregnancy and his upcoming album.

"Why not?"

"It's complicated. The short version is she became romantically involved with a musician she worked with."

He shrugs. "That's not so bad."

"He's married."

He chuffs. "So she's a homewrecker?"

"I don't think so." I had the chance to observe Blake with

Mindy, months ago, before the story became public fodder. He touched her like she was his. I shrug the memories away. "Blake is still with his wife. There's more to the story than what the press is sharing, I'm sure. Besides, he is the one who broke a promise to someone. Mindy isn't married."

"Touché. I'll give you that point." He shifts in his seat, reaching for the bottle of water at his side and taking a sip. "So you think maybe if you send this Piper girl some songs, she'll share it with her sister, and then if this Mindy gets a job again, she'll call you?"

I grimace. "It's a long shot."

"It's longer than a long shot. But it's what you got." He rubs his hands together. "Which one are you gonna send her?"

"Should I send more than one?"

He shrugs. "I think it will only take one."

The one song I've played for him. "The one about Kevin."

He nods.

I look up at the ceiling, focusing on the old water stain in the far corner. "That's the hardest one to share."

He rests one heavy hand on my shoulder. "Which is why it's the best."

I tilt my head to meet his eyes. "I'm going to have to go home next month."

"I understand."

I can't keep doing this. I'm out of options, and money. Why I ever thought this would work in the first place is beyond me. I think my brain was burned out after med school and residency and working in an ER.

I told my parents and Granny Bea that I'd try for a year. One year to give it my all, and now the time's almost up. If I could get over my stage fright, I might be able to get some low-paying gigs at bars or make money busking and stay longer, but I can't. I've tried.

I push myself to stand. "Dinner later?"

"Only if you let me cook since you brought me lunch." He raises the sandwich he's halfway through eating.

"Fine. But it better be low sodium." I grab my guitar and head toward my room.

He chuckles. "You're worse than a mother hen."

"You know it," I call out before unlocking my door and disappearing into my closet-sized room.

I rest the guitar against the wall and grab my laptop from under the bed.

I open the file with all my audio recordings and a blank email and drag Kevin's song over. Then I key in the address Piper gave me and type out a quick note.

After a slight hesitation, I add my phone number under the signature. You never know, but my expectations are tempered by recent experience.

I've had my hopes up so many times, and every time they've been smashed into oblivion. This is my final Hail Mary. It's almost relieving in a way, knowing that this is all almost over. I gave it my best as I promised, and now I can go home and . . . I don't know. Figure out what to do with my life.

Maybe I should do what my parents want and get a job at a hospital, but the thought leaves me hollow.

I'll miss Walter, but there's not much else to miss about New York.

Except for a certain prickly A&R director. I think about Mindy's embarrassment and her crankiness, and I can't help but smile.

Chapter Five

MINDY

"Will you pass me the peanut sauce?" I ask Piper.

She hands over the porcelain dish before skewering a piece of chicken with a gold-plated fork. "When are you going back to Whitby?"

It's been almost a week since my disastrous non-interview with Last Chance Records. I've spent the entire time reconciling myself to the fact that I have to move back home and trying to view it as an opportunity instead of a failure.

But now, eating dinner with Oliver and Piper under a gleaming crystal chandelier surrounded by opulence, failure is a weight pressing me down, making it hard to breathe.

"As soon as I can rent out my apartment. You interested?" I ask, half kidding.

I don't want to rent out my apartment at all, but Piper would at least be better than a complete stranger. When I bought my own place five years ago, it was like I had truly *made it* in New York. It's a symbol of my success. Now it's like I'm giving up on all my dreams.

I doubt Piper is interested in renting anything since she sleeps at Oliver's almost every night. Honestly, I think she stays with me now and again out of pity and to make sure I don't lapse into a totally incoherent state of depression.

I can't blame her for preferring his place over mine. Oliver owns an entire building near Central Park. It's like a palace.

She glances over at Oliver.

One corner of his mouth tips up. "You might need somewhere to go when you need to get away from me."

A crease forms between her brows. "I never want to get away from you."

He waves a hand. "You know, those incredibly rare occasions when I'm being an overbearing ass."

A masculine voice speaks up from the doorway. "You mean those incredibly rare occasions called every day that ends in a Y?"

Oliver frowns at Carson as he enters the dining room. "You're back already?"

"Don't be so thrilled to see me. Hey, Mindy, Piper." Carson shucks off his gray suit jacket, slinging it over the back of the creamy cushioned chair, and then drops into the chair next to me. "What are we eating?"

"Chicken satay, peanut sauce, rice, salad." I point out each dish to him.

"Sounds fantastic. I'm starving." He glances around the table and then down at his tie and vest. "And over-dressed." He loosens his tie with one hand while grabbing a few chicken skewers with the other and plopping them on his plate.

Despite the luxurious surroundings, we're all wearing jeans, even Oliver, who used to live in his three-piece suit. The change in his attire, and attitude, is all thanks to Piper. She definitely smoothed out at least some of his rough edges.

Piper stands, grabbing the bottle of wine nearby to pour some into Carson's empty wineglass. "The date didn't go well?"

"Men are the worst." Carson reaches over, tipping her hand to get her to fill it up more.

"Hear, hear," I lift my stem. "Present company excluded, mostly."

Carson laughs as we clink glasses.

"What happened?" Piper asks.

"He showed up, we had a drink, and he was meh," he makes a face. "And so I left. What were you talking about when I came in? Is Oliver being an ass again?" He dishes rice onto his plate.

Oliver gives him a narrow-eyed look but doesn't respond.

I bite back a smile. Even though Carson is technically Oliver's employee, they act more like siblings. "I was asking Piper if she wants to rent my apartment while I'm in Whitby. Temporarily."

Carson perks up. "I can rent it."

"Really?"

Oliver scowls. "You don't want to live here anymore? What's wrong with here?"

"It's not that I don't enjoy residing in the whole east wing of your building, but it might be a good thing for me to have my own place. I've intruded upon you and Piper long enough."

"It's only been a few months." Oliver frowns down at his plate.

"It's been almost six months."

Oliver's tone gets crisp. "Do you find the accommodations lacking?"

Carson sighs. "It's not about that."

"Then what is it about, exactly?"

Piper reaches across the table and pats Carson's hand. "What Oliver is trying to say is that he worries about you and he likes you living here, and showering people with food and shelter is his love language. But if you need to move out, he understands and he only wants what's best for you."

"I know. He's a real dick. We can all talk about this more later." Carson tilts his head in my direction. "So, Mindy, what are you going to do in Whitby?"

"You could stay here, Mindy," Oliver tells me, shooting a glare at Carson. "We apparently will have some space soon."

I bite my lip to stop the laugh wanting to erupt. "Thank you, Oliver, I would love to stay in your mansion while I look for work outside of the city, but I promised Finley I would come to visit. I can come to stay with you after that, though." Since I may be a homeless wretch for a long while I may as well keep my options open.

Oliver nods, shooting Carson a glare that says, *See? How hard is that?*

Carson ignores Oliver and gives me a sympathetic wince. "Nothing going here?"

"Nope."

Piper dabs her mouth with a cloth napkin. "You'll find something. Labels should be lining up around the block for the chance to hire you. You have a gift. You have a sixth sense for finding artists who will be successful. Your track record is unparalleled."

"Yeah, I guess." Not that any of that helped me keep my job with Rebel Records.

Piper taps a finger on the table, her lips pursed in consideration. "Did you give any thought to starting your own label?"

I shrug. "I don't know, not really."

Which is a half-truth. I thought about it, the same way you might think about winning the lottery, finding a vinyl of Prince's *The Black Album*, or meeting Tom Hiddleston and having him fall madly in love with you.

It's a fantasy.

I would need startup capital. I would need some decent equipment, a space for recording, and people to deal with the legal aspects, accounting, producing . . . not to mention finding actual decent artists that would be willing to take a chance with someone who has none of the above and a shitty reputation to boot.

An image of Luke pops into my head, his dimpled smile, shaggy hair, and easygoing personality. He has the charm and presence to pull it off, maybe, but the fact that no one has picked him up yet despite his obvious persistence makes me wonder if he has the chops.

Being a musician is hard. Not only do you need to craft killer hooks and riffs and catch the interest of listeners, but you also need to be appealing, emotionally vulnerable, and authentic. That's what makes the fans stick around.

Carson taps a finger on the table. "Maybe you should think about it. You've got the experience."

Piper nods, sitting up straighter. "He's right. You've had your hands in literally everything from concept to launch for a ton of artists and their albums. Why not find your own talent and use your existing contacts and resources in the industry to launch your brand-new label? It could be whatever you wanted, and I bet you would crush it."

I poke at a piece of lettuce with my fork. "I don't know. Maybe."

Piper lifts her brows and gives me the sister face, the one that says she's going to hound me until I acquiesce to her demands.

"I'll think about it," I relent.

"Here, here." Carson lifts his wineglass.

Chuckling, I clink my glass against his and we drink.

The conversation moves on to easier topics.

We talk about the weekend camp coming up in December, which Oliver is going to be present for since it's the soft opening of the kids camp he owns with Finley. They are planning some kind of winter forest science thing for kids. I half listen.

Through it all, the idea of starting my own label sticks in my mind like lint stuck in honey.

What if I went for it?

More importantly, what if it worked out?

The next morning, I'm in bed staring at the ceiling as it brightens with the encroaching day, lamenting my life choices, when my phone chimes with a text.

I pluck it from the nightstand. It's from my former assistant, Ally.

Did you see the Page Seven article?

She's been keeping me in the loop, businesswise, ever since I left Rebel Records. She's the one who told me when they extended Blake's contract, offered Vacation Mustache more money, and basically rewarded him for the same mess that got me fired.

Her text is immediately followed by a link to the article.

The headline reads "Blake Bonham on his New Album: 'My most personal project to date.' "

My stomach lurches. I sit up in bed so quickly that I'm almost lightheaded.

Oh, shit.

I click the link against my better judgment.

The album title is *Revelations*.

My teeth clench. I resist the urge to chuck my phone across the room.

This is so typical.

I skim the article, which waxes on about how Blake is finally "getting vulnerable" with his listeners and "really opening up old wounds." The author waxes on about how Blake's tumultuous past year, full of *mistakes* and learning experiences, gave him the opportunity to really dig in and inject emotional authenticity into his lyrics.

Motherfucker.

Mistake?

Is that what I was to him?

It shouldn't hurt, but it does.

Why is it that men can spin the stories of how they cheat and lie and all kinds of shitty behavior and everyone's like, "They're so deep and vulnerable!" But if a woman sings about her relationships, it's all judgment and criticism: "Why can't she be more creative, write about something else, date less, or *be* less?"

Blake and I both made a mistake, except while I got fired and lost my life's work, he got more money, a better contract, and critical acclaim.

Anger burns in my gut.

My phone buzzes in my hand.

I click on it.

It's an email from Piper, and the subject line is all caps: "MINDY LISTEN TO THIS."

I tap it to open the message.

• • •

I know I'm not some kind of musical genius like you are, but I think this is good. Actually, I think it's really good. Take a listen and hear for yourself.

<3

P

I toss my phone onto the comforter and flop back into bed, covering my head with my pillow.

I don't want to listen to any songs. I don't want to think about my career or what I'm going to do next or the fact that while Blake is spilling his guts on his next album for what will likely be a massive profit, I'm the one with the open wound and bleeding bank account.

I definitely don't want to listen to a song from some stupidly attractive cowboy who's intelligent and considerate and has a dimpled smile and worn jeans that sit perfectly on his narrow hips.

If he can sing, though . . . God, he would be so easy to market. I could make the world fall in love with him. People would be charmed by him. He has that thing, that vitality.

But the fact that he's so appealing immediately puts me on the defense. I don't want to work with someone I'm attracted to.

The thought stops me in my tracks. What am I doing? What am I thinking, that I'm never going to be able to work with an attractive male musician again? And why? Because of Blake? I can't let him ruin my future.

When did I become this whiny, mopey creature?

I throw my pillow, shove the blankets off, and stand.

I'm not a quitter. I'm not someone who hides under her covers and cowers from the world.

I'm smart, organized, talented . . . . I will not be beaten by a bad man and a sexist industry.

No one wants to hire me? Fine. I'm going to do this. I can find some acts, start my own successful label, and tell the world to go screw itself.

Marching to the bathroom, I shower and get dressed before moving into the kitchen to make an egg-white omelet.

While I'm pulling a pan from the cupboard, I make a mental list.

I'll eat, stretch, maybe go for a run, and then get to work on . . . my eyes flick over to my phone, lying silent and dark on the counter.

I turn my back to it, grabbing eggs from the fridge along with some pre-washed mushrooms and peppers.

I put everything out on the counter and stare down at the phone.

I'll listen to it. It's only one song.

I open Piper's email, click on the audio file, and set the phone back down while I work on chopping the veggies.

A few chords sound, the rich notes filling the air. It's good. Simple. Appealing.

At first there's just the strum of the guitar, and then he starts to sing.

His voice is deep, husky, slightly gravelly.

My ears prickle. My knife stills halfway through slicing a pepper.

The melody is upbeat and catchy, and the lyrics are solid.

Every night I see you in my dreams
But every morning I wake up to reality
I'm trying to move on, but I'm stuck in the past
I'm drowning in sorrow, and it's hitting me fast

The memories we made, they linger on
But sometimes I wonder if it's a mistake to hold on
Perhaps I should let them slip away like sand
Leaving me with nothing but empty hands

The melody shifts and slows near the end when he breaks into the bridge.

The things that we carry
Make us sink like a stone
To the bottom of the waters
Yet still we don't know

We think if we keep it close
We will have some control
But we stay stuck in the muck
And the only way to move forward
Is to let it all go

. . .

I blink in surprise. The lyrics are . . . surprisingly deep. Sad. Unexpected. It doesn't always work, mixing a cheery pitch with deep lyrics, but when it does work, it's incredible.

My skin tingles, goose bumps breaking out on my arms and the back of my neck.

He's not bad. Actually, he's pretty damn good.

My heart thumps harder, food forgotten. A few minutes ago, my thoughts were running on pure bravado. But now that I've heard this, we might actually have a shot at something.

What if I really did this?

My mind calculates the possibilities, rushing through ideas and thinking through what I would need. How much do I need? I consider what I have in the bank, what I have in savings and retirement. What would I be willing to invest to give this a true shot?

I finish prepping my food, half engaged in the process, listening to the song again and again.

The smell of smoke jerks me from the spell of the music. I gasp and yank the pan off the stove, turning off the burner with a shaky laugh.

Pull it together, Mindy.

It's only one song, but he must have more.

Once I'm done eating, I pull out my laptop and start crunching numbers, making a list of what I might need and who owes me favors.

I craft a contract, one that would offer less money upfront in exchange for a better split on the royalties.

I can work on scrounging up a few producers who might be willing to take a similar deal and work on anything else he's got, craft some songs that are deep like this but with commercial appeal.

Piper was right. I've done all this for years. I know how it works. I just need to take the formula I've memorized and replicate it for myself.

It would be a lot of work, but I'm used to that. Work is what I'm good at.

A frisson of excitement zings through me.

I pick up my phone, scrolling back to the email Piper forwarded me from Luke. His number is at the bottom.

I stare at it for a long time, considering, then I put the number into my phone and open up a text message.

Hi, Luke, it's Mindy Fox. I listened to your song, and I was wondering if we could discuss it. Maybe later today or tomorrow?

I bite my lip, waiting. Rue the day I have to wait on a man to text me back. Again. Reminds me of the hours I spent waiting around for Blake to dump me.

Hi Mindy. Thank you for reaching out. I'm open today. Tell me when and where.

. . .

I grin and resist the urge to shoot my fist in the air. My thumbs move quickly over the keys, and then I hit send.

Think Coffee on 8th by Jackson Square. 3 p.m.

Chapter Six

Luke

I stare down at my phone, shock rooting me in place.

She wants to talk. To me. About my song. *Today*.

What does that mean? Did she actually like it? What if she wants to hear me play in person? My stomach clenches, the oatmeal I just downed threatening to reappear.

I won't bring my guitar.

But then she might want to hear me sing a cappella. That would be so much worse.

Wouldn't it?

I have to meet her. This is why I'm here. This is why I gave up eight years of grueling work, to chase this dream.

If you pass this up because of fear, you're more of a dumbass than I thought. Kevin's voice echoes in my head. My lips quirk. He would kick my ass.

If Kevin taught me anything, it's that life's short. If

you aren't learning and growing and changing, what's the point?

I reread Mindy's text for the seventh time.

Think Coffee. There are a few of them scattered throughout the city. I pull up the map on my phone to route my way there. The 2 train will drop me at 12th and Greenwich, which looks to be the best course of action.

I have a couple of hours, at least. If she had suggested tomorrow, I probably wouldn't have been able to sleep tonight. My heart is already pounding so hard I'm surprised my shirt isn't lifting in front of my face with each pump. It takes me a full minute to key in my response.

I'll be there.

I review the three-word text thirty times before pressing send.

Holy shit.

I need to get ready.

"Walter." I call his name as I head down the narrow hallway. "You're not going to believe this."

He's sitting in the recliner in the common room, an old paperback in his lap. His furry gray eyebrows lift, and he looks at me over the rim of the glasses pushed down to the bottom of his nose.

I pace in front of the TV, blocking his view of

Antiques Roadshow. "She wants to meet with me. To talk about my song."

"Who?"

"Mindy Fox."

"The homewrecker from the other week?"

"She's not a homewrecker."

"Fine, fine." He takes off his glasses and squints at me. "Is that what you're wearing?"

I glance down at my jeans and flannel. "Yeah?"

"Don't you own a suit?"

"We're meeting at a coffee shop. I'm not wearing a suit."

He grumbles something about kids these days. "You better get in the bathroom before the couple in 2B wakes up. Yesterday they were in there for two hours."

I give him a thumbs-up and make haste toward the communal bathroom.

Even after taking extra care to shave, putting on double the deodorant, and taming my wayward hair, I make it to Think Coffee twenty minutes early.

Pushing open the glass door, the scent of coffee hitting my senses like I've run into a wall of it.

I glance over at the ordering counter, curving off to one side, and consider whether I should order something or wait for Mindy.

After a few seconds of hesitating near the door, an incoming family forces my hand and I take a seat in a dark booth near the front where light streams in through the windows.

And then I wait and try to remember to breathe.

Seven minutes later, Mindy pushes open the front door, dressed in gray slacks and a black peacoat.

She spots me immediately and a relieved smile crosses her face. "You're early." She stands behind the chair across from me, setting her briefcase on the marble-topped table.

I stand up to shake her hand. "You are, too."

Her grip is firm in mine. "Better three hours too soon than a minute too late."

The words are familiar. I search my memory bank. "Shakespeare?"

Her eyes widen slightly with surprise. "Yes. My dad used to say it. He was big on respecting people's time. He wouldn't work with contractors who showed up late, even if it was only ten minutes."

"What did he do?"

She takes her coat off, draping it over the back of her chair. "He owned a rental cabin business upstate, in Whitby. We still own the property. My sister and brother are still there along with my sister's boyfriend. They've turned it into a nonprofit camp for kids."

Now it's my turn to be surprised. "That sounds amazing."

"It is." She glances behind her, toward the ordering counter. "Did you want some coffee or something?"

"Yeah, sure. I haven't ordered yet because I wasn't sure what you preferred." And I didn't want to down a coffee and have to pee as soon as she arrived or get too jittery since my anxiety levels are through the roof.

"That's fine. I'll get us something."

I take a step, and she puts out a hand. "It's my treat, I insist."

An argument rises to my lips, but the tension in her shoulders and the way she's gripping the back of the chair hint at her own nerves. Maybe she needs a minute. Maybe she needs the control. "An Americano is fine."

One corner of her mouth twitches upward in a semblance of a smile. "Got it. Be right back."

The kids who were in line before have disappeared, so it doesn't take her long to get our coffees.

She returns, setting a brown disposable cup in front of me.

"Thank you." I pick it up and blow on the top before taking a small sip.

"You're welcome." She sits and opens her briefcase, pulling out a manila folder, a faint tremble in her fingers.

"Like I mentioned, I listened to your song. I thought it was very good."

My mind buzzes with competing thoughts: I guess we're jumping right into it, combined with *holy shit* she likes my song.

Since it wouldn't be appropriate to jump up and down screaming, I nod. "Thank you. Thank you for listening at all."

I don't know what else to say. I can't believe we're even having this conversation. A month ago, hell, two hours ago, I was thinking I'd have to throw in my chips and return home. Now . . . maybe not?

She leans forward, resting her elbows on the table, her hands cupped around her coffee. "Can I ask what inspired it? What do the lyrics mean to you?"

The scent of her wafts over me, something with bright floral notes. She smells like spring. I breathe her in, and my mind scatters in different directions. One part of me contemplates if she tastes as good as she smells. Another part of me considers how to reply to her question while also berating the part that's hung up on her scent.

This isn't a date. It's business.

I drive my thoughts to the song. It's not exactly easy to talk about. I told Walter about what happened with Kevin, but that was after knowing him for nearly six months, and it was a late night when I'd had too much coffee and couldn't fall sleep. We'd been alone and lonely and did a bit of soul sharing.

Mindy waits, her expression reflecting patience and understanding. She's worked with many artists. I'm sure she's heard it all. Life is messy. Art is our way of making sense of the chaos. And I know she understands grief.

I have to be honest with her even if it's an old wound that is still deep enough to draw blood with the merest swipe. I have to get accustomed to questions like this. If I experience even a modicum of success, it's going to come up again.

"When I was young, I had this friend Kevin." I look down into my coffee cup. "He died when we were both sixteen. He . . . killed himself." Even though the song is about his death, it's difficult to admit how he died, how much he was struggling, and how little I was aware of it. I was his best friend and didn't help him.

A loaded silence descends. I resist the urge to scrub my sweating palms on my jeans.

What is she thinking?

When I finally meet her gaze, instead of pity, there's a glint of respect.

She takes a breath. "I'm really sorry. I know how—" she breaks off, her gaze shooting to the side. She swallows and meets my eyes. "My sister Aria died when she was fifteen. To lose someone close to you, and so young. . . it changes you on a molecular level that's hard to explain to people who haven't experienced it."

Surprise and relief root me to my seat. "Yes."

She gets it. I knew she would. I knew she must have experienced something tragic based on the interview I'd read, but I didn't know the depth of the loss. Her sister. Fifteen.

"When I first listened to it, I thought it was about a lost love, a romantic love interest or something, but then, I caught on that you were opening it to other interpretations. Which is great, because really the listener can apply whatever meaning they want. A lot of people will be able to relate to it."

I nod and rub at a smudge on the table. "It's about making mistakes, losing someone too soon. It's about the guilt and the confusion that cling like a second skin and weigh us down, preventing us from moving forward."

She doesn't speak for a few long seconds.

I look up. Our eyes lock, and recognition shoots along the connection between us, two soldiers comparing battle scars.

Her eyes are beautiful, dark, bright with intelligence. With a decisive nod, she speaks. "I have a proposal for you to review." She severs the connection, pulling a stack of paperwork out of the folder in her hand.

She sets it in front of me, bound together by a gold binder clip latched at the top.

I scan down the first page. There is a lot of legalese: the *initial contract period, Outfoxed Records agrees to produce master recordings consisting of songs written and performed by*, and then a blank spot for the artist's name. "Are you . . . is this an offer to sign me? To a label called Outfoxed Records?" A smile tugs at my lips. "I like it. The play on your name." Not to mention the deeper meaning, how she's outfoxing those who have underestimated her.

"Yes." Her chin lifts. "I'm going to be upfront with you. No one in the industry will hire me, and I'm sure you're aware of the reason why. I understand if you don't want to work with me because of my reputation, but I need to know now if that's a hard line for you. I will give you time to review the contract, but since you met with me, I'm assuming it's not going to be an immediate no. I'm not sure if my notoriety will help or hinder this endeavor, but I can promise you that no one will work as hard as I will to launch a successful album and, hopefully, a long-term career."

I tap a finger on the table. "I know your reputation, and you just confirmed it."

Her lips tighten.

Before she gets the wrong idea, I continue. "You're honest, persistent, and you treat your artists with fairness and consideration," I add.

Her shoulders relax a smidge, barely noticeable if I wasn't so tuned in to her every movement.

"We can go over the contract now, and then if you want to have a lawyer or someone else look it over before you make a decision, that's perfectly acceptable. However,

I do ask to have an answer in a week. If you pass, I need to start exploring other options."

"That sounds fair enough."

She nods and pulls out another bundle of paperwork from her briefcase. "I have a copy here, so you can take that one with you. I also have some questions for you, and I'm sure you'll have some for me." She takes a breath, shuffling the papers and getting them in order before continuing. "How many songs do you have ready for development?"

I think about the answer, shuffling a list in my mind, the notes running through my head. "Twenty in a notebook, another ten in my head, most in various stages of completion."

She purses her lips. "We can work with that."

"It's been difficult to create since I've been in the city."

A lame excuse but the truth.

"How long have you lived here?"

"Nearly a year." I shuffle the paper in my hand, trying to focus on the words on the page. There are sections for costs, dates and location of the recording sessions, licensing, distribution, copyright, royalty rate, among others.

"This is a better rate than industry standard." I point at the percentage on the page. Most artists get about 13%-16% royalties. This shows 30%. Even big artists with established fan bases don't get more than 18%.

"We're both taking a risk here, and I wanted the contract to reflect that. You'll notice there's no sign-on money. I don't have the capital for that, so instead I'm offering a higher rate on accrued royalties. I will take care of all production costs, including room and board while we're in development. In addition, you'll see in Subsection E, the type of music recorded, the artistic vision for your album will be a mutual decision."

Another surprise. Most labels offer limited creative control to their artists.

I read through the section that outlines our production schedule. "We're not recording in the city?"

She shakes her head. "We're going to my family's property, the one I told you about earlier."

I reach back into my mind and pluck out the name. "Whitby."

"Yes. It's quiet and remote."

"Even with the kids camp?"

"No kids, at least not yet. They completed construction recently and they'll be running a short winter camp, but that's not for a couple months. I have top-of-the-line equipment being delivered to Whitby by the end of this week and a producer confirmed for about three weeks from now."

I digest that information and then offer, "I have some recording equipment, but it's midgrade."

"Bring it. It's always good to have backup."

We sit in silence for a few minutes while I peruse the document, trying to absorb everything on the page. Every few seconds, I lose focus and have to reread.

I'm intensely aware of Mindy's regard. Not that she's staring at me like a creep or anything. She's sipping her coffee, making notations on her copy of the contract, but there's something about her that captivates me. It's like an invisible string wrapped around my midsection, tugging with an almost delicate pressure and yet strong as a steel chain.

On page four, one of the bolded headings snags my attention: *Public Performances.*

My gut clenches. The anxiety that had been ebbing away as our conversation progressed spikes through the ceiling.

I knew singing in front of people would be inevitable, and yet I've managed to mostly avoid it for the past year. I want to be a songwriter. I want people to listen to my songs and hire me to write—not sing.

Mindy is the only person who's even cared enough to listen.

I have to sign this.

But there will be no backing out. No more excuses. No more *I'll try again tomorrow.* I have to make the commitment and see it through.

"Tell me what you envision for your first album. Do you have any thoughts on what the feel of it should be?"

"I would like it to be acoustic, mostly. I want the focus to be on the lyrics."

She considers me for a second and then nods. "I was thinking the same. You have a specific sound that fits with the acoustic rock market, similar to Jack White and maybe The Head and the Heart."

Before this gets any further, I really need to tell her about my not-so-little problem.

"You know, I really want to be a songwriter."

Her forehead creases. "But you have a great voice. Why wouldn't you want to sing your own songs?"

She's right. It's a ridiculous question. Who wouldn't

want the fame and adulation that come along with singing in front of a crowd?

Me. It's me.

"I'm not really in it for the applause. Attention makes me a little uncomfortable."

She shrugs. "So you're not Lady Gaga. Who is? Once you've proven your worth as a songwriter, you'll have people knocking down your door for a chance to work with you. But we have to get your name out there first. They have to hear it and know you can create something marketable."

I nod and return to reading the contract. I already know this. I've learned over the past year that a singer who doesn't write is a lot easier to sell than a songwriter who doesn't sing.

The terms are all aboveboard. I've done enough research on what a typical label offers, and although I'm not getting a sign-on bonus, the royalty rate and marketing she's committed to are more than most artists get. Of course, I understand her reasoning—we're both taking a big risk, but considering my . . . limitations, she's taking the bigger risk.

I need to tell her the truth, but the words cling to my tongue, refusing to budge.

I'll shove them out quick, like ripping off a bandage. It's five words, max.

I have crippling stage fright.

After taking a fortifying sip of coffee, I open my mouth. "I'll do it. I'll sign."

Wrong five words.

Her eyes widen. "Really? Are you sure you don't want

to read it over more, have someone else double-check, like an attorney?"

"I'm sure." I have an almost perfect memory, which was very helpful during medical school. One more read-through when I'm not being hammered with the force of her presence, and I could recite this thing in my sleep.

"That's wonderful. I mean great." She smiles then, but calling it a mere smile is like calling the vastness of the universe *big*.

It's a true grin, one that reaches her eyes and sets her entire face alight. Having its force directed at me is like being struck by lightning.

After a minute of being blinded, I return to my body.

" . . . timeline is tight, but I think if we work together on really fine-tuning at least sixteen songs for a decent LP before the producer arrives, we'll be able to pick the best and then knock out the album in a week or less. We won't need a lot of overdubs or vocals because your voice is so strong."

I clear my throat. "Thanks. That sounds great. So, when do we leave?"

Chapter Seven

Luke

A week after my fateful meeting with Mindy at Think Coffee, we're driving to Whitby. We left the city behind over an hour ago with our suitcases, my guitar, and recording equipment loaded in the trunk.

"Tell me more about this kids camp. What made your sister decide to change up the family business?" I shift in the plush leather passenger seat of the Cadillac Escalade and angle myself toward Mindy.

"It's complicated." She changes lanes, glancing over her shoulder before returning her eyes to the road. She's dressed down in jeans and a long-sleeve black T-shirt that caresses all her curves.

I've never seen her dressed so casually. All of our encounters up to this point have been professional. She's always dressed up in perfectly tailored suits and immaculately applied makeup, hair salon fresh. Now she's . . .real.

It's more than a little intoxicating. I can barely keep my eyes focused on the pastoral settings rushing by the windows because my gaze is constantly drawn to her profile: her pert nose, her firm chin, the way her hair tucks behind her ear and traces to her jaw, as if the strands can't bear to be parted from her skin.

The drive has been lush with reds and golds and bright yellows, a tapestry of fall. But I'm not sure any of it is as lush as the thickness of her bottom lip.

Get a grip.

I can't let this fascination with Mindy Fox—and her lips—affect our mutual goals.

"I'm sure I can keep up." Plus I need a distraction, and not just from her mouth. I'm already anticipating how it's going to go when I inevitably have to sing her more of my songs—which I promised to do shortly after we settle in.

On top of everything else, saying goodbye to Walter this morning, even temporarily, was brutal. He acted like it was no big deal, like he would be just fine without me. He even said it—*I was fine before you moved into this dump, I'll be fine after*—but there was a glint in his eyes that belied his words. Who's he going to talk to? Who's going to bring him sandwiches and make sure he takes his blood pressure medication?

"It used to be Fox Cottages, which was basically a bunch of short-term rental cabins."

I push my worries to the side and turn my focus to Mindy. I am intensely curious about her, her past, her family, all of it. My eyes trace down the soft curve of her neck to her shoulder.

Stop gawking.

I direct my attention out the windshield in front of us.

"The buildings were old and outdated, and after some of the nearby ski resorts updated their facilities, it got harder and harder to attract customers. Finley did her best to keep things afloat, but once rents were down it was bleeding money—which of course she never shared with the rest of the family. Finley has a tendency to carry the world on her shoulders." She shakes her head with a sigh.

"She's the oldest?" I ask.

Mindy nods. "She's a year older than me. Anyway, Oliver had been pressuring Finley, sending a bunch of his business lackeys to get her to sell to him. He managed to buy up all of the parcels around ours, but she kept rejecting him." Her lip quirks. "Sometimes rather forcefully."

Oliver, I learned this morning, is Piper's boyfriend and the owner of the car we're currently in. Apparently he has more than a few vehicles lying around to loan out.

"Why didn't she want to sell?"

Mindy taps the steering wheel with a finger, contemplating her response. "After Dad died, we all signed the property over to Finley. She was the most invested in keeping it alive. It was her coping mechanism. She and Jake were the only ones who stayed. I couldn't—it was hard to be there, after everything."

I swallow, resisting the urge to reach over and touch her, to offer comfort. I understand more than she can possibly realize. "I get it. After Kevin died, about a year later, we moved away. It was a relief. It was too hard to remember. I would catch glimpses of him around every bend."

We share a glance and something in my chest squeezes and releases before she looks back at the road.

She clears her throat. "Then, Oliver sent in Archer."

"Archer is Finley's boyfriend, right? He lives there now?"

She nods. "Yep. Archer is a master negotiator. He can close any deal. He was tasked with convincing Finley to sell to Oliver, but instead he fell head over heels for her." The corner of her mouth quirks. "Oliver and Finley eventually came to a joint ownership agreement—something laid out by Archer to make both of them happy. Finley didn't have to move or sell our family property, and Oliver got the camp he'd been gunning for."

"Everyone wins."

"In this case, yes. Most importantly, my sister is happy. My brother, though—"

Her phone dings.

It's resting in a holder on the dash, and the notification snags my attention. The actual text conversation isn't visible, only the sender's name.

Blake.

There's no last name, but it doesn't take a genius to figure it out.

A muscle in her jaw twitches. She reaches over and pushes a button that turns the screen black before gripping the steering wheel with both hands like she expects it to jump out of the car.

Curiosity tugs at me. Are they still in contact with each other? She hasn't said anything about it other than alluding to her damaged reputation last week. I had the impression they weren't a thing anymore, especially considering all the media attention around his wife's pregnancy and the fact that Mindy's still strangling the steering wheel.

"What were you saying about your brother?" I ask, a not-so-subtle attempt to distract.

"It's nothing." The words are delivered wrapped in frost.

I fall silent, not wanting to push.

An invisible barrier erects itself between us, growing thicker and thicker with each passing mile.

I'm staring out the window, contemplating what will happen when I finally have to sing in front of her. Will I throw up, pee my pants, or black out? The choices truly are endless, and all lead to my inevitable humiliation.

She clears her throat. "This goes without saying, but I've had bad luck in the past mixing my work with . . . other, more personal parts of my life, so we have to keep everything as professional as possible." Her jaw is set, but there's something vulnerable in the way she's holding herself, in the rigid line of her shoulders. Like she's waiting for my judgment of her history. My eyes drift over to the phone on the dash, the screen still dark.

Or current events.

"Should we put it in the contract?"

She almost smiles. One corner of her mouth twitches and she pretends to consider it. "That's not the worst idea."

A crack forms in the wall between us. A small one.

"Don't worry. I would never do anything to compromise our working relationship. You're the only person who wants to work with me. I would never do anything to ruin things with my one fan."

"Thank you. And I'm sorry. I don't mean to make anything weird or uncomfortable, that's the opposite of what I want. We're going to be working together really closely over the next month and beyond, and I want us to be friends."

I nod. "I understand. I appreciate your honesty. I want us to be friends, too."

She clicks on some soft music and the miles pass in relative silence, but at least the strain has left the car.

She slows down as we approach the town limits and the sign announcing Whitby, population 1,803.

We pass a barn-shaped hardware store and drive slowly through a town center boasting an idyllic row of shops along Main Street: a bakery, a grocery store, a restaurant, a barber, and a few others before the buildings thin out and nothing but soaring pines line the road, stretching out in front of us.

A few miles outside of town, Mindy slows the vehicle, and we turn onto a paved driveway. A rustic wood sign faces the street: "Camp Aria," it reads, in bright blue cursive lettering.

The narrow road forks, and we head to the left, curving up an inclined drive. Outside my passenger window, the road to the right narrows and tapers into a cobblestone street lined on either side with quaint, colorful cottages.

The view is brief, and seconds later Mindy brings the SUV to a halt.

I peer up at the asymmetrical structure looming over us.

The wooden porch has been painted a light bluish-gray color and appears relatively new, a contrast to the building surging up behind it.

I step out of the car, stretching my legs and peering up at the house. It's a large two-story home, built with a variety of materials like dark wood and red brick, topped with a splash of stucco. I've barely had a chance to take it all in when a figure comes speed-walking around the corner.

It's a guy with dark hair, maybe a couple of years younger than me. His clothes are covered in mud, and he's holding a red rag around his hand, held up in front of his chest.

He winces, and I zero in on his tense shoulders and the strain bracketing his features.

Wait. That's not a red rag. It's stained with his blood.

Chapter Eight

MINDY

"Jake?" I call out, coming around the side of the car and jogging over to him. He's muddy and disheveled and my stomach turns at the blood seeping through the cloth wrapped around his hand.

"Are you okay? What happened?"

Luke's footsteps tread behind me.

Jake glances over my shoulder and then shakes his head. "It's fine. I just cut my hand."

"You're covered in mud," I say.

"Gee, thanks. I wasn't aware." His tone is dry.

"Jake." I put on my big-sister voice, but it has little effect.

"Can we talk about this inside? I need to get cleaned up and see if this thing needs stitches."

I resist the urge to growl at him. "Fine. Let's go check

out your hand. Jake, this is Luke Fletcher." I follow Jake up the porch steps, gesturing to Luke behind me.

Jake dips his head in Luke's direction. "Hey, man."

"Nice to meet you," Luke replies, following us into the house. "I can take a look at that cut if you want. Do you have a first-aid kit?"

We walk inside and then through the front office.

"I think there's one in the kitchen," Jake says.

An interior door leads us into the main part of the house and through the open living area. Off to one side, the staircase leads up to the bedrooms. We pass by the giant dining table on our way to the kitchen.

New flooring stretches into these rooms, and the kitchen has new granite counters and gleaming white cabinets. I barely recognize it. At least in the living room, the ancient wood paneling still covers the walls. Even though it's old and dated, it's familiar and somehow comforting.

Jake moves to the sink, unwinding the wrapping around his hand.

I follow right behind him, peering over his shoulder.

He twists his head to scowl at me. "Will you stop hovering and grab the first-aid kit? I think Archer put it in the cupboard over the fridge."

I huff but turn around to comply.

Before I can take more than a single step, Luke holds up a hand. "I can get it. You'd probably have to climb up on the counters to reach."

"Thank you." I spin around to Jake and move to his side. "Let Luke look at it, he's a doctor."

Jake frowns down at the sink. "I thought you said he was a musician."

"I am a man of many talents." Luke sets the first-aid kit on the counter and pops it open, assessing the contents. He nods at Jake. "Run that bad boy under some warm water to clear off the blood and I can assess how deep the laceration is. What did you cut it on?"

Jake flicks on the sink and slides his hand under the water, washing off the blood, some of which has dried to a dark brown. He hisses quietly. "An old tractor."

"When did you last have a tetanus shot?"

"I'm not sure. I think I was in high school. Maybe a senior?"

Luke slides on a pair of rubber gloves. "They're good for years."

"Then I'm golden." Jake turns off the faucet.

Luke holds out a hand. "May I?"

Jake nods and gives him his hand.

Luke examines the wound, probing it gently with one of his glove-covered fingers. "Have you been applying pressure?"

"Yes."

"How long ago did you injure it?"

"Maybe ten, fifteen minutes."

I take a step closer to them. "What tractor did you cut it on?"

Jake glances over at me. "The old run-down piece of junk over in that field bordering Bernie and Estelle's place. Which now, I guess, is all our property."

I wrinkle my nose at his mud-splattered clothes. "How did you get all dirty?"

"Oh, you know, I decided to stop on the way home for a relaxing mud bath."

I snort out a laugh and then give him my best I'm-your-big-sister-don't-prevaricate-with-me tone. "Jacob."

He lifts his free hand. "I fell off the tractor, cut my hand, and fell in a puddle. You really think I want to give you a play-by-play of my most graceful moment?"

I sigh.

He turns his attention back to Luke. "Will it need stitches?"

"It's stopped bleeding, so probably not. I'll irrigate it a little before I patch you up, make sure there are no lingering bacteria."

"Why were you out at the tractor?" I ask Jake.

Jake winces as Luke sets his hand over the sink and uses a bottle of saline to rinse it out. "Piper called the other day, and I told her I would get more pieces off it for something she's working on."

Luke chats easily with Jake, discussing Piper and her upcoming art show.

Now that I know Jake isn't in any real mortal danger, some of the tension in my body releases.

Luke patches him up, his movements confident and capable, and my thoughts slip back to the drive here, heat flushing through me when I recall my little speech about keeping things professional.

I had to say *something*. He was mere inches from me for three full hours, just lounging there like some kind of golden lion, all relaxed and self-assured, asking me questions and gazing at me like he actually cared about the answers.

It uncoiled something inside me, a dark, nebulous current of wonder and longing. It was very . . . alarming.

Almost as alarming as receiving a text from Blake, a message that was a timely reminder of all the very good reasons I shouldn't be having personal conversations with my very attractive client. There is too much on the line. I have too much to lose.

Blake hasn't reached out to me at all since everything ended.

As much as I dread eventually reading his message, a small part of me is burning with curiosity. Why now? What does he want?

I tune back in to Luke and Jake's conversation, Luke telling him to keep the bandages on for a few hours and clean and apply ointment before he goes to sleep.

Jake winces down at his muck-splattered shirt. "I really need to shower."

"Try not to get water into it. Tape a bag around it or something."

"Got it. Thanks, man."

"No problem at all."

Jake rubs the back of his head with his good hand. "You want food? There's sandwich stuff in the fridge, and we also stocked food in the cabin if you'd rather head that way to get settled."

"That's a good idea." I look over at Luke for confirmation. "That way we can get to work after lunch and get a few hours in."

Some emotion resembling horror flickers across his face, gone so fast I must have imagined it. "That sounds great."

"You'll be over where cabin twelve used to be, down at the end of the line." He points to a side entrance. "Keys are there, the one with the Garfield keychain. Oh, and take one of the golf carts, too. They're all parked by the storage shed. That way Luke can get around the property without having to walk for miles."

"Perfect. Thanks, Jakey. Where are Finley and Archer?" I ask.

"Doing laundry." He shudders. "Do not try to find them. That way lies trauma."

I chuckle. "Thanks for the warning."

He salutes, exiting the kitchen and heading upstairs to shower.

I grab the Garfield keychain and a set of cart keys and we exit out the side door.

Once it's shut behind us, I turn to Luke. "Thanks for helping bandage him up."

"It's nothing."

I hand him the keys to the golf cart and gesture over to where two of them are parked, just across the drive in a small dirt-packed lot. "Follow me. We can unload your things, then meet up again in a couple of hours after we've settled in to get to work."

"Sounds good."

Making my way around the side of the house, I grab my phone out of my sweater pocket as I walk.

I hesitate before opening it. Maybe I shouldn't even read it. Maybe I should delete it and then block his ass.

What could he possibly want from me now?

Curiosity gets the best of me.

I miss you.

My feet bring me to a screeching halt before I run into the driver's door of the SUV. I stare down at the three words, my heart hammering in my ears.

What the hell?

I slam into the SUV, tossing the phone onto the passenger seat, then shut my eyes and take a deep breath to calm my racing blood and relax my suddenly ragged breathing.

Luke is parked at the corner of the house, waiting for me to precede him. Our eyes lock through the windshield and he waves, oblivious to the storm going on inside me.

Putting the car in drive, I head back down the driveway the way we came in.

My body vibrates with tension.

How dare he?

It's like he knows, somehow, that I've moved on. This is supposed to be a fresh start, a new opportunity, a chance to follow my dreams on my terms.

I have zero intention to reply, not even to tell him to fuck off. I want nothing to do with him. I'll just ignore his ass. A good ghosting is exactly what he deserves.

Around me, the property I grew up on has been transformed, but I can barely concentrate to take it all in through the red haze of anger clouding my vision.

No. I won't let him ruin this. I take a deep breath and focus on my surroundings.

Where there used to be dilapidated bungalows and

run-down cottages, there are now brightly painted cabins and chalets. Everything has either been refurbished to a glossy shine or razed and rebuilt. New trees and bushes dot the spaces between the buildings, adding pops of fall colors, from deep reds to bright yellows. The cobblestone driveway makes the space feel like we've stepped into some kind of fairy-tale camp.

It's truly incredible.

Pride for my family pushes through my irritation and frustration.

Cabin twelve is all new construction. What used to be a sagging one-room A-frame is now a Craftsman bungalow painted a cool gray with red accents, sporting a pitched gable roof, a covered porch lined with tapered columns, and a cherry wood door.

I click a button to pop the trunk, and Luke is already there, grabbing his bag, the cart parked behind me.

I run up the porch to unlock the front door.

"Thanks." He passes by me into the house. His scent blows by with him, the same aroma that taunted me on the drive here. Like sandalwood and soap. It's simple, not like Blake and his exotic overpriced cologne.

Stop thinking about him.

My gaze dips to Luke's firm rear, outlined perfectly in his jeans as he walks into the kitchen, to the left of the entry.

Damn. Don't think about that, either.

I shut my eyes. I will not exchange one mistake for another.

Spinning around, I head back to the SUV.

Hauling the recording equipment into the cabin gives

me a few minutes to pull myself together and calm my irritation. By the time we're done, I'm ready to have a normal conversation.

"This is a nice setup." Luke stuffs his hands in his pockets, his eyes trailing over the open-concept living and kitchen areas. The galley kitchen is small, but the appliances are up to date, the counters are pale granite, and the cupboards match the cherry wood front door. There's an island between the kitchen and the living room with three cushioned bar stools.

The living room is sparsely decorated, with one overstuffed couch and chair bordered by end tables and facing a gas fireplace.

A spiral staircase between the two rooms curves up to an open loft, where the edge of a comforter peeks out.

"Do you need—"

The stomp of footsteps running across the patio derails my question, the front door flies open, and my sister bursts into the room, throwing her arms around me.

"You're here!"

Behind her, Archer shakes Luke's hand. Archer is as broad as a tank. His giant mitt engulfs Luke's more slender fingers. They move into the kitchen, where Archer points out where he can find supplies.

"I am here."

Finley pulls back, her hands still clutching my shoulders. "I'm so glad you made it. I have so much to show you, and we have so much catching up to do. You have some time today, right? I haven't seen you in months."

She smiles, but the tension strains her features. Her back is ramrod straight, her shoulders rigid.

"What's wrong?"

Her smile brightens. "It's nothing. I just," she glances over her shoulder at Archer and then lowers her voice, "I need some sister time. We talk on the phone, but it's not the same."

"I know. You're absolutely right. We can hang out now." I have to make time for Finley. I'm sure she wants to vent more about Jake, not to mention the massive amount of work she's been doing to get this place in order for the upcoming camp, and who knows what else.

Yet, despite the inevitable stress from all of it, she looks fantastic. She's practically glowing, even dressed in ratty old overalls and a faded long-sleeved flannel, her hair pulled back in braids with a beanie on her head to ward off the chill.

"Can I show you around now, or did you want to settle in back at the house first?"

Before I can come up with a reply, Archer strides over and gives me a side hug. "We've cleaned out your old room. We could turn up the heat in the cabin next door if you'd rather stay there? At least until your producer friend arrives."

"No, it's fine. I want to stay in the house with everyone." I turn to catch Luke's eye. "We should probably put off our work until tomorrow then."

Relief glimmers on his face. "That's fine. I can write out some of the songs I have up here." He taps the side of his head.

Is he relieved to get away from me?

I flick the thought away. It doesn't matter.

An hour and a half later, Finley has dragged me from one side of the property to the other, showing me the facilities.

"I am so impressed with everything you've accomplished. I can't believe how quickly all of this was built." I gesture to the art building we just exited.

She beams. "It helps that my not-so-silent partner is rich and lets me do nearly anything I want."

"This is going to be a great place for kids to escape, have fun, and learn skills."

We get back into the golf cart and she heads us back toward the house.

Not only is there an ice rink, a paintball course, fire pits, and a vast amount of wooded property for the kids to explore, but they have a whole restaurant-grade kitchen for meal preparation that also has stations where the kids will be taught how to cook and prep their own food. They have a garden area for spring, so some of the fruits and veggies can be grown on-site. There is another small building outfitted with a kiln and art supplies for painting, drawing, and sculpting.

"How has Jake been doing?" I ask.

Except for the cut on his hand, he seemed normal and healthy to me when we arrived, but we only spoke briefly and mostly about his injury. Not to mention my eyes were drawn more to the doctor than to the patient.

I swallow and shove the thoughts aside, focusing on Finley's response.

"Better. I think. He's been really helpful with work and whatnot around the camp, but I'm not sure if this is what he wants to do with his life." She worries her bottom lip. "I'm not sure he knows what he wants to do. He's just sort of aimless."

"He's also only . He doesn't have to know anything yet."

She huffs out a short laugh. "Taylor is only twenty-six. You never cease giving her all kinds of shit for her wandering ways."

I wave a hand. "That's different. Jake has a purpose here and contributes even if it isn't his ultimate life goal to help you run the camp. Taylor chooses the life of a mooching vagabond." I don't want to talk about Taylor, so I change the subject. "Have you asked Jake what he wants to do?"

Her nose wrinkles. "You know how he is. It's hard to get much out of him. Except, well, there was one thing that was kind of surprising I did need to talk to you about." She brings the cart to a slow stop and cuts the engine.

If she's pulling over, it must be serious.

"What is it?"

She shuts off the cart and shifts to face me. "While everyone is here, after Thanksgiving, and after you have things sorted with Luke, we were thinking we can take a day to go through Dad's room and clear some of it out."

I stare at her, surprise winging through me. "Really? Everyone is onboard with this? Even Jake?"

She nods. "It was his idea."

"Wow." I'm stunned.

We rarely talk about Dad anymore. I can't believe Jake wants to sort through his things.

Both Dad's and Aria's rooms have remained untouched and unused since they passed. Jake can't even bring himself to say Aria's name out loud. Maybe he is doing better.

Finley reaches out, putting a hand on my arm. "He's right that it's time for us to move on. Past time."

"What about," I lower my voice, "Aria's room?"

She shakes her head. "Not yet. But we need to move forward in some way, for all our sakes. Don't you think?"

I nod. "Absolutely. Of course, I'll help however you want me to."

She squeezes my hand. "Thanks, Mindy."

Chapter Nine

Luke

Mindy will be here in fifteen minutes and I've already sweated through two T-shirts.

I tug a fresh shirt over my head, moving the phone back to my ear.

"Now, just take a few deep breaths," Granny Bea tells me. "You have nothing to be concerned about."

I have everything to be concerned about.

Calling Granny Bea is an attempt to distract myself, but so far she has only decreased my anxiety by about five percent.

"Talk to me about something else. Anything else." I pace back and forth in the living room in front of the couch.

"Over Thanksgiving, I'm counting on you to make sure I don't drink too much and insult your father."

My lips quirk. "Gran, you haven't had a drink since last century."

"Doesn't mean I won't start up again. If anyone can drive me to it, it's your parents."

"Are you sure it wouldn't be me driving you to it? And all my bad decisions?"

Granny Bea didn't so much as blink when I gave up my job as a highly paid ER physician and moved to New York City to be a penniless songwriter. My parents thought I had lost my mind.

Maybe I did.

She huffs. "No. You're young. Stupidity is expected. Following your dreams is anything but stupid. Once you reach middle age, there can be no more excuses. Your parents put more emphasis on having bragging rights than on your happiness."

A light knock halts my steps mid-pace.

My heart flips and lodges itself in my throat. "I have to go. Mindy's here," I manage to croak. She's five minutes early. We are supposed to start at .

"Luke." Granny Bea's voice slips into a seriousness I've only heard twice before in my life: once when Kevin died and the second time when I left medicine to pursue this madness. "You're an incredible songwriter. You're talented and you know how to sing. She wouldn't have wanted you otherwise. Why don't you tell her the truth?"

I ignore the question. She's going to figure out the truth right now. "I have to go, she's waiting, but thanks, Granny Bea. I'll call you later. Love you."

"Love you, too."

I slip the phone in my pocket and open the door.

Mindy's wearing dark jeans that mold to her hips, tan boots with furry edges, and a light T-shirt under a zip-up sweater, the hood pulled up over her head.

The mere sight of her shoots a bolt of lust straight to my center that's almost enough to overpower my nerves.

"Are you ready to get started? I'm so excited." She clutches the strap of a canvas messenger bag, unaware of my inner turmoil, and passes me on her way into the house.

I shut the door, hanging onto the knob for a few seconds, taking a deep breath before I turn around. I can do this.

"I can't wait to hear your other songs." She's already set her bag on the coffee table. Shrugging off her sweater, she drapes it over the back of the chair set to the right of the sofa.

She pulls out a laptop from her bag and powers it on. "I want to hear everything you've got, and I'll make a list so we can decide which ones to work on before the producer arrives in two weeks."

She's rested, excited, eager, almost glowing. It's like she's taken off the cloak of responsibilities and the things weighing her down. She's in her element.

I'm ready to throw up, pass out, and possibly expire from supraventricular tachycardia, if the racing of my heart is any indication.

Grabbing my guitar from where it's resting against the side of the couch, I sit and try to remember to breathe.

I grip the neck, attempting to mask the tremors in my hands.

Why is it that in a life-or-death situation I remain calm

with the steadiest of hands and the greatest self-assurance, but give me a guitar and sit me down in front of a near stranger and my composure cracks into pieces?

I strum a few chords, my fingers missing the mark twice, then I halt, take a deep breath, and try again. The second attempt is better, for a few seconds. My fingers won't cooperate, as they've turned into sausages topped with marshmallows. I have to do this. Sweat beads along my hairline.

I sing, but my voice cracks and wobbles, unable to hit the right pitch. I cut off abruptly. "I'm sorry. I can't do this."

Mindy's brows are drawn in confusion. "What do you mean?"

"I can't sing."

She frowns. "What are you talking about? I've heard you sing. Those recordings you sent me . . . ." Her eyes widen, alarm blanching her face. "Was that someone else? Did you fake—"

"No, no, no." I rush to assure her. "It was me. I'm sorry." I blow out a breath and set the guitar to the side, running both hands through my hair and holding my head. "I misspoke. I *can* sing; it is me singing on the recordings I sent you. It's only that, I have to be alone or I just-I can't." My hands release my hair, clenching in my lap. "I have a problem with singing in front of other people," I finish. The words emerge stilted and awkward.

She sits back in the chair, her mouth popping open. "Other people? Like, at all?"

My stomach twists itself into knots. "I've sung in front of my parents and Granny Bea, but I know them really well. The only other person I've been able to play in front of is Walter."

"Who's Walter?"

"He lives in the building I was staying in, in New York."

She stares at me, emotions flickering across her face. Concern, confusion, worry, and then she leans forward, elbows on her knees, fingers rubbing at her temples. "Why didn't you tell me?"

"I should have. I thought I could do this."

"You thought? Past tense?"

"I think I can. I know I can, I just might need a little . . . time."

She stands, moving in front of the couch and pacing the same line I had been tracing all morning. "We don't have time, Luke, we have deadlines."

I groan, flopping back against the couch. "I know. I've been trying. Every day I went to the park and watched buskers. I tried to play in less populated areas of the park, but every time my throat would close up, my palms would sweat, nausea would overwhelm me, and I couldn't do a damn thing about it."

She stops pacing and blows out a breath, eyes falling shut for a couple of seconds before opening again. "That's all very Eminem *8 Mile* of you, but it's okay. We can work on it." Her words are positive, but her voice is getting higher and squeakier with each passing word. "Barbra Streisand has crippling stage fright; did you know that?"

"No."

Her head bobs. "She went blank in front of 150,000 people in Central Park," she releases a short, nervous laugh, "and she was not able to recover. She left the stage, just bailed. If she can survive that, you can survive this." She points at me.

"I am definitely not Barbra Streisand."

"No. And you're not going to be playing in front of thousands of people, at least not initially. I've booked you much smaller venues. You're a new artist. We aren't ready for Madison Square Garden. But there are things we can do to mitigate your anxiety. Streisand had a rider that stipulated total blackness in the audience so she couldn't see them. That helped. We can do something like that, we can stage that. And more. We can work on this."

I blink. "We can?"

"How did you practice? To be able to play in front of Walter, I mean." Her hands clench at her sides.

Oddly, my heart rate has slowed the slightest bit, as if releasing the burden of carrying around this secret, without the world collapsing on me, has done some part in reducing the pressure in my chest. I swallow, my mouth still dry. "He would listen to me play from the hall outside my door where I couldn't see him."

She grimaces but nods. "Right. We can do that. I can do that. Then we can slowly have you play around other people."

"Okay. I'll do whatever it takes, I promise."

Her eyes search mine for a few seconds. "Is this why you asked about songwriting?"

I dip my head in acknowledgment. "Yes. That's always been my end goal."

"Right. Right. We can work with this. But you will need to fulfill the terms of your contract."

"I will. I promise."

She presses her lips together and then blows out a breath. "We can start slow, but it's going to be hard. I need you to promise me you'll do the very best you can. Can you do that?"

"I can. I'm sorry again. I know I should have mentioned it sooner—"

Her hand slices the air in front of her. "We can't look back. We have to move forward. Even if you had told me, honestly, I still would have signed you."

"Really?"

"This isn't a deal breaker. Besides," she sits next to me, "I need you. Or someone else with equal parts desperation and talent. And you have talent, Luke, don't forget that." She reaches over, her hand a slight weight on my forearm, gone after a brief second of contact.

Despite the apprehension of the past fifteen minutes, her simple touch triggers a shock of awareness, zipping up my arm before spreading heat through the rest of me.

Pull it together, Luke.

"Thank you for being so understanding. I hope you're also very patient." I glance around. "Any ideas on where you can hide from view?"

Chapter Ten

MINDY

I can't believe I'm sitting on the floor in the kitchen, out of sight, waiting for Luke to play for me. This is not how I envisioned this going.

The day started out great. Finley made breakfast. I ate eggs and pancakes with my family for the first time in months. Jake was his silly, goofy self. Archer and Finley were annoyingly in love. It was fantastic.

Plus, I've been looking forward to working with Luke since I first listened to him sing.

My ears perk up when he plucks at the strings and jaunty notes flick through the air. It sounds better than his attempts when I was in the room with him.

He plays for a few minutes. Then a few minutes more. The tune is fun. Peppy. A little more complex than the chords from the other song I listened to. It sounds almost like a sea shanty or something.

I shift on the sofa pillow underneath me.

He's playing but not singing.

More time passes.

This might be bad. This might be very, very bad. What if this doesn't work?

I put on a brave face for Luke's benefit—this has to work. We've both signed this contract. We have to make this happen. There's no choice.

Part of me wanted to yell at him, but a much stronger part just couldn't. His face was miserably adorable, brows furrowed, eyes dark with guilt. It would be like shouting at a puppy. There's something about Luke that makes it hard to hang onto any kind of anger. He's so authentic and somehow charming. Even in his mortification he was boyishly earnest.

The chords are getting stronger, more assured.

Please don't let this all be a giant mistake.

He sings. Low, at first, almost inaudible. Then louder.

His voice breaks, but without a pause in the strum of the guitar, he starts over. Again and again. Even when his words stutter and stumble, he keeps going, he keeps trying.

The persistence is promising. I have to trust that he meant it when he said he would fulfill the terms of the contract. Failure is not an option.

Then he finally sings.

It will all be okay
As long as you pay pay pay
Give us all your money

Plus your blood sweat and tears
Don't worry about morals or scruples
No need for that nonsense here

I cover my mouth with my hand to stop the surprised laugh from escaping. He's still playing. The song changes, the tune morphing between one chord and the next into one of the songs I've already heard.

He keeps going, segueing into new songs, different bits and pieces. I prop my head back against the cabinet, shut my eyes, and listen, letting his voice flow over me.

The stress of the past half-hour ebbs with each passing moment. His voice is truly incredible. Low and soothing, it's like a deep velvet stroke brushing against my skin.

I pick up my laptop and start jotting down notes.

When the last chord strikes and his voice tapers off, silence permeates the room. My ass is numb, but I'm a lot more hopeful about this collaboration than I was thirty minutes ago.

"Mindy?"

"Yes. I'm here." I push myself to stand. "That was great."

Relief rolls over his face, his shoulders dropping as the tension releases. "Thanks."

I walk over and sit back in the chair, picking up my laptop. "How do you feel?"

"Like I've been run over by a truck. But also relieved." He scrubs a hand over his jaw.

My eyes trace over the movements.

God, he has great hands. Strong forearms, too.

I clear my throat and click something on my laptop that opens a window I don't need. "How many songs was that? I think about fifteen?"

He nods. "The first one isn't a real song, though. It's just something I came up with during residency after staying awake for three days."

I click rapidly, trying to get to the screen I need without appearing distracted. "We need five more to work on, then we can let Jerry help us choose the top sixteen for the LP."

"I have most of them written down in here." He reaches over to the side table and picks up a leather-bound notebook, handing it to me.

I flip through it, noting the bold strokes, his penmanship neat and meticulous. "You have nice handwriting. I thought the ability to scribble was a requirement for the medical profession."

His mouth twitches. "One of the many reasons I wasn't a good fit."

I want to know more, want to ask why he left medicine, what were the many reasons? But instead, I press my lips together.

"Music can be healing, too," I say instead.

"That's true. It has definitely been a type of therapy for me. I struggled a lot after Kevin died, and I don't think I would have come through it without writing."

I nod, understanding more than he can possibly realize. After Aria died, I had so much guilt. Music was how I coped, along with throwing myself into my work.

Shaking the thoughts away, I focus on the present. Time to get back to business.

"Let's rank what you have by most complete to least. Then we'll work through them, one at a time, and get them as ready as possible for recording. That way we can make the best of the time we have with Jerry." Jerry can be a bit scattered and likes to dive down musical rabbit holes. When I've worked with him in the past, I've found it's best to be as organized as possible to keep him on track.

"Sounds like a plan." He smiles and the dimple appears in his cheek, making my stomach flip.

I swallow hard.

Just business.

Chapter Eleven

MINDY

The next week flies by in a flash despite the fact that our days are long and grueling and often last fourteen hours.

We even work during meals, eating and talking and bouncing ideas for lyrics and arrangements off each other. When we're not seeing to our basic needs, Luke practices playing for me, at first while I'm hiding in the kitchen, but after a day or two, he's able to sing with me sitting only a few feet away without issue.

Thank God.

It's great but also getting harder and harder to maintain my façade of keeping everything purely professional. I should have known better. Working side by side with artists is often incredibly personal. Music is emotion in rhythm. Songwriting is all about sharing bits of yourself, of shared human experiences. A sense of awareness hums between us, growing stronger and stronger with each passing day.

Not to mention the way coiled heat tenses in my belly every time he sends me a lopsided smile.

It doesn't matter.

We're working on song number seven when Jake comes barging into the cabin. "Knock, knock," he calls out, walking into the kitchen, arms loaded with grocery bags. "I come bearing sustenance."

Luke's playing cuts off abruptly, like a mute button being pushed.

I stand up to take one of the bags from Jake and set it on the counter. "Calling out 'knock, knock' as you walk into someone's home isn't the same as actually knocking," I tell him.

"I couldn't knock—my hands were full."

"Then how did you open the door?" I ask.

He lowers his voice. "With my mind."

I roll my eyes and poke through the contents of the bag. "Is there any more?"

"No. But before I forget, Finley wants you both to come to dinner tonight. Archer is making his famous lasagna. It's not great, but he makes enough to feed everyone in the county twice over, and I'm sick of eating the leftovers."

Luke and I share a glance.

"I'm not sure we have time," Luke says.

"Mindy," Jake pulls out a loaf of bread and points it at me, "stop turning Luke into one of your mindless workaholic drones."

I smack him on the shoulder. "I'm not. I was just

going to say we'll be there. As long as you're okay with that, Luke? I think you've earned a break. We don't want to burn out. Besides, rest nurtures creativity."

He nods in agreement. "Okay. Then I'm in."

~

We pull up to the side of the house right at five o'clock. Finley is standing outside the side door on the stoop, arms crossed over her chest, concern creasing her brow.

Jake passes her into the house first.

When Luke walks by, she smiles distractedly. "I'm glad you could come."

He enters the house in front of me. Then she meets my eyes and stops me with a hand on my arm. "There's something I didn't tell you about dinner."

"That sounds ominous. Are we dining on the souls of our enemies?"

She doesn't so much as smirk.

It must be bad. I frown.

A familiar voice calls from inside, the volume increasing as they move closer. "Did you move the plates? I can't find them in the cupboard by the—oh." Taylor stops in the open doorway, her eyes locking with mine.

I flick my gaze to Finley, who's biting her bottom lip, her cheeks flushed.

"Really?"

Finley grimaces. "I'm sorry."

"What, you didn't tell her I would be here? I mean, I'm her favorite punching bag, and you couldn't even give her a heads up to make sure she brings her boxing gloves?" Taylor props a hand on her hip.

She wants to fight, the urge outlined in the hard set of her jaw, the fire in her eyes.

It triggers a responding blaze in my gut along with a sharp arrow of guilt that I tug out and cast aside. I've been holding onto my anger at Taylor for so long I can't let go of it. It's become a part of me, the sticky glue holding all my shattered pieces together.

Finley rubs her temples. "No fighting, please. Can we have a nice family dinner?"

I shrug. "Maybe you should have found a nicer family."

"Hardy, har, har." She glares at me, then flips a pleading gaze to Taylor.

Taylor lifts her hands. "I'm not saying a word if she doesn't."

"Fine," I say.

"Fine," Taylor repeats, slightly louder.

Finley looks back and forth between us. "Good."

Taylor rolls her eyes, spinning around and stalking deeper into the house.

In the kitchen, Archer hands a bowl of freshly grated parmesan to Jake, who takes it into the dining room.

I shut the door behind me and pull off my jacket to hang it on the coat rack.

"Did you find the plates?" Finley calls.

"Yeah. Luke has them. We're setting the table now," Taylor calls back.

Luke says something, the words unintelligible over the sound of Archer and Finley in the kitchen and the humming of the fan over the oven, but his voice is a recognizable tug in my midsection.

So is Taylor's responding giggle, but for entirely different reasons.

I clench my jaw shut to prevent any kind of growl or curse from emerging and focus on Finley. "Is there anything I can help with?"

"No, I think we got it covered."

We head into the dining room where the others are taking their seats around the chunky wood table.

"Can I get you anything to drink?" Finley asks Luke. "We have lemonade and tea and water, and that's about it." She gives him an apologetic wince. "Sorry, we don't keep any alcohol in the house."

"It's my fault," Jake says. "I'm the troubled child of the family. Will you pass the garlic bread?"

Luke hands him the platter of bread. "It's fine. I don't drink either. Lemonade sounds great, thanks."

Archer sits at the head with Jake, Luke, and Taylor all lined up down his left and an open spot on his right for Finley.

When Finley returns with a pitcher of lemonade, I take the seat next to her.

Once we're all seated and passing around food, Finley glances over at Luke. "I hope you'll be able to join us for dinner more while you're here."

"We'll see," I tell her. "We have to get the lineup set and polished as much as possible before the producer arrives next weekend."

Taylor coughs, the sound forced.

"What?" I ask.

She stabs a tomato with her fork. "I didn't say anything."

My jaw clenches. "You didn't have to."

Finley clears her throat loudly. "So. Luke, Thanksgiving is in a few weeks. Are you planning on staying here for the holiday? We would love to have you. Piper and Oliver are coming for the weekend, and Archer's friend Mason is flying in from LA, so we'll have plenty of food."

"I appreciate the invitation, but my family is in Corning, so I was going to head home that morning. I'll be back the day after, though."

"Oh, that's only a couple of hours away. Do you have a big family?" She sprinkles parmesan on her lasagna.

I reach for the salad bowl at the same time as Taylor. She tugs and glares at me.

I roll my eyes and let her have it. She's so childish. When will she grow up?

Luke wipes his mouth with his napkin before replying to Finley. "Big enough, my parents, grandma, and sisters, and my sister's family."

"How many sisters do you have?" Jake asks.

"Two."

Jake lifts his fork in triumph. "I win. I have four."

Luke purses his lips. "What do you win, exactly?"

Jake considers the question and then frowns, the fork lowering. "Trauma and annoyance, mostly."

Taylor reaches behind Luke and smacks Jake on the back of the head.

"Hey." He grabs her hand.

A small scuffle punctuated with giggles and laughter

ensues, Luke ducking to get out of the way of their flailing hands.

"Hey, children," Finley taps her fork against her glass. "Settle down."

"She started it." Jake grins and then shoves a giant bite of lasagna into his mouth.

Finley sighs, ignoring him. "Taylor, you're staying for Thanksgiving, right?"

"Yes. I'll be here for at least a week. I'm going to the Sasquatch Festival in Canada a couple of weeks after."

"How long will you be there?"

One shoulder lifts in a half-shrug. "Only a few days."

"Who's playing at Sasquatch?" Luke asks her.

She beams at him, her body angling in his direction as she rattles off a list of indie rock bands.

I take a drink of my water and tune out their conversation, working to maintain a neutral expression.

It doesn't bother me that Taylor is flirting with Luke. If he wanted to date her, he could. It has nothing to do with me, because I have sworn off musicians forever, and that has not changed in the past week despite the fact that Luke and I have been working closely together and the more I get to know him, the hotter he gets.

If I need any convincing, the multitude of texts that have come in from Blake Bonham over the past week are proof enough that it's a bad idea.

I miss you.

Please call me.

How are you?

Can we talk?

A litany of three-word messages that all lead to the same reaction: annoyance and anger.

Taylor rests a hand on Luke's arm, laughing at something, and my eyes zero in on where she's touching him, a sudden impulse to reach across the table and rip her fingers away pulsing through me.

Irrational. Ridiculous.

This is not normal. I breathe in through my mouth and then slowly release the air through my nose. I will be cordial, at least for Finley's sake. She's gone through enough and—

"—Mindy?"

I look over at Finley. "What?"

"Do you know her?" Finley asks.

I take a sip of my water to mask my inattention. "Sorry, know who?"

Taylor's fork clatters, but when I glance over, she's staring down at her plate, her hand wrapped around the handle tightly enough to make her knuckles white.

She thinks I'm being intentionally rude. I want to explain that I was spacing out, and it's not about her, but I know she won't believe me.

"Laila Mae," Finley says, drawing my attention back to her. "She's a singer. Taylor is friends with her."

"Sort of," I answer.

Taylor shifts in her chair, glancing over at Luke before continuing. "I'm friends with her manager, Ursula. I've met Laila a handful of times, but she's really nice, really down to earth, and an incredible musician."

"I know Ursula. Not well, but we've met a few times. And I know of Laila," I admit. "She's really talented.

Incredible at marketing. Her fans are dedicated because she's very open about her life, and her songs have an almost story-like quality to them. I think they call her fandom the Laities?" I pronounce it like "ladies."

Taylor's eyes narrow, like she's waiting for me to keep going, tack on some scorn and derision.

When I don't, she continues. "Anyway, when I get back after Thanksgiving, Finley, I'll stay a few weeks if that's okay? I need to have some work done on the van, and Veronica agreed to let me bartend a few nights a week for some cash."

I press my lips together, holding back an irritable comment. *When is Taylor going to grow up, stop mooching off her family, and get a real adult job?*

"What?" Taylor's voice is a whip, reaching across the table.

I jerk up.

She's staring at me, hostility outlining the rigid set of her lips, the gleam in her eyes.

Crap. Did I say that out loud? I'm sure I didn't.

I scan the room. Jake is stuffing food in his face, Archer and Luke have their eyes trained down at the table, and Finley is glancing between us and biting her lip, probably ready to leap across the table to pull us apart if needed.

"What?" I ask. "I didn't say anything."

"You don't have to, you made a face."

"No, I didn't."

"Yes, you did. I saw it. I'm not blind. I know you think I'm some kind of flighty loser because I'm not stuck day after day in some corporate hamster wheel, and I stay with my family sometimes. Well, you know what? I'm not the only one who's had to come home to stay for a spell, now am I?"

"Taylor," Finley says, her voice sharp.

Taylor slashes a hand in her direction. "No, Finley. It's my turn to say something. I've dealt with snide comments and contempt from her for years."

No one needs to ask who "her" is. She's still glaring at me like she wishes she could cut me with her eyes.

"It's funny how some people are so judgmental about other people's life choices, and then they go and make the shittiest choices possible. Like sleeping with a married man that, hey, they also work with." Her voice is as sharp as a blade. "Some people will knock you for spending any time living at home, and then what do you know—they have to live at home. It's like," her eyes lift skyward, as if searching her memory, "what's that word, when people get exactly what's coming to them?" She snaps her fingers. "Karma."

Taylor isn't wrong. I have been terrible to her. We've been terrible to each other.

That doesn't mean I'm going to sit here and admit that in front of my entire family and Luke. Hot embarrassment sweeps through me. I'm lightheaded with the heat of it.

I set my napkin down. "I'm sorry. I can't do this." I push my chair back and half jog out of the house, through the front office, down the porch, out into the cold night, the brisk air stinging my heated cheeks. I wish I could run away from the past just as easily.

Chapter Twelve

Luke

Shocked silence permeates the air, the aftermath of released tension echoing through us like the reverberation after a bomb has gone off. The unease is so thick I could reach my hand out and grab it.

Finley is the first to speak. "Taylor, I—"

Taylor stands with an abrupt force, her chair screeching across the wood floor. "Don't start with me. You have no idea what she's put me through. She deserved all that and then some." She stalks out, going into the kitchen. A few seconds later, the side door slams.

Finley's eyes fall shut. She rests her elbows on the table, her hands clenched together in front of her face like she's praying. She blows out a breath. When she opens her eyes and looks over at me, they're rimmed in red. "I'm really sorry about all of this, Luke. They have some history, you know, things to work out. It's complicated."

"It's fine," I say, not sure how else to respond.

Archer reaches over, rubbing Finley's shoulder. "Do you need—"

She shifts away from him, shaking her head. "I think I have to—I'm sorry, excuse me." She puts her napkin down and exits. Her footsteps thump up the stairs a few seconds later.

Archer stares after her, concern etched into his expression.

After a second, Jake shrugs and reaches across the table, grabbing Mindy's plate and spooning the rest of her pasta onto his dish. He then picks up Taylor's and repeats the movement. Then he picks up Finley's.

Archer cuts him a sharp look. "Are you serious right now?"

"Oh, sorry." He lifts up Finley's plate. "You want to get in on this?"

Archer presses the fingers of his right hand to his temple. "No. What is wrong with you?"

Jake shrugs. "Hey, when you grow up in a household with a lot of siblings, you eat what you can, whenever you can. People think girls eat less, but that is not true, especially when there's five of them. You should have seen them when they were teenagers. They were like a pack of starving, perfume-drenched wolves in crop tops."

I can't help but laugh, and after a second, Archer chuckles as well.

"I know what you mean," I say. "My sister Vanessa could outeat a grown man when she was thirteen, even though she didn't weigh more than 80 pounds soaking wet."

Jake grins at me. "I'm not even surprised. I'm telling you, it's a teenage girl thing. When Aria was—" Like a switch being thrown, he cuts off, the words chopped midsentence. The smile drops, his face going blank. The happy, joking guy who was sitting there a second ago has completely disappeared.

"Jake—" Archer starts.

Jake stands. "I've got to—I'll check on Finley."

He disappears, jogging up the stairs.

Baffled, I look over at Archer.

His eyes fall shut, his fingers steepled in front of his face, elbows on the table.

"Is he okay? Did I say something wrong?"

"Yes. No." He opens his eyes, his hands falling onto the table. "I don't know."

"I feel like I've been dropped in the middle of a story and missed the first half."

Archer rubs his temple. "That's the first time Jake has said her name out loud since," his hand waves in the air, "since she died, as far as I'm aware."

"Ah."

We sit in silence for a minute while I have an internal struggle with what I should do. Should I stay? Should I go? Concern for Mindy nibbles at me, pressuring me to go out and find her and make sure she's okay.

Archer stands. "I'm going to check on him. Feel free to stay, or," Archer's head tilts toward the front door, "if you want to check on Mindy, we can clean this up later."

"I'll get the dishes started, at least. I don't mind."

"Hey, thanks. And thanks for coming over, and I'm sorry about. . ." he gestures vaguely.

"It's not a problem." I lift my brows and nod to the stairs. "Good luck."

Archer heads upstairs.

I push my chair back and stack plates, piling silverware on top. In the kitchen, I load as much as I can into the dishwasher, working quickly. The need to race after Mindy to make sure she's all right is like an itch under my skin.

Once the dishwasher is loaded up and running, I grab my coat from the rack and Mindy's —since she went out the front, she left it behind—and slip out the side door.

Jumping in the golf cart, I head back down the drive toward my cabin at a snail's pace. I don't want to miss her in the darkness, so I keep my eyes peeled.

Halfway there, I come to a halt outside of one of the sitting areas, flames flickering in the fire pit. She's standing in front of it, holding her hands out to the fire.

I park the cart off to the side and pocket the keys as I approach. "Do you want some company?"

"I don't care." Her tone is brisk, icier than the breeze winging through the trees around us.

She's embarrassed. I know it's not about me, but I had hoped at this point we could be honest with each other. Working on my songs together has been like opening up a tender, fragile part of myself and trusting her not to drop it. I had hoped the trust that was building between us was mutual.

I rock back on my heels. "Did you want your coat?"

"I'm fine."

It's going to be a cold walk back to the house, but I'm

sure she knows that. I walk over, place it on the bench near her, and then turn to leave.

I make it three steps.

"Wait, Luke."

I twist around.

Her arms are crossed over her chest, her eyes downcast. "I'm sorry about dinner. I know that couldn't have been comfortable for you. And then I left you there. I'm sorry. That was . . . messed up."

"I have sisters, too. Our official family motto is: Well, that escalated quickly."

She laughs, the sound short and abrupt but real.

I duck my head, staring down at my boots.

"Do you want some s'mores?"

I glance up, trying to read her expression, limned with the flickering flames, but she's carefully blank.

"Yeah. That would be great."

She walks over to a nearby outdoor cabinet, opens up one of the tall cupboards and pushes on a puck light. "What kind of chocolate do you want?"

I follow her, peering into the opening over her head. "You have more than one kind?"

"Yeah. You've never had s'mores with a peanut butter cup? Or a caramel chocolate bar?"

"I've never even thought about it." I rest my hand on the edge of the cabinet door. Her back is a few scant inches from my chest. The top of her head comes up just under my chin like she's a perfect fit.

"You've been missing out." She grabs a box of graham crackers and stacks a package of candy bars and a handful of napkins on top.

"Clearly." I reach over her to snatch the bag of marshmallows from the top shelf.

She twists around to look up at me, her shoulder brushing against my arm. "Oh." She startles at my nearness.

I step back. "Sorry."

I'm crowding her like some kind of lurking creep. *Keep it professional, jackass.*

She clutches the s'mores fixings against her chest with one arm and smooths back her hair with the other. "It's fine. What's your favorite?"

I clear my throat.

Don't say she's your favorite.

"Favorite?"

She frowns up at me. "Candy bar?"

"Oh. Right. Let's start with the peanut butter cup."

"You got it." She hands me a couple of roasting sticks before shutting the cabinet.

We head back to the fire pit, where the flames have dropped to glowing embers.

"Will you put another log on that?" she nods to the fire pit. "They're under the bench over there."

I do as asked while she stages the goodies on the bench, laying out a napkin and then opening up the package of graham crackers first.

I sit a few feet down and open the marshmallows.

She sorts and stacks the crackers and chocolate methodically, her movements quick and efficient.

When she finishes, I hold out one of the roasting sticks topped with a fresh marshmallow.

She takes it and meets my eyes, hers luminous in the

yellow glow. "I am really sorry I left you alone with my family after that . . . scene."

"You already apologized."

She sits, extending her marshmallow into the fire and giving me her profile. "I know. I need to apologize again, at least more times."

"That's an oddly specific number." I sit next to her, put my roasting stick in next to hers, hovering over the flames.

"What happened after I left?"

"Taylor took off out the side door. Then Finley went upstairs. Then Jake stole everyone's leftover food, but before he could eat it, he said Aria's name and bolted from the table like it was on fire."

She gasps, turning toward me, eyes wide. "He said her name?"

"Yeah. Archer mentioned maybe he hasn't in a while."

She shakes her head. "No. He hasn't, not since she passed."

We sit in comfortable silence for a minute. An owl hoots in the distance while the fire crackles in front of us.

After a minute, she pulls her marshmallow from the flames, standing up to put together her s'more.

"Are you ready for yours?" She sets hers on the bench wrapped in a napkin.

"Yep." I pull my stick from the flame.

She holds out the pieces and uses them to scrape the marshmallow off my stick, squishing it all together and handing it to me.

We sit next to each other, eating in sticky silence.

When we're done, she tosses her napkin into the fire. "Aria and Jake, they were twins."

I can't read her profile, cast in shadow.

"That's rough." I finish my treat, wiping off my hands and chucking my napkin in the fire on top of hers.

"Yeah. It gets worse. He was with her when she died."

My heart aches, the s'more turning into lead in my gut thinking about what he must have gone through. What he's still going through.

"Not long after she died, our dad got sick. Jake took care of him. It helped distract him from the reality of Aria's loss, but then after Dad died . . . ." She stands suddenly, moving to the fire, holding her hands out in front of her.

She swallows, the delicate muscles of her throat bobbing with the motion. "A couple of years after Aria passed, Taylor came to stay with me. I had just graduated from college and Taylor had just graduated from high school. She came so we could celebrate." She crosses her arms. "She told me—" her eyes fall shut. "She came to me for comfort. She admitted a mistake she had made. It had to do with Aria. What she told me made me really angry. It was a big mistake. A lethal mistake." She opens her eyes, her gaze pleading to understand.

I nod.

"I lashed out at her, and we had a huge fight and . . . I don't know." Her arms drop to her sides. "She wants to be absolved. She wants me to tell her it's not her fault and that it's all okay, but I can't do it. And now, I don't know if we can ever forgive each other. Every time I see her, I get so angry I can barely think straight." She frowns. "Am I a terrible person?"

"No." My answer is instant and unequivocal.

"How do you know that? You don't know the whole story. I left out a lot of details."

"Your feelings are valid, even the bad ones. It's okay to feel angry. It's okay to be upset. There's nothing wrong with experiencing the gamut of human emotions, even the negative ones. The trick is to understand where they're coming from. Is your anger masking something else?"

She stares at me for a long minute. "I don't know." The words are whispered so softly if her mouth hadn't moved I might have questioned if she even spoke. She clears her throat and speaks louder. "It's just—I-I wish I could be around her without feeling so wretched. It's like I can't control it."

I understand all too well how grief can trigger uncontrollable anger. "When people we love die, we feel helpless."

She walks back over and sits, no more than a foot away. "Yes."

"When Kevin died, I blamed Granny Bea. I was incredibly angry with her."

She shifts slightly, angling in my direction. "Your grandmother? Why?"

"She's not really my grandmother, she was Kevin's. I felt like she should have known. She should have seen it coming. I didn't understand that I was actually mad at myself, because *I* should have seen it coming. I had so much guilt I couldn't deal with it. I had to project it onto someone else. Which I did, onto more than one person."

"What happened?"

I lean forward, resting my elbows on my knees. "When I went back to school, one of my good friends pretended like nothing had happened. He said nothing about Kevin because he was worried that bringing him up would upset me, but instead, the fact he didn't bother to ask made me irate. Later that day, another friend stopped me in the hall to see how I was feeling and talk about Kevin, and I almost decked him." I shake my head, chuckling softly.

She leans closer, her hand resting on the bench between us. "A tad conflicting."

"Exactly. I realized then that the irrational anger I felt toward everyone was covering up my other emotions. Grief tosses our entire world into turmoil, and anger is safer than guilt and fear. Anger is easy to use as a shield when someone you love is suddenly gone and you have to deal with the fact that you have no control over the world around you. It's all just . . . meaningless."

She's staring at me, eyes wet. A tear slips down her cheek, and she dashes it away with a hand. "It is."

Our eyes lock, the moment stretching between us, a mutual understanding. Mindy has a lot of hard edges on the outside, but they mask so much pain. I want to take it all away and somehow make it better, gather her in my arms, and tell her it will all be okay.

But I don't have the right.

Her hand covers mine. "I'm so sorry. I gave you that

whole spiel about keeping things professional, and here I am, vomiting my private life all over you."

It's only natural for me to flip my hand over and link her fingers with mine. "Anytime. I've been through it, and I've been through the therapy. And the rehab."

She doesn't pull away, her eyes searching mine. "Rehab?"

"I tried to escape for a while after Kevin died. I've been sober for ten years."

"You were so young." Her eyes are compassionate when she leans into me, her shoulder pressing into mine.

"We both were."

Her warm gaze, the press of her body, and the floral scent of her skin all hit me like a physical blow shooting straight to my gut, spreading heat through me that can't be attributed to the fire burning in front of us.

The world tilts beneath me.

The moment before the fall.

And then I open my mouth and say, "I have to go."

Chapter Thirteen

Mindy

"I don't know if I like this phrasing." Luke tilts his notebook in my direction.

The moment before I fall

I skim over the line, taking in some of the other lyrics. Words have been erased and rewritten so many times, the paper is thinning.

The wind whispers in my ear
  Heart beating fast, adrenaline rush
  Feel the weight of the world, it's too much

. . .

"What about a stronger word for fall? Something like, plummet, maybe?"

His eyes brighten. "I like that. Let me try it." He sets the notebook on the coffee table in front of us, leaning over to scribble more notes.

Then he picks up his guitar and strums a few chords, humming along, trying to harmonize the sound of the lyrics with the beat and the pitch.

The past few days have been a frenzy of work, development on Luke's old songs, and hashing out this new one. The idea struck him the other night, the same night I fought with Taylor at dinner and we made s'mores and held hands and I almost threw myself at him and then he took off running.

Well, more or less. I understand what it's like when the muse hits. He helped me put out the fire and dropped me off at the main house before racing to the cabin for his notebook and guitar.

That was the first time I'd ever spoken about what happened with Taylor, and even though I left out a lot of details, he knows more about the rift between us than anyone, even Finley. I can't figure it out—what made me tell Luke, what made me want to open up, like the words were just sitting in a cage, waiting for him to come along and unlock them.

Maybe it's because of practically living with each other over these past couple of weeks, the shared vulnerability, the closeness that comes from working together so intimately—but I've done this before with other artists.

With Luke, it's different. It's easy, but there's an undercurrent of something else. Something more.

Luke shifts on the couch next to me, angling his knees in my direction. "I want it to be like, the fear of the fall but also feeling safe at the same time." He taps the pencil on his bottom lip. "Feeling secure and unafraid in the face of jumping into the unknown—that sort of contrast. Does that make sense?"

"It does."

He keeps strumming on his guitar, humming a little and playing with the pitch.

When he first shared what he was working on, this song about falling in love, I couldn't help but wonder—since it came to him when we were holding hands—is it about me?

But it can't be. That's ridiculous. Even if it was, it doesn't matter. I'm not going to ask, because it *can't* mean anything. He's my client. My one and only client. I've gone through this before. Work has to be my sole focus. I can't sleep with another musician, let alone one I'm working with.

A little harmless fantasizing never hurt anyone, right?

How can I not fantasize? Especially when he's sitting next to me, his thigh inches from mine, his fingers strong and sure on the strings of his guitar, his voice a low rumble that tugs at something deep in my stomach.

I can't believe I didn't notice his potential the first time we met.

Of course, at the time I was intensely focused on Blake since it was right around the time we started our *affair*.

That whole period of time is a blur now. I was stuck in that moment between dreams and wakefulness when everything is a little soft and warm, and I was wrapped up in all things Blake. I had more energy. Food tasted better. I was falling in love.

It's exactly what Luke's song is about.

It's exactly why I need to ignore the temptation Luke presents just by existing.

I pick up the notebook, reading again through the lines he's piecing together.

The alternating verses might be better with a soprano to contrast his baritone.

"Could this one be a duet, do you think? Since you're considering the contrast to the lyrics."

His fingers pause on the strings, his gaze lifts to mine, brows shooting up to his hairline. "You want to take a stab at it?"

"Yeah, sure."

He strums his guitar and sings the first couple lines and then gestures to me and I sing the next.

His mouth pops open and then he grins. "You have an amazing voice."

Flustered, I drop the notebook onto the coffee table. "I can carry a tune. I was in a band, in college."

His head cocks. "Why didn't you pursue a career as a singer?"

I cross my legs, leaning toward him. "I prefer working behind the scenes, finding talent, bringing an album to life, and then basking in the afterglow of how music touches so many people's lives."

His eyes search mine. "Is that what made you get into music?"

I shrug. "Yeah. Mostly. Music is such a unifying force. It's embedded in our cultures, in our very DNA."

His entire face brightens. "That's so true. Rhythm is part of our everyday life, the thump of our hearts, the measure of our breaths, it's all music." He considers me, his bright eyes scanning my face before adding, "It can also be a safe way to deal with feelings because there's like a gap, a filter between you and the emotion. Like reading someone else's story."

I lean toward him, the words resonating inside me, luring me closer. "That's it, exactly. There's nothing more magical than a building full of people all experiencing the same connection and understanding."

He adjusts the guitar in his lap, shifting it out of the way so the body isn't pressing against my knee. "You always knew you wanted to be in the music industry?"

"For the most part. I double majored in music management and business administration."

His brows lift. "Ambitious."

I smirk. "Well, it's not med school."

He grins back at me and neither of us speaks for a few long, lingering seconds.

My stomach trembles, my skin tightens.

His thigh presses against mine. When did we move so close?

His gaze drops to my mouth.

Unthinking, I lick my lips.

"Do you want some water?" He stands with so much speed, the breeze from his guitar gusts by my face.

"Uh, yeah. Sure. That would be good." I can't even

speak properly, my body still reeling from . . . whatever that was.

He gives me a dimpled smile that ignites the blood in my veins. My mouth goes dry.

He cannot bring me that water fast enough.

Pull yourself together, Mindy.

He comes back with two glasses and I down half the glass in one chug.

My phone rings.

Saved by the cell. "Oh, it's Jerry. Probably calling to confirm for this weekend." Finally. I've been trying to reach him all week.

I answer the phone and stand. "Hey, thanks for returning my call. I just wanted to confirm your arrival time—"

"Mindy, I'm sorry."

My heart sinks into my toes, unease making my stomach twist. This isn't going to be a good call. "What are you sorry for?"

"I can't help you with this project." He says the words in a rush, like he's ripping off a bandage.

And just like that, I go from happy and slightly turned on to pissed the hell off.

The walls of the cabin close in on me, blackness crowding my vision. I stalk outside onto the front porch, taking a deep breath in a vain attempt to gather some serenity into my lungs. "Jerry, you owe me. We agreed. You gave me your word." I knew I should have gotten something in writing. He was out of town when we first spoke—he hates email and refused to do an e-sign, he's old-school that way—and he told me he would sign the contract when he got here. We've worked together so many times, this is how it always goes, but he always came through. I thought I could trust him.

Besides no one else would even take my calls.

"I know. I'm really sorry. Something came up and my hands are tied. You understand?"

What I understand is that Jerry is worried about being associated with me since I'm on the naughty list. He expressed a little apprehension when I wrangled him into this, but he owes me. He's a prima donna. He's notoriously difficult to work with because of his perfectionism, and I hired him when others wouldn't. He's eccentric, but he's talented.

And now he's giving me the brushoff.

I take a deep breath and hold it in. I have to remain professional even though what I want to do is scream and stomp my feet and act like a toddler.

"No. I don't understand. We had a deal, and now you're breaking that deal."

"Mindy, I'm sorry. Let me explain."

Frustration pummels me. "I have to go. I have a lot of work to do."

Before he can reply I hang up and stalk to the edge of the patio, gripping the railing and gazing out into the trees, the mountains soaring up behind them in the distance. Blood roars in my ears. Despair wraps cold arms around me.

"Are you okay?"

I spin around.

Luke leans against the door frame, his eyes penetrating.

No.

"I'm fine."

"That was our producer?"

I nod. "We've run into a little bit of a hiccup." I force a smile.

"Is there anything I can do?"

Against my will and better judgment, my eyes scan down his lean form, from the shirt outlining his broad shoulders, down to the jeans hugging his trim hips.

Not helpful.

"No. We'll keep to the same schedule. I'll find someone else."

I will not let this impede our forward progress. I can't.

Even though it feels like I'm sinking into the thickest, darkest quicksand and it's rushing up over my legs, about to suck me into the abyss.

I can't catch a break. I'm a total fuckup. How the hell am I going to find someone on such short notice?

Straightening my shoulders, I tug a confident expression around me like a suit of armor.

"It's not a problem. Don't worry. This doesn't change our plans." I infuse my voice with all the confidence I can muster. "Everything is going to be fine."

"Everything is not fine. What am I supposed to do now?" I ask Keanu Reeves.

I'm lying in my childhood bed, hugging my pillow and staring up at a magazine photo I stuck up on my wall when I was a teenager. I can't believe that little piece of tape has been gripping the wall securely for 16 years.

"You're the only one who's stuck around for me, Keanu."

I've lost it. This is where I finally crack. What the hell am I going to do? We could record the songs ourselves, but I'm not a producer. This album is my one shot to get my career back. We have to put out the best possible product.

My mind sorts through options and possibilities, but Jerry was my last-ditch effort.

Damn it, Jerry.

After the phone call, I couldn't focus. I couldn't be around Luke without the truth of how dire our situation actually is spilling out of my mouth, so I told him I needed to make some calls. I came back to the house to talk to Finley, but she's not here. No one was here—except Taylor, who was downstairs painting her nails—so I booked it upstairs and have been trying not to have a total panic attack ever since while lamenting all my problems to Keanu.

He's such a great listener.

Finley isn't answering her phone. She was giving ice skating lessons today, but they should be over by now.

Maybe she's still at the rink.

Taylor isn't downstairs when I head back out, but the lingering scent of nail polish remover hangs in the air. We haven't spoken since dinner the other night. Over the years, we've become experts at evading each other.

I walk down the drive and cut across behind the cabins to get to the skating rink.

Pushing open the thick steel doors to the building, I'm greeted by a gust of chilly air. It's almost colder inside than it is out. Under the cathedral ceiling, standing in the middle of the rink, Archer comes into view. He's in his sneakers, watching Finley while she skates around him.

I make my way around the walkway that hugs the barrier wall of the rink.

The swish of her blades cutting into the ice echoes in the cavernous space.

Her movements are confident and smooth, gliding across the ice like she was born with the blades strapped to her feet. My heart twists. She was born to do this.

At eighteen, she placed fourth at Nationals, missing the Olympics by one since they send the top three.

Four years later, she placed first in Sectionals. We all knew she would be heading to the Olympics. It was her year. The other competitors couldn't touch her.

Then Aria died a week before Nationals. Finley came home to take care of Piper and Taylor and Jake. I would have left college, too, and come home to help, but she insisted I stay and finish school. I was in my last year.

She gave up all her dreams for us. For me.

"Do that thing where you spin in the air," Archer calls out.

In one fluid movement, she turns so she's skating backward, facing Archer. "Like an axel?"

"Yeah, or that other one." He waves a hand. "Salad chow."

Her laughter, bright and effervescent, reverberates through the chilled air.

Despite the fact that my world is falling apart—again—I smile at the sound.

I stop, leaning my elbows on the partition.

Finley's speed increases as she flows across the ice, one foot sliding effortlessly in front of the other. In one seamless movement she dips and spins, and my heart lodges somewhere in my throat.

It's not only her talent, but also her presence on the ice. She's pure joy. I can't take my eyes off her.

Neither can Archer.

Open adoration emanates from his every pore as he watches her. He really loves her.

A pinch of jealousy twinges in my stomach. It's not that I'm not over the moon for Finley and Archer, because I am. I love Finley more than anything, and her happiness means the world to me.

I thought Blake would be the person to look at me like that, like I hung the stars and moon.

An image flashes in my mind of Luke from the other night when he shared about his anger after Kevin's death, the way the light from the fire played over his features and the depth of understanding in his eyes. I slice at the thoughts. That way lies madness.

Finley spots me and waves. "Hey." She skates over, coming to a skidding halt in front of me, a smile spreading on her face. "You want to go get lunch? Taylor is meeting me here in a few—" her brows dip, the smile disappearing. "What's wrong?"

I never could hide my feelings from Finley.

I shake my head, my eyes darting to Archer, walking toward us.

She glances behind her as Archer approaches the railing. "Hey, Mindy."

He scans her face and then says, "I'm going to go meet Jake at the paintball course. I'll see you back at the house?"

She nods, tilting her head back.

He leans over to brush his lips against hers.

I gaze over at the bottom row of seats to the right.

"Bye Mindy," he calls out over his shoulder, exiting the rink through one of the half-door exits on the other side.

"Bye."

Finley tilts her head to one side. "Let's go over to the bench."

She takes off and I follow the path along the railing and meet her at the sitting area.

She plops down on a bench, leaning over to tug on the laces of her skates. "Tell me what's going on. You look like someone ran over your signed vinyl of *Abbey Road*."

"Jerry bailed. The producer."

Her eyes widen. "He was supposed to be here this weekend. The cabin and everything is ready; I turned on the heat this morning."

"Not anymore. So we won't need that cabin. Feel free to shut it back down."

She picks up a couple of fuzzy slipperlike towels from the other side of the bench, tugging first one and then the other over the blades of her skates. "Can you get anyone else?"

"He was the only one who agreed. I called a dozen different people who owed me before trying Jerry, and they all had other obligations." Or they completely ignored my existence.

She leans her elbows on her knees. "Did you try anyone who doesn't already owe you one?"

I huff out a laugh. "It's not worth it. No one else will help me. They won't want to risk being ostracized."

"How do you know until you ask? Or maybe you can do what you did with Luke: find a producer who's looking to make their mark."

Exasperated, I lift my hands in the air and then drop them at my sides. "Where? How? I need someone I know is good, and I need them now. I want to put out the best possible product."

She bites her lip, reaching out to pat my arm. "Do you want to join us for lunch?"

"No."

A flicker of relief passes across her eyes.

The corresponding sting in my heart is immediate and completely irrational. Finley is sick of the animosity. Hell, I'm sick of it, too. Taylor is the last person I want to be around today, so I have no reason to be upset they're having lunch without me. I don't have time for lunch.

I need to work, or start calling people, or doing *something*.

"You know, I've tried every producer I know. But I might have a few audio engineers on my list I can reach out to. Maybe something will shake out."

Staying active and focused will get me through this. It's just a rough spot. It's not my first, and it won't be the last. I'll do what I always do and fight my way through it.

Chapter Fourteen

Luke

"Hey, Luke!"

I squint in the direction of the voice calling my name.

"You want to help us out for a minute?" Archer waves his hand, gesturing me over.

He and Jake are standing by a squat storage building to the side of the paintball course. A door on the side is open, revealing stacks of dark clothing and large black guns hanging up on the wall.

Mindy might need some time alone anyway. She tried to play it off like things are fine, but the tension thrumming through her body and her ashen face said otherwise. I wish she would open up to me, but who am I kidding? We work together. Our relationship can't be anything more.

Even though the inexplicable twinge in my chest indicates otherwise.

Shoving those thoughts to the side, I change my trajectory, swinging open the short chain link fence, and jog over. "Sure. What do you need help with?"

"Target practice." Jake hands me a tactical vest. "You want to be the clay pigeon?"

Archer sighs. "We're testing the paintball equipment."

I shrug the vest on. "Cool. I'm in."

"Here, take these, too." Jake hands me kneepads and a helmet.

Archer hands me a gun. "Your ammo is red, Jake's yellow, and mine's blue."

"Hey Archer," Taylor calls out, walking by. "Is Finley still at the ice rink?"

He nods. "Yep. Mindy's there with her."

Taylor makes a face. "Thanks for the warning."

I finish strapping on the kneepads and put the helmet on.

"What are you guys doing?" She's stopped at the fence, one hand lifted to block the sun from her eyes.

"We're testing the paintball equipment," Archer repeats.

She lifts her brows. "Testing, huh?"

"It's a safety thing," Jake adds. "We need to make sure all the structures they installed are weight bearing to avoid, you know, accidental injury. It's for a liability, uh, procedure."

"It's standard protocol," I add.

Jake grins at me and then makes a small movement and yellow explodes across my chest along with the brunt of the impact.

Archer bursts out laughing.

My mouth drops open and I glare at Jake. "Hey! You shot me!"

"Game on!" he yells, sprinting for a nearby wall.

Taylor is forgotten as the battle begins.

I take aim and red paint bursts against the faux rock wall, barely missing Jake's retreating back as he ducks out of view.

I take off running for a nearby shell of a building, ducking down underneath an open window and leaning my back against the wall. I take a minute to catch my breath before peeking up into the opening.

Everything is perfectly still and quiet, not even the hint of a black vest rustling in the breeze.

I duck back down, out of sight. My ears strain for any hint of movement or footsteps.

A bird caws in the distance. The wind picks up, scattering dried leaves, and I almost jump out of my skin.

I can't sit here forever, waiting for their inevitable attack. I peer out of the opening again and a blast of blue splatters the wall right under me.

Dropping back out of sight, I leave my hiding spot, staying crouched down and hugging the wall. The lip of Archer's helmet gleamed when he shot at me. He's hiding to the north of me, behind a propped-up wooden wall.

Assessing the course in my mind, I devise a strategy to make my way around the south edge and approach him from the rear in a surprise attack.

I'm hunkered down and hiding behind a tree when loud reports pepper the air no more than fifteen feet away.

"I got him!" Archer yells.

I glance around. "Where?" I mutter. I lean out farther,

peering around the trunk to get a better view, when something punches me in the back.

"Damn it."

"Sucker!"

I look up.

Jake climbed into the tree and is sitting on a thick branch about six feet in the air, lifting his gun in victory and shaking it. "I can't believe you fell for that, it's the oldest trick in the—oof!" He wavers, losing his balance and falling backward with a thud.

"Oh shit." I sprint the few steps over to him, tossing my gun to the side.

He's breathing, but it's a little labored. I grab his wrist. His pulse is fast but nothing too concerning.

"Jake, you okay?"

Archer kneels on his other side.

Jake blinks his eyes open. "What happened?" he croaks.

"I think you had the wind knocked out of you. How do you feel? Does anything hurt?"

"Terrible. So much pain." He groans.

Archer holds up his middle finger a couple of feet over Jake's eyes. "How many fingers am I holding up?"

Jake lifts his head and focuses on the digit. "Saturday." His head flops back to the ground.

Archer gives a quick nod. "Yep. He's fine."

Jake twitches on the ground.

Concerned, I lean over him, but the concern ebbs when it becomes clear that he's laughing. Only a chuckle at first, but it's infectious. Pretty soon we're all consumed by the hilarity, practically crying.

"You're such a dick," Archer says, smacking Jake on the shoulder.

"You fucking love it, asshole. When's lunch?"

A few minutes later, we're sitting on a giant tire, our legs hanging into the center hole, eating sandwiches Archer procured from a cooler they had stashed over by the storage closet.

"How's all that," Jake waves a potato chip in the air, "song stuff going?" He pops the chip in his mouth.

"Good." Except for the whole we might not have a producer thing, but I trust Mindy to resolve it. She won't let me down, not only because she has just as much riding on this as I do, but because she's good at her job.

"You should play for us," Archer adds, tossing me a bottle of water from the cooler at his feet.

I catch the water and an immediate rejection flies to my lips, but I bite it back before it can escape. This might be exactly what I need. I've been playing in front of Mindy without issue, but we need to expand my circle if I have any hope of playing in front of a roomful of strangers. "That's . . . actually a really good idea. I need to practice playing in front of people." I swallow and waffle for a second before deciding to level with them. "I have a little problem with stage fright."

Jake takes a bite of his sandwich and chews. "Yeah, we know."

Archer nods. "Finley told me."

"And Archer told me," Jake adds. "No one keeps secrets around here."

"You get used to it," Archer says.

Jake takes a swig of water. "Wait, wait." He holds up a

finger. "Except for when Piper was in an abusive relationship and just avoided all of us for months and wouldn't tell us anything."

Archer dips his head in acknowledgment. "Right. Oh, and whatever is going on with Mindy and Taylor."

Jake chuckles. "Yeah, good luck getting that out of them. They are like vaults."

Pleasure uncoils inside me with the sudden understanding that Mindy shared a piece of something with me that she hasn't shared even with her family.

Jake keeps going. "Let's not forget that time Finley never told anyone about this place almost going bankrupt until it was almost too late."

Archer waves a hand. "Okay, okay, so maybe they *do* keep secrets but never other people's secrets. Only their own."

Jake purses his lips in thought. "That's true. They love talking about everyone else. You know, sharing other people's shame."

"I'm not ashamed about my stage fright. It's just an anxiety I have to deal with."

Jake claps me on the back. "I know my handsomeness and general allure can be very intimidating, but you have nothing to worry about except for the not-so-silent judgement I will be rendering before, during, and after you perform. Sing for us, my man, and by the time we're through with you, you will be feeling all kinds of shame, and maybe some self-loathing, too."

Archer barks out a laugh. "You know, that's actually a good idea. We can heckle you until you cry like a toddler without his binky. Then you'll have experienced the worst and you will no longer have to fear it."

Jake grins. "We'll be so terrible, nothing else could possibly compare. You will dread no one and nothing like you will dread us."

I chuckle. "You know, it's just crazy enough that it might work." If anything, the memory will make me laugh instead of throwing up or peeing my pants. "Maybe we can meet later?"

Archer lifts his brows. "Why not now?"

"I don't have my guitar. It's back in the cabin."

"I'm done eating." Archer chucks his trash into the bag at his side. "I'll go grab it while you yahoos finish up." He pushes himself off the tire, jumping to the ground and jogging off.

"So," Jake shoves a final bite of sandwich into his mouth, ignoring the napkin next to him and rubbing his hands on his pants. "Why even pursue this whole singing thing if you have such bad stage fright?"

I crumple up the empty bag of chips in my hand. "I made a promise to a friend."

His brows lift. "Must be some friend."

"He was my best friend."

Jake's gaze sharpens. "What happened to him?"

My use of past tense didn't slip by him.

I take a bite of my sandwich and consider how much to share. Blunt truth might be the best option. Jake's been through his own hell, and I think he needs honesty. The same way Mindy uses her anger toward Taylor as a shield, Jake uses humor and a blasé attitude toward everything.

"Suicide. He was sixteen."

His mouth pops open in surprise. "Jesus," he curses.

"No, his name was Kevin."

His answering smile is fleeting.

"After Kevin died, I struggled for a while. I made some really bad decisions."

He grunts in acknowledgment. "I'm sure Mindy's told you all about my problems and bad decisions."

"She didn't. It was sort of obvious the other night at dinner."

His lips purse in thought.

"I've been sober since about a year after Kevin's death, so a little over ten years," I add.

His head shoots up, eyes wide. "You were so young."

"And stupid. I wanted nothing more than escape. So I fell into drugs and booze and anything I could get my hands on. Thankfully, it wasn't for an extended period of time but long enough to realize I could never go down that path again."

"How did you do it? How do you keep doing it?"

"I don't know, man. There's no easy answer. I wish I could say it gets better, but I can't promise anything. Every day is different. Every person is different." I think about it, considering my words before I speak. "One thing that helped is something my therapist taught me. Life is always going to be hard."

Jake rolls his eyes dramatically. "Gee, don't hit me with the inspirational sunshine and rainbow quotes all at once."

I chuckle. "There will always be pain and loss and things outside of our control—like death. There's no such thing as a perfect life. No one is happy all the time—our brains would probably explode or something. There will always be some bad shit and some good shit. What we can do is develop tools to get through the bad times, knowing they will be temporary, and then take the time to sink into the happy moments as they come."

He blinks at me. "That's hella deep man."

I chuckle and shrug, finishing off the last of my sandwich.

Jake jumps down from the tire, chucking his trash in the bag. "People don't understand. My sisters and Archer, they try, and they mean well, and they lost a sister, too, but it's not the same. They don't get it."

I hop off the tire and throw my trash away. "If you ever need to talk, I'm an okay listener."

Jake nods, not meeting my eyes, squinting in the direction Archer walked off.

After another minute, he gestures to one of the walls. "Want to hide and then when Archer shows up we can shoot him in the ass?"

"Absolutely."

Twenty minutes later, they haul me and my guitar over to a low wooden platform by one of the fire pits. In front of the makeshift stage, about a dozen twenty-foot logs have been trimmed and sanded into bench-style seating.

I stand in the middle of the stage, the strap of my guitar a comforting weight on my shoulder.

Surprisingly, I'm not that nervous.

Or not surprising, considering my audience is a couple

of dirty guys in paintball gear lounging on wooden logs and eating popcorn.

"Booooo!" Jake jeers.

Walking toward the front of the stage, I lift my hands. "Really?" I haven't even started playing yet.

"Do you know any Beatles songs?" Archer shouts.

I grin and play the intro to "Blackbird."

"Now do Beyonce," Jake yells. " 'All the Single Ladies'!"

I chuckle and take a seat at the center and let my legs hang over the edge, strumming the intro to the song Mindy and I have been working on the most, the first one she listened to.

"This is terrible," Jake yells. "My ears are bleeding!"

"Who hurt you?" Archer adds.

The most remarkable thing happens. Instead of wanting to vomit or run away, I want to laugh, and I do, my hands still moving across the instrument with perfect motor memory, but attempting to sing is impossible because I can't stop the humor from spilling out of my mouth.

With anxiety, you're always picturing the worst that could happen, but now that they're making it happen, it's not scary at all. It's actually rather ridiculous.

They were right. What am I so afraid of? What's the worst that could happen? A crowd heckling me just like this? Maybe this will help the next time I have to get up in front of strangers and bare my soul.

I replay the intro a few times until the mirth has settled, no longer at risk of eruption, and then I shut my eyes to block them out and sing.

A few minutes later, I open my eyes.

At some point during my little performance, Taylor joined them, sitting on the other side of Jake. She sets her phone in her lap—*was she recording me?*—and then jumps up clapping. "That was incredible," she shouts. "You killed it!"

"Dude. You don't actually suck." Jake thrusts a fist in the air.

Archer whistles. "Encore, encore!"

I hop off the stage and head over to my adoring fans. "Stop it, you're making me blush." I wave a hand in an aw-shucks motion.

Taylor's phone pings and she glances down at it, her eyes widening. She reaches out, grabbing my arm. "You are not going to believe who just listened to your song."

Chapter Fifteen

Mindy

I spent all afternoon yesterday and then another three hours this morning locked away in my room calling, texting, and emailing everyone I've ever met that might be able to help me get out of this muddle. In the past twenty-four hours, I've begged, pleaded, and nearly cried, and the result?

Nothing.

No one will work with me. Not that I expected anything different, but desperation drove me to the limits of my contact list.

We're absolutely fucked, and even worse?

I need to explain all of this to Luke.

The conversation plays out in my mind. I'll tell him the truth. He'll be kind, considerate, and understanding, and I'll be a giant ball of shame and disgrace. He will be absolutely in his right to terminate our contract considering I can't fulfill my terms.

I can't believe this is happening.

Then again, maybe it's for the best. I can't deny the attraction between us, and maybe it's better to end things now before I do something truly horrible like throw myself at my only client and ruin my own life. Again.

It's midday before I gather the courage to come clean to Luke. I have to tell him we have no producer and I won't be able to get one in order to meet the deadlines outlined in our contract. It's a breach of contract, and not only could he then break our agreement, he could also could sue me.

Luckily, I make it out of the main house without running into my family—everyone must be out and about —and I'm glad. I can't face them right now.

I knock on Luke's door and fidget on the doorstep, my heart in my throat by the time he answers.

"Hey. I'm glad you're here." He steps back to let me in.

He's dressed in jeans and a sweater, his hair is a little mussed, and I might be distracted by his effortless appeal if I wasn't ready to throw up because of the conversation looming between us.

I stalk into the living room, turning around to face him when his footsteps sound behind me. "We have to talk."

He speaks at the same time. "I have to tell you—" He stops and grins. "Sorry, ladies first."

I can't sit. I'm too wired. I wave a hand. "No. Please, you go first."

It's not exactly like I'm in a hurry to talk about how I've totally fucked up.

"Yesterday I played for Jake and Archer, and I was barely nervous."

"That's wonderful." I guess this is something he can hold on to after I tell him my news. At least his time here wasn't a complete and total waste. He was able to work through some of his issues so he can go be a great musician for some other label that's much more together than I am. I must not look very enthused because he's eyeing me with skepticism.

"No, really. It's incredible."

He ducks his head. "Thanks. So did, uh, Taylor find anything out yet?"

I stare at him blankly. Taylor? "What do you mean?"

A crease forms between his brows. "Didn't she tell you?"

"Tell me what?"

He rubs the back of his head. "When I was playing, she recorded a bit of it and emailed it to her friend Ursula, the one she talked about the other night over dinner."

The shock hits me upside the head. I drop to the couch, staring up at Luke. "She did what?"

His smile falters. "I'm sorry. I thought you knew. She said she would tell you." He sits next to me.

"Tell me what, exactly?"

A torrent of knocks hammers at the front of the cabin, making me jump.

Luke springs up to answer the door.

I'm still reeling, unmoving on the couch, when Finley comes charging in. "There you are. I have the best news."

Her face is flushed with excitement, and she's out of breath.

"Taylor sent a clip of Luke's song to Ursula, and Laila Mae wants to work with him."

I stare up at her. "What? Why would she—"

"Apparently," she cuts me off, raising her voice to prevent my inevitable meltdown, "Laila's been working with some producer who's really good—Damon Lewis—and he would be willing to help produce Luke's album."

"What? Why?" I blink, shaking my head. "What?"

I couldn't be more surprised if Finley had told me Archer sprouted the head of an elephant and now wants everyone to refer to him as the Count of Monte Cristo.

Damon Lewis? He's huge. He won three Grammys last year.

I'm completely dumbfounded. Numb with disbelief. "That can't be right."

Finley grins. "Isn't it great? This will be the perfect solution."

I shake my head. "There is no way anyone, let alone *Taylor*, could convince someone like Damon Lewis to work with a brand-new, unpublished artist on such short notice."

"Well, he does want to work with Luke since he's been working with Laila and she's the one who listened to Luke's song. And then she convinced Damon to come out here with her, but it wasn't difficult to sway him."

There must be some mistake. "With her?"

"Yes, all three of them, Laila, Damon, and her manager, Ursula."

"When?"

"In a few days. A little later than Jerry would have been, but still with plenty of time to get something done, I hope?"

My eyes flick over to Luke.

His eyes search my face. "Are you okay with all this? We don't have to do it if you don't want."

He somehow reads me in a glance when I can barely muddle through the mixed emotions myself.

And just like that, I sit up straight, lift my chin, and pull my shit together.

"Yes. We do."

I can't believe he would even ask. I can't believe he would put my feelings over his career—my stupid, immature, and petty feelings.

There's no way I can let anything stand in the way of Luke's success, especially my personal troubles with Taylor.

How can I be so concerned with being *professional* while simultaneously acting like a child?

Blake would never have put me first.

If anything, I was dead last unless he needed something from me.

The thought is depressing and humbling, but at the same time, I'm grateful he's out of my life. Well. Mostly. Except for the one-sided texts that continue to roll in nearly every day. I push that thought aside and focus on the present.

"Do you have contact information so I can talk to someone in order to flesh out the details?"

Finley pulls her phone from her pocket. "Let me see." She thumbs something in.

"Are you texting Taylor?" I ask.

"Yeah."

Irritation tumbles through me, not at Finley, but at myself.

"Is she at the house? We can just go up there and talk to her." I stand. "You don't need to be the middleman."

She throws a glance at Luke before eyeing me curiously. "Are you sure?"

"Of course I'm sure." I try to temper my tone, but the words are still snappish.

Have I been so awful? I don't even want to think about it, because obviously, I have.

I can be courteous and speak with Taylor like a grown-up.

"She's with Jake up at the pond. They went to practice fishing and ax throwing."

"Fishing and ax throwing?" Luke's brows lift in question.

Her eyes roll heavenward with amused exasperation. "Jake has been insistent on practicing before Oliver comes for Thanksgiving in order to 'crush him like the worm he is.' " She makes air quotes with her fingers. "Every time Oliver comes to stay with us Jake gets majorly competitive."

Finley's phone pings. She lifts it up to glance at the screen. "They're still there. We can take my cart. I'm parked out front."

Finley drives, Luke sitting next to her in the passenger seat, and I take one of the seats facing backward. The wind is chilly, but I don't mind the cold sweep of air across my cheeks and the back of my neck.

The drive is short, and I use the limited time to gather my emotions and shove them down into a box.

I will play nice because it's the right thing to do regardless of my tumultuous emotions about Taylor and how she's all tied up in thoughts of Aria and my own guilt.

We stop near a cluster of pine trees, and I jump off the cart, landing on the hard-packed dirt and kicking up a small puff of dust.

Jake and Taylor are over by the pond, the water a flat pale-gray slate under the cloudy sky. They're sitting about ten feet apart on folding chairs, holding onto fishing rods.

"Hey." Taylor waves with her free hand, her smile bright.

I take a deep breath and follow Finley and Luke, keeping my eyes down so I don't trip and practicing my deep breathing exercises.

If Taylor makes any snide comments or rubs her assistance in my face, odds of which are likely to be certain, I have to keep an iron grip on my self-control.

"Catch anything?" Finley asks.

"I've caught three," Taylor says.

"She's been lucky," Jake grumbles.

"Practice not quite making perfect?" Luke teases Jake.

Jake puffs up his chest. "I'll whoop your ass up and down this beach, Fletcher."

A smile tugs at the corner of my mouth in spite of my chaotic emotions. Of course, Luke has already charmed Jake into being his buddy.

I clear my throat. "Why is Damon Lewis agreeing to

work with us?" The words come out sharper than I intended.

Taylor's eyes are wary. She glances over at Finley and then at me, lifting her chin slightly before answering. "Damon has been working with Laila on her next album, but she's been in a bit of a rut, creatively." She tilts her head toward Luke. "I sent the video of him singing to Ursula, and she shared it with Laila, and I guess she totally flipped." She grins over at Luke. "I already told you this, but she just loved it so much, all of it, your voice, the song, your presence."

He smiles back at her, the dimple making an appearance.

I grit my teeth.

Taylor continues, keeping her gaze on Luke. "She wants to work with you. Maybe do a couple of duets or something, for her album and for yours. She feels like she's in this liminal space, and working with other artists and the flow that comes from a nexus of creators working together might help her get her groove back, so to speak. I can give you her number. She wanted to talk to you."

Luke takes a few steps closer, standing next to me. "Mindy and I can call her together if that's cool?"

Taylor glances over at me and her smile dims. "Yeah, whatever."

She pulls out her phone.

"We'll need to hash out some of the logistics," I say to Finley, while Luke is keying the number into his phone. "Where can they stay?"

She taps her chin. "The cabin we were going to give Jerry, right near Luke's, has two bedrooms. Maybe Laila and Ursula can stay there, and we can find another cabin for Damon."

"We'll talk to them and I'll let you know. Thanks, Finley."

I glance up. Taylor is watching me with guarded eyes.

I open my mouth to tell her thank you, gearing up to push the words out of my mouth and convince her of their sincerity, and I truly am grateful, but Luke speaks before I can.

"Thank you for doing this. Really."

"Yes, thank you." My words are a lame echo of Luke's heartfelt sentiments.

Taylor's brow lifts in question, her lips pursing.

Dammit. I'm trying to be genuine.

"I mean it." The words launch themselves out of my mouth, the volume overly loud.

"We get it," Jake leans forward, yelling toward me.

"You're not funny," I tell him.

"I'm kind of funny, right, Luke?"

Luke considers this. "Kind of funny . . . looking!"

"Oh, ho, ho! That was literally the lamest comeback I've ever heard. Wanna go throw some axes?"

"Yeah. Just for a minute."

They saunter off in the direction of the cluster of trees nearby.

Once they're out of earshot, Taylor sighs. "Listen, I'll help however I can, but I'm not doing this for you, I'm doing it for Luke." She spins on her heel and stalks after Luke and Jake.

"Isn't this exciting though? We're going to have real

celebrities here." Finley grabs my arm, shaking it as she jumps up and down.

"I'm glad you're happy."

"Don't worry. It will all work out."

I really hope she's right.

Chapter Sixteen

Mindy

Four days later, I'm in the kitchen of Luke's cabin with Ursula and Damon, reviewing the contract for the production elements. We hash out some of the details while Luke and Laila are in the living room working on songs together.

"Play me the one you were talking about last night, the one you said could be a duet." Laila's smoky voice is distinctive, her presence impossible to ignore. She's friendly, charismatic, and exudes a sense of confidence that's nearly palpable despite the fact that she can't be a day over twenty-two.

"I only have some of the lyrics ready."

"That's fine. Let's hear it."

They're sitting on opposite sides of the couch facing each other, holding guitars in their laps.

They've spent the morning warming up, jamming to get a feel for the other's style.

Luke had no discernible struggles playing in front of her. Maybe it's because they spent all last evening—they arrived yesterday—chatting about music and getting to know each other.

Maybe part of his ease is due to the fact that when Laila first came in this morning, she sat down and began playing before Luke even had a chance to grab his guitar. She was completely unselfconscious when she missed a few chords or stumbled over words, laughing at herself and belting out silly children's tunes like "Baby Beluga" and "The Hokey Pokey" to warm up her vocal cords. Laila is a whirlwind of sunny smiles and bright, flowy clothing.

I'm happy he's getting this experience. I'm happy his anxiety is fading, but some part of me is almost . . . proprietary.

"I like it," Laila says when Luke finishes the first verse. "What if the male vocals are all about falling and—" she strums a few intro chords, already able to play the song after watching him play it once, "—the female lyrics can be about not falling. Like being stable and grounded."

She keeps playing the song, then she sings.

Keep my feet on solid ground
You've got your head all in the clouds
I won't let anything knock me down
Even when the darkness comes around
I'll stand tall, with my feet on solid ground.

. . .

She grins at him and then shrugs. "You know, that kind of thing."

Luke's responding smile is blinding. "Wow. That was incredible. Was that an A chord?"

They bend toward each other, the movement damn near synchronized. It's been like this all morning. They are in the zone, completely immersed like no one else is here.

Damon taps on the keys of his laptop. "I'll email the finalized agreement to you now."

"Thanks."

Damon is the epitome of indie sleaze, pulling together '90s grunge flannel with a fur coat, skinny scarf, and jeans, somehow making it appear effortless. "Mastering the final audio might take two weeks, or a smidge longer since I'll be working with Laila to get some recording done on her next album—we hope." He tosses Ursula a pointed look.

Ursula leans against the counter next to me, casual in jeans and a plain long-sleeve T, sporting a no-nonsense boyish hairstyle. She's gotta be in her thirties, only a few years older than me, at most. "She's been in a funk. But check her out now."

As one, we examine the couple in the living room, who are still completely focused on each other.

Damon grins. "I don't think I've seen her this engrossed in months. We may get more than a couple of tracks out of them if they keep at it like this. But for now, let's plan on two duets, one for each of their albums."

I nod. "Understood." We might get pushed behind our schedule a couple of weeks, but it's okay. I will take anything I can get at this point. Damon is giving us fantastic rates, considering his accolades, he could easily charge thousands of dollars.

"I hope they keep it up," Ursula murmurs. "Usually once she gets in the zone there is no slowing her down, let alone stopping her."

Damon nods his agreement. "I set everything up this morning, so we're ready to get started on the songs Luke has ready. Whenever Laila needs a break, we can steal him away. He's got a great sound, and if you have enough songs polished and ready, we may be able to get them all done before Thanksgiving."

"That sounds perfect."

"If we need to come back for a couple of days after the holiday to finish things up, that will work with her schedule," Ursula confirms.

Boisterous laughter in the living room catches my attention.

Laila's head is thrown back in mirth, and Luke's face is practically glowing with whatever hilarity is passing between them.

Damon and Ursula exchange a look.

"Luke and Laila," she says.

"They're perfect," Damon murmurs.

"Perfect for what?" I ask, even though I know exactly where they are going.

Ursula waves a hand. "Oh, come on, look at that chemistry."

"If they don't end up hooking up, I will eat my favorite silk necktie. And it's Gucci."

I bite back the automatic and extremely vehement *no way* begging to erupt out of my mouth.

This isn't a bad thing. Laila has a huge following. If we hint at a romance, it will trigger more interest in both their albums. I know this, and yet the thought of spinning it to the press makes me physically ill.

Because of Blake. Of course it's because of Blake and not because I'm majorly attracted to Luke myself.

I'm not romantically interested. I can't be interested. At all. Ever.

Maybe if I keep thinking it, it will come true. Manifesting disinterest.

Ursula holds up her phone.

"What are you doing?" I ask.

"Getting some clips for her social media. Her fans will eat this up. We've been having to repost old videos because she's been in such a slump. She has over a million followers. This will be good exposure for Luke, too," she adds.

"That's wonderful. Thank you. I can see why she has such a dedicated fan base. She seems really great."

Not to mention talented and gorgeous.

"She is great. One of the best artists I've ever worked with." She taps on her phone and then slides it into her back pocket. "I have a couple of clients seeking new representation in a couple of months when their contracts expire." Her dark brows lift. "One of them is Duncan Santos."

I barely restrain my mouth from dropping open. Duncan's first album, which came out earlier this year, was a massive success. "He didn't have an option to extend?"

"Nope. We negotiated a twelve-month term, one album, with C&C Records."

Interesting. Most labels add options to extend, especially if the record does very well, as his did. No one wants to lose a cash cow. It was smart of him to negotiate a shorter term. It's always good to have choices and not be stuck with a label that might be hard to work with.

"Can I give him your number?" Ursula asks.

"Of course." Getting someone like Duncan, with an established fan base, massive talent, and credibility, someone who's already proven their worth, would be a huge boon. I wouldn't have to worry about producers flaking or ignoring me if I could sign someone like him. They would be coming to me.

Ursula flashes me a grin, but then her head dips before she lifts her eyes to mine. "Just one warning. He might ask you about," she waves a hand, "some of your past history and how that might impact any work you would do for him."

It's like being kicked in the teeth. "Oh."

Will I ever escape my past?

She winces. "He asked me about it already, when I told him we were coming here to work with you and Luke. If you speak with Duncan, I just wanted you to be ready. He will ask if working with you would prevent him from being able to pursue any collaborations with Rebel Records artists or venues they frequently work with, you know, that kind of thing."

I swallow and nod. "It's a valid question. Thank you for letting me know."

Gritting my teeth, I turn away from her to observe the musicians in the living room.

Luke and Laila laugh together again, nearly falling over on each other this time.

My head starts to pound at the temples.

Fuckity fuck rocket.

"Do you want the porch light on?" Finley asks, haloed in the light emanating from the open doorway.

"No. I want to look at the stars."

She hugs her sweater around her tighter and clicks off the office light before walking out onto the porch, meeting me at the railing.

I've been staring out into the darkness and thinking.

Finley clears her throat. "We're having a bonfire tomorrow night by the pond. Laila and Ursula are staying."

I've been out here on the porch for twenty minutes, at least, contemplating going to talk with Luke since we wrapped up recording for the day a few hours ago . . . but I'm not sure if it's the wisest choice.

"Really? I thought they would be leaving tomorrow." Thanksgiving is only two days away.

"They were really excited about roasting hot dogs and s'mores. I thought Laila would be more . . . I don't know, fancy?" She chuckles, putting a hand on the railing and turning to face me. "Damon is going to Boston for the holiday, so he wants to leave tomorrow, but Laila and Ursula are driving to the city, so they decided to stay an extra night and leave Thanksgiving morning. That's when Luke's driving home, too, right?"

I nod. "Yeah." He's taking Oliver's SUV to his parents' as we planned.

"Piper and Oliver will be here midmorning, and Mason is coming with them. They're picking him up at the airport on the way."

"Sounds good." Mason is a childhood friend of Archer's, and although I've only met him once, last Easter, he's basically part of the family now.

"How is everything going with the album?"

I grip the railing a little tighter. "Really great. We're almost done, actually. Just one more duet to record."

Damon and Luke recorded more than half the song list in a matter of days, faster than I thought would be possible because everything just clicked. It happens that way sometimes.

"Luke and Laila really jive well together."

I try not to flinch. "Yeah, they do."

Finley's head tilts. "Does that bother you?"

"Why would it bother me?" My voice is entirely too high-pitched to be believable. I clear my throat. "It's great for Luke's career, and mine. They have chemistry, creative chemistry."

Maybe other chemistry, too. Maybe they are hooking up. I don't know if she's sneaking over to his cabin at night, but it's entirely possible.

The videos Ursula uploaded of Laila and Luke totally blew up.

The most popular one ended up being a clip of them bantering after they had finished a set. Laila says to him, "That was gorgeous."

Luke replies, "I might throw up."

Laila bursts out laughing.

That sound bite went viral, people using it to create their own videos using the clip in a variety of skits and jokes.

The comments on the uploaded videos also exploded, half of them making observations about their chemistry, how cute they are together, and one even insisted *if they don't get married and have a million babies I will* along with a dozen skull emojis.

I shut my eyes and mentally heave the thoughts away. I can't think about them together for too long. It gives me an ulcer. I mean, it's wonderful they get along so well and work together like they were born to do this. But . . . there is no but. There shouldn't be a but.

I've already received numerous requests for interviews with Luke from magazines and various press outlets, and I've scheduled most of them around the launch date. Working with Laila is building buzz around his album in a way I never could have anticipated or initiated on my own.

We've also planned for an intimate show a week after Thanksgiving. We got it set up to take place in Whitby, at Veronica's. She agreed to close the place down for the event—a bonus to growing up in a small town and knowing the owner since I was born—and we've invited a bunch of industry people, critics, publicists, and journalists.

It will be a small venue, the perfect size for an exclusive gathering to get even more buzz circulating, but not so much of a crowd that it stirs up Luke's stage fright. I hope. Laila will join him for a duet, which should help.

Before Laila and the crew showed up, it was like Luke and I were in our own little bubble. Now that bubble has burst. I haven't been alone with him for even a minute since they arrived.

Luke's album is sure to be a success because of Laila. I should be thrilled. I am thrilled.

But I miss him.

It's ridiculous. I see him every day.

"Are you going to stay up much longer?" Finley asks.

"A little bit longer. I'll lock up before I go inside."

"Okay. Goodnight." She gives me a side hug and then goes back into the house.

I stare out into the night, contemplating the winking stars overhead. I want to walk over to Luke's.

The problem is, I don't have any real professional reason to go see him. I just want to be around him without all the distractions and other people, especially Laila, who is really so sweet I can't even truly hate her despite all my best intentions.

I squeeze the railing once before turning around to head inside.

"Mindy."

I'm so obsessed, I'm hearing his voice now.

"Mindy, wait."

Hold on. It is Luke's voice. I spin around.

Luke jogs up the porch steps, coming to a halt within touching distance. "Hey. I'm glad you're still awake."

I drink him in, dressed in dark sweatpants and a zip-up hoodie. The faint moonlight exposes a hazy outline of his features.

Keep your eyes up. "Is everything okay?" I ask.

"It's great. I wanted to see if we could chat for a minute. I feel like we haven't had a chance to talk in ages."

Damn if he isn't reading my mind. "Yeah. Of course."

The high-pitched blare of a cellphone ringing cuts through the night.

"Oh, sorry." I tug the offending object from my pocket. I frown at the name glowing on the screen. "It's Carson," I murmur, and then explain to Luke, "He's renting my apartment. Sorry, I need to take this."

Hopefully he's not dealing with a burst pipe or something.

Luke nods, shoving his hands in his pockets.

"Hey, Carson," I answer.

"Mindy, hey, sorry to be calling so late."

"Is everything all right with the apartment?"

"Oh, yeah, no, that's all fine. I thought you should be aware of a, um, visitor who was just here and looking for you."

Confusion puckers my lips. "Who?"

"Blake Bonham."

My eyes fly up to Luke's. He's watching me, concern dipping his brows.

I shake my head in disbelief. "What was Blake doing there? What did he say?"

Luke's eyes widen.

Carson sighs. "Well, first off, he was completely hammered."

My hand flies up to my head, rubbing near my temple. "Shit. Did anyone else see him?"

"I don't know how many people *saw* him, but half your neighbors, some random pedestrians, and that homeless guy always panhandling on the corner definitely *heard* him."

I groan. "What did he say?"

"The words he said weren't always clear, but there was a definite theme of how much he loves you and misses you."

I blink. "What?" Blake never told me he loved me. I don't think he's capable of loving anyone other than himself. "Did you talk to him?"

"I told him you didn't live here anymore and to go away before I called the cops. That got rid of him pretty quickly."

I blow out a breath. "Thanks, Carson, for getting rid of him and for letting me know." I'll have to set an alert on my phone for any news being leaked about this. This is all I need, more media scrutiny involving me and Blake when I'm getting ready to launch a new album and kick-start my career.

"Anytime, babe. Talk atcha later."

We hang up, and I shove my phone back in my pocket.

"Are you okay?" Luke asks, stepping closer.

"I'm fine." Am I though? Frustration and irritation twist in my stomach. "This is just, so typical."

"What do you mean?"

I wave a hand. "Blake. He's so self-absorbed. He showed up at my apartment drunk. He's been texting me lately, too."

Luke considers me, his head tilting to one side. "Do you want to talk about it?"

Surprisingly, I do. "It's a lot to unpack."

"I have time." He gestures over to the porch swing off

to the side, and after a second, I nod.

Once we're settled on the cushioned seats, I consider where to even start.

"I thought I loved him. But now, I'm not sure. Nothing about Blake is real. He's so sucked into fame, and the optics of that, I'm not sure if he even knows who he really is. I knew that before we ever got . . . involved, but I didn't care."

Luke shifts on the seat next to me, stretching his arm along the back of the chair behind me. "He's been in the spotlight for a long time."

"That's exactly it. Having millions of adoring fans seems like it would be amazing, but it really fucks up your self-image. His whole life has been this never-ending parade of ego-inflating moments, one after the other. He's so used to everyone adoring him, telling him yes to everything. He forgets he's a mere mortal because the world keeps telling him he's a god."

Luke dips his head in acknowledgement. "It's especially damaging if that fame begins in childhood, when your brain is still developing."

I nod. "It's easy to confuse fame with love. But the general public doesn't really know Blake. They love a version of him, the version he's created, the one he chooses to share. It isn't real."

"Being superficially enamored of someone's best qualities isn't the same as loving them despite their worst."

I sit back in the seat, the motion setting it to rocking back and forth slightly. "Yes. Honestly, anyone who survives childhood celebrity status without going stark raving mad is a miracle." I blow out a breath. "With Blake, when we first met, we were just friends, but he pursued me relentlessly. Maybe because I said no. But over the years, we got to know each other, and we became friends. At least I thought we were. I trusted him. He told me that he and Jeanette were separated, married in name only for years, and I believed him." I shake my head.

"Why wouldn't you?" he asks softly.

I shrug. "I don't know. In hindsight, I feel like I should have known better. It wasn't the first time I had been hit on by a musician, but Blake was more difficult to ignore. He was tenacious, pursuing me for three years before I gave in to his charms. And then I got burned."

"And now he's showing up at your apartment. Would you go back to him?"

I bark out a surprised laugh. "What? No. Never. That ship has sailed. I'm still a little mad at him, but I think what I feel is more . . . irritation. And pity. I don't think he's happy."

"Are you happy?"

I gaze up into his shadowed face. "I . . . I don't know. I'm trying to be."

"I guess that's the best any of us can do." He extends a leg, setting the swing to a gentle sway.

"Thank you for listening."

"Do you want me to go?"

I lean my head back, my neck resting against his arm behind me. I should tell him to leave. He needs his rest, and I don't need to be developing tender feelings for another musician.

"Stay, for just a little bit?"

He nods, and we rock back and forth in silence.

Chapter Seventeen

Luke

The sun is kissing the horizon when Laila and I make our way up and over the hill to where the bonfire is being held.

It's a little cool, but the fresh air is energizing. The past week has involved a lot of sitting or standing around and very little time for exercise other than vocal.

Laila skips ahead on the packed dirt path, spinning around in a circle, her arms spread wide. She stops and faces me, arms still extended. "Don't you just want to live here forever?"

I chuckle at her exuberance. "Forever is a long time."

She sighs and jogs back to me, linking her arm in mine. "It is, but this place is like . . . magical."

"You only think that because you found your inspiration here after having writer's block for an eternity."

She laughs. "Maybe. But I think it's more than that.

It's the fresh mountain air, it's quiet that only comes from being surrounded by nature, and it's the energy of the people who live here. Like it's one of those mystical places, you know, Sedona or Mount Shasta or something. I feel so vibrant." She squeezes my arm. "I'm so glad we met. It was kismet, Taylor sending Ursula that video."

"Maybe it was," I murmur.

We went from being unsure if an album would even happen to what feels like near stardom overnight. *We.* Mindy and I. Of course, it's my face and voice that have been plastered all over the Internet, but she was the impetus.

I wanted to kiss her last night so badly it was like a physical ache. I still want it so badly I can almost taste it—taste her—on my tongue.

"It was definitely kismet that led you to Mindy," she adds, nudging me with her elbow. "There is so much built-up tension between you two I could jump on it like a trampoline."

"It's not like that."

But I want it to be.

The errant thought strikes like a lightning bolt.

This isn't the first conversation we've had like this. Laila's been teasing me about Mindy since about day two. She's convinced we make calf eyes at each other every time the other isn't looking.

"So you've said." She rolls her eyes, clearly unimpressed at my blatant lie.

"Even if there was something between us, you know I can't do anything about it because of her past. You know what she's been through."

She snorts. "You are not Blake Bonham, and I mean that in the best possible way. He's a total piece of shit. Don't worry." She smacks me on the shoulder. "I'll talk to her."

"Please don't."

"Relax, Romeo. I won't even mention you. It will just be a little girl talk to assure her that she doesn't need to let her past dictate her future."

"I'm not sure—"

Pounding footsteps sound behind us along with a feminine peal of laughter and the distant hum of golf carts.

"On your left," a deep voice calls out.

I twist around. A man runs toward us, over six feet tall, wide as a tank, a slighter figure propped on his back, arms wrapped around his neck.

Wait. Is that Mindy?

They pass by, Laila and I stepping to the side to get out of their way.

"Sorry!" Mindy calls out when they're a few feet ahead.

Laila laughs. "Who was that?"

"I think it's Archer's friend Mason?" Jake mentioned him the other night. Archer doesn't have any living family, the closest he's got are his two childhood friends Oliver—Piper's boyfriend—and Mason, who flew in from LA and drove in with the couple.

On the heels of Mason and Mindy, two golf carts come up the path. We move to the side so they can pass.

The first one stops next to us. "You two want a ride?" Jake calls out. "We have extra seats." He gestures behind him. Archer and Finley are with him on the first cart, and the cart behind them is loaded up with Oliver, Piper, and Ursula.

"We're good, thanks." Laila waves at everyone.

"Suit yourselves," Jake waves. "Last one there gets chucked in the pond." They take off, kicking up dust in their wake.

A couple of hours later, the sun has set and we're all sitting around the fire, roasting hot dogs and drinking hot cocoa and tea. The buzz of conversation, interspersed with the periodic bubble of laughter, fills the air.

No one was chucked in the lake since the last one there was technically Laila, and Jake can barely manage a full sentence if she's within ten feet of him. He's a little star-struck.

Finley is telling Ursula and Laila about the upcoming winter camp weekend. Oliver and Piper disappeared somewhere fifteen minutes ago.

Mason and Mindy are huddled together on the other side of the fire, talking in low voices.

Jake and Archer are arguing with Taylor about whether mashed potatoes or stuffing is the best Thanksgiving side dish.

"Mindy, help me out here," Jake calls out.

"With what?"

Jake lifts a hand. "Sweet potatoes are disgusting, right?"

Mindy considers the question. "They make decent fries, terrible mashed, though."

"See?"

Taylor shakes her head. "Hello, consider the source! I win."

Mindy frowns. "What's that supposed to mean?"

A taut pressure fills the space, silence descending on the glowing circle of faces.

Taylor and Mindy have been under a sort of fragile truce since Laila and Ursula arrived. It probably helps they haven't been around each other much, but when they have been in the same room, at least it's been civil.

Taylor rolls her eyes. "Nothing. Stop being so sensitive."

Mindy's mouth pops open, but then she shuts it, leaning toward Mason to tell him something in a voice too low for the rest of us to hear.

"Do you have something you want to share with the rest of us?" Taylor asks, her voice rigid.

Mindy stares at her, letting the silence sit for a few long seconds. "Believe it or not, it's not always about you."

Jake stands up. "Anyone want to throw around some axes? Only those not actively contemplating murder may apply."

The strain pops like a soapy bubble on the breeze, and Jake, Archer, and Ursula move over to the nearby coppice of trees, where they keep the axes locked up in a storage trunk.

Taylor huffs, moving over to sit by Finley.

All this, and the night has just begun. It should be an interesting evening.

Chapter Eighteen

Mindy

"What do you know about Oliver's assistant?"

I lift my gaze from the flickering fire to scrutinize Mason, the sniping conversation between Taylor and I still taking up residence in my head. I should have known the tenuous truce between us wouldn't last. "What, you mean Carson?"

"Yeah."

I grin, happy for the distraction. "What do you want to know, Casanova?"

"Is he single?"

"As far as I know. He had a bad breakup over the summer."

His eyes brighten. "Oh yeah?"

"You might want to check with Piper, though." I glance around. Where is she? Oliver is also missing in action. Okay, I definitely don't want to know what they are getting up to. "I haven't heard Carson talk about any new men in his life, but she's closer to him than I am."

He shrugs one massive shoulder. "It probably doesn't matter. It's not that it could go anywhere. He lives in New York, right?"

"Yeah. He's renting my apartment right now, actually."

"He's pretty cute."

"He is. Maybe a holiday fling?"

Mason's cheeks flush. They would make a cute couple. Too bad they live on opposite sides of the country.

"Maybe, but I doubt it." He claps his hands on his knees. "You want any more food?"

"Nah, I'm good."

"I'm gonna get another dog or two." He pushes himself up, heading over to the cooler by Finley to grab more food.

Seconds after he vacates the spot next to me, Laila plops down.

"I really wanted to thank you for everything you've done for me."

"Oh. Um, you're welcome." Really she's done more for me and Luke, but I don't have it in me to gush all over her.

"I mean it. I'm so glad you found Luke and decided to start your own label. If it wasn't for you, I'd still be in a total black hole nightmare, creatively speaking."

I nod. "I'm very glad everything worked out."

"I should call Jerry and thank him for being a flake," she chuckles.

"He had his own reasons. I'm just grateful my . . . " I

pause, considering the most delicate way to phrase it, "past didn't affect your decision to work with Luke."

Laila leans closer, her shoulder touching mine. "Blake's a total piece of shit."

A startled laugh erupts from my throat.

She shrugs, unapologetic. "Everyone knows it, they just kiss his ass because he's rich and famous. You know how it is."

"Thank you," I say, surprised at my own sincerity. Also surprised to realize that I like Laila. She's a good person. She would be good for Luke.

"The only people who would judge you for your past are probably assholes. Don't let Blake or anyone keep you from going after something that could be amazing."

I stare at her. She can't mean—

"If you ever need anything, for Luke or anyone or even yourself, I mean it, please reach out to me. I may not be as illustrious as Blake, but I have my own cachet."

She nudges me with her shoulder, and I catch a whiff of her rose and amber perfume. Damn it, why is she so sweet? And smell so nice? She makes it impossible to hate her.

"Do you want more hot cocoa?" she asks.

"Yeah, sure."

An hour and three cups of cocoa later, I have to pee so bad my back teeth are floating.

"Finley, can I get one of the cart keys? I need to use the restroom."

"I'll go with you. I need to grab more firewood. Anyone else need to use the facilities?" she calls out to the group.

"I have to go, too, I'll come with you," Taylor says.

"Great," I murmur. "More fun family times." If I didn't hate peeing in the woods, I'd just go squat behind a tree.

Finley gives me her mom stare, the one that says *be good and keep your trap shut*.

I know she's right. This isn't the time or place, but Taylor started it earlier with her picking a fight with me over sweet potatoes, for crying out loud.

But for now, she's being civil enough. We get into the golf cart, taking our seats without issue.

When we arrive at the house, Finley starts loading up the open seat in the cart with firewood, and I head upstairs to use the bathroom, letting Taylor take the closer one downstairs.

When I finish, Taylor is sitting on the couch, waiting for me.

I try to pass by into the kitchen, and she stands, stopping me. "Look, I know you're going to be pissed at me for all eternity or whatever, but can we set it all aside and pretend to be adults for one day? For Finley and our family?" Her tone is laced with superior condescension.

Don't let her get to you. "I don't know, Taylor, can we? You haven't exactly been holding back."

She shakes her head. "You're the one who won't let go of the past."

Is she serious right now? Frustration bubbles inside me, mixing with the anger that's been covering up guilt. My guilt. The toxic mixture forces words to bubble up, and I lash out. "You should have stopped them."

Her mouth pops open.

There's a moment of fraught silence while she registers my words, her eyes widening, fists clenching at her sides.

We haven't talked about this since she first told me, years ago, about the night Aria died. We've fought about everything under the sun but never discussed the source.

Her voice shakes when she finally speaks. "I never should have told you anything. I thought I could trust you."

I ignore the shard of guilt slicing me in the gut. "Why didn't you stop them? Why didn't you say anything?"

She throws her hands up. "Why would I have stopped them? They were going home, where they should have been. I don't even know how they found out about the party."

"Probably from listening to you."

Her jaw drops. "You don't think I feel guilty about it every day?"

"You should feel guilty."

Her head jerks back, as if I landed a physical blow. "What do you want from me? What do you expect me to do? You don't think I would do anything, give up anything, give up everything, my own life, whatever it took, to go back and change that night? But I can't, Mindy. I can't change anything, and neither can you."

A choked sound grabs our attention, both of us turning toward the source of the sound in the kitchen.

Finley's eyes are wide and gleaming as she glances between me and Taylor.

"Taylor. It wasn't your fault." Her voice is shaking with emotion.

Taylor huffs. "Tell that to the ice queen."

Finley's eyes move to mine, confusion creasing her forehead. "You've been blaming Taylor for Aria's death? That's what this has been about this whole time?"

Shame floods me, uprooting a knee-jerk reaction of denial. "You don't understand."

She spreads her hands. "So explain it."

My whole body is a knot of tension, a volcano ready to erupt. "Taylor saw them that night. She saw Aria and Jake at that stupid party. She's the reason they were there to begin with. She should have taken them home. Instead she told them to leave and then they—" The words get clogged in my throat. We all know the rest of the story.

Finley bites her lip, her expression a mixture of concern and disbelief.

Why isn't she angry?

"It wasn't Taylor's fault. It wasn't anyone's fault."

I shake my head in denial. It has to be *someone's* fault.

Finley continues. "We've all suffered. It's been ten years, and we're all still suffering." She blinks and two twin tears track down her cheeks. "She wouldn't have wanted this. She wouldn't have wanted to be the cause of this."

Taylor stalks past Finley, out the side door, slamming it shut behind her.

On numb legs I walk over to the couch and sink down onto it.

Finley moves to my side, placing a soft hand on my shoulder.

"I can't go back," I tell her. I don't know if I'm talking about the bonfire or something else.

"I know."

My body is going numb along with my emotions.

"Do you want me to stay?" Finley asks, her voice low.

"No. I need some time alone."

"Okay." She squeezes my shoulder and then leaves. I listen to the cart hum to life and then the crunch of leaves under the tires as they drive away.

I sit there for I don't even know how long before irritation itches at me, making me get up and go outside.

I have to get out of here.

Where could I go? I can't just leave. Luke is taking the SUV to Corning tomorrow for Thanksgiving so . . . I'll be trapped.

I pace back and forth in front of the house, unsure what to do with myself. I can't stay here. I can't sit across the table from Taylor tomorrow and eat turkey and pretend like nothing is wrong.

I need to get out of here, and I really only have one option.

I pack an overnight bag and then walk briskly through the camp. I make it to Luke's cabin and let myself inside.

Sitting on the couch, I rest my head back to stare up at the ceiling.

What am I doing here? What am I going to tell Luke when he arrives? I have to tell him something. I can't go back to the house tonight, not if Taylor is going to be there and not if Finley is going to look at me like that again, with so much concern and pity.

I jolt up when a thought strikes like a bolt of lightning.

What if Luke comes back with Laila? What if they come here to—?

I cut the thought off before I make myself sick.

I stand up. Surely I can break into one of the other cabins. It might be a little cold, but they keep them warm enough to prevent the pipes from freezing.

I'm almost to the door when it swings open.

Luke blinks. "Hey. What are you doing here? Is everything okay?"

"It's fine. It's just . . . I, you know, everything with Taylor." I stare down at my hands fidgeting in front of me. I clasp them together and then meet his steady gaze. "I can't stay up at the house. Can I stay here? I'll sleep on the couch."

He shuts the door behind him, taking a step toward me. "Of course you can stay here but you're definitely sleeping on the bed. I can take the couch."

I bite my lip. "Are you sure?"

"Absolutely." His brow creases. "Do you want to talk?"

I shake my head. "No. I just want to go to sleep."

He nods. "No problem. Let me get my things from upstairs."

I stand in the entryway while he winds his way up the steps. I'm being incredibly selfish, putting him out like this, but I don't know what else to do. I can't go back to the house. I can't offer to share the bed. Knowing Luke, I'll never convince him to let me take the couch.

When he comes back down, he's holding a pillow and blanket, and he's changed into sweats and a T-shirt. "Do you need anything?" he asks.

"No. Yes. Just one more thing. Can I go with you tomorrow?"

His brows lift to his hairline. "You want to come home with me for Thanksgiving?" his voice has gone up three octaves.

I wince. "I know it's last minute and it's probably weird and rude and you can say no, and I'm so sorry I—"

"Mindy, it's fine. Of course you can come."

"Are you sure? Your parents would be okay with that?"

He huffs. "My mom will be thrilled. My sisters will love to have someone they can interrogate about me." He points at me. "Don't say I haven't warned you."

"An interrogation would be relaxing compared to spending the day with Taylor."

He nods thoughtfully. "Family can be hard."

"Some more than others."

He reaches out, gently setting his hand on my shoulder. "Don't even worry about it. Try to get some rest. Things will look better in the morning. If you need anything, I'll be the one snoring on the couch."

Despite the stress of the past hour, a smile pulls at my mouth. "Thank you."

I go upstairs with my overnight bag and get ready for bed quickly, sliding into sheets that smell like Luke, like clean soap and sandalwood.

He is so tempting.

I am such a mess.

Chapter Nineteen

Luke

The first hour of the drive to Corning is silent, but it's not uncomfortable. It's still early, the sun barely cresting the horizon. We woke up at six and were on the road by seven.

I insisted on driving, in case she wanted to sleep, but so far, she's been staring out at the slowly brightening world outside her window.

"Are you hungry? I brought some granola bars." I tilt my head in the direction of the bag in the back seat.

"I'm okay. Thanks."

Well, that conversational gambit went nowhere. I frown. Her face is drawn and pale, the thin skin under her eyes smudged a light purple. I had hoped to distract her from the worrying thoughts dancing behind her eyes, but so far nothing's working.

I'm racking my mind for ideas on how to provide some diversion when she speaks.

"You said it will be your parents, Granny Bea, and your sisters at dinner?"

I squint into the rising sun. "And my nieces and nephew."

Mindy pulls my sunglasses out of the center console and hands them to me. "Your sisters are both married?"

"Thanks." I slide the sunglasses on. "My sister Vanessa, she's only two years older than me, she's not married. She's a massage therapist and lives in Boston. Lynn, the oldest, is six years older than me. She's divorced, for a couple years now. She has three kids, but her ex-husband, Daniel, will be there, too. They own a restaurant together and all still live in town. It was an amicable split."

"That's unusual."

I nod.

"Full house, then," she adds.

"It usually is." The last time I came home was Christmas, nearly a year ago. I can't believe it's been that long.

"How old are the kids?" she asks.

I think about it for a second. "My nephew, Adam, is twelve, Diana is nine, and Cassie just turned four."

A smile ghosts over her mouth. "Those are good ages."

My eyes dip to her bottom lip, wondering for the umpteenth time what it might taste like. "Yeah. They are a handful, but they keep things interesting."

She looks back out the window and another silence descends.

After a few minutes, she shifts in her seat, her knees angling in my direction. "Your parents are still married?"

"Yep. Over thirty years."

"That's incredible."

"They met in high school."

"Wow." Her gaze is a physical stroke against my jaw line. "My mom took off shortly after the twins were born"

The twins. Jake and Aria.

I glance over at her. "How old were you?"

She waves a hand. "I don't know. Six or seven."

"That's young."

"Young enough that I don't remember much about her." She pauses. "I remember her being sad a lot. She had dark hair and a necklace with a phoenix on it. But I don't remember her face or the sound of her voice."

"You don't have any pictures?"

She leans her head back against the seat. "No. Maybe Dad got rid of them."

My chest aches. "It must have been hard for you when she left."

"Harder on Finley. And Dad. He did the best he could, but there were six of us. I helped Finley as much as I could with our siblings, but . . ." she shrugs.

Of course, she thinks she wasn't enough. "You were just a child."

"So was Finley. She's a year older than me." One corner of her mouth curls up. "She was born old, though."

"You never heard from your mom again?"

"Nope."

"You never tried to find her?"

"Don't see why I would care to locate someone who didn't care enough to stick around."

I want to dig into her past and uncover whether any of

these early life experiences are at the core of why she's built up so many walls, but I don't want to pry, either. She's already shared so many of her vulnerable pieces.

An hour later, we pull up to the split-level ranch house, flanked by skeletal trees dusted with snow. I take in the familiar red brick and white siding. I glance over at Mindy, wondering what she thinks of my childhood home.

"I apologize in advance for anything my family says."

She blinks. "What do you mean?"

"They can be loud and obnoxious and a bunch of busybodies."

A wry smile twists her mouth. "It's like you haven't spent the last month dealing with my drama-ridden family."

I unbuckle my seatbelt with a grimace. "It's different when it's your own. I've been able to act all high and mighty, but now you're going to realize the truth."

"And what's that?"

"We're all a mess. Some people are just better at hiding it."

She chuckles, and for a second the shadows in her eyes recede. Delight fills me at being the one to put the light back in her face, even for a moment.

We get out of the car, and I halt Mindy at the trunk. "Let's go in first. We can grab the bags once we figure out where Mom's gonna put us."

She bites her lip. "I hope it's not a trouble for her to accommodate me last minute."

We head up the sidewalk, between the hedges. "Are you kidding? She loves this stuff." I stop in the middle of the walkway and face her. "But if she breaks out the album with my old report cards, run." I turn and jog up the concrete steps.

She frowns, about to ask more, but I push open the mahogany front door and call out. "We're here."

The announcement is heralded by the stomping of multiple feet on the hardwood flooring.

"Uncle Luke!" Cassie is the first to make it into the entryway, throwing herself at my legs. Her hair is in pigtails, one braid coming lose. She has a streak of chalk on her forehead, and when I reach down to hug her, something sticky and red transfers from her hands to mine.

The small room bursts at the seams with people. My mom embraces Mindy in greeting. Mindy is frozen stiff, her movements jerky as the rest of the family follows suit, welcoming her with hugs and sometimes cheek kisses. I probably should have warned her about all the affection. From what I've observed over the past month, Finley is the most demonstrative of the siblings. Mindy is generally more reserved.

I don't have a chance to rescue her from their attentions because Adam is excitedly telling me about how he's been practicing drums, and Diana is tugging on my hand, wanting to play Uno. I'm suffused with guilt for how big they've gotten while I've been gone, like a physical manifestation of my lengthy absence.

Mindy gets dragged into the living room, presumably where Granny Bea is prepping for football, and Dad and Daniel press me into service in the kitchen. It's our year to cook.

After handing me a bag of potatoes to wash and peel, I get to work while Dad chops onions and herbs at one counter and Daniel preps the bird for the rotisserie at another.

"I can't believe how big the kids are," I tell Daniel.

"Tell me about it. Adam's almost a teenager."

"He'll be driving soon," Dad says.

Daniel clutches at his chest with a grimace. "Let's not think about that."

"How did everything go with recording the album?" Daniel asks.

I give them the highlights about the business side of things, how we finished recording my first album—words I can hardly believe even as I speak them. Then Daniel asks questions about Laila and Damon and the contract I signed with Mindy. Dad stays mostly silent, only nodding and grunting occasionally. My parents still haven't accepted the fact that their son, Dr. Luke Fletcher, gave up the prestigious title.

Once the bird is cooking, I escape to the living room to make sure Mindy is doing okay. She's sitting on the dark blue couch between Granny Bea and my sister Vanessa. My mom is in the recliner on one side of the sofa, and Lynn is lounging in the loveseat across from her.

The flat-screen hanging on the wall has the game playing, the volume low.

"Don't look at us like that, we're just talking to Mindy." Vanessa shoots me a glare, flicking her dark hair over one shoulder.

I eye Mindy for signs of torture. "Interrogating, you

mean?" She doesn't look tortured. She's smiling, the movement reaching her eyes, so it must be sincere.

"Of course not," Mom clucks at me.

"We're bonding," Granny Bea says, "so make yourself scarce for at least more minutes."

"Are you sure?"

Mindy nods at me. "It's fine. No interrogation here. It's more like they're divulging all your embarrassing childhood stories so I have something to blackmail you with later."

I groan and cover my face with my hands, and they all laugh, the devils.

"See? We're awesome," Lynn says.

Vanessa lifts her brows at me. "You've never brought someone home with you."

"I told you, we work together," I say.

"He's rescuing me from my family," Mindy adds, a hint of flush to her cheeks.

Lynn grimaces. "We really can't promise this will be any better."

Mindy chuckles. "So I've been told."

"As long as you've been warned." Granny Bea pats her on the leg.

Vanessa jerks a thumb at me. "Now scram. We were about to tell her about the time you swallowed a dime and cried for an hour."

I lift my hands in surrender. "Okay, okay. Have fun."

I follow the sound of yelling and find the kids in the den playing board games. They rope me into a few rounds of Clue, and then I'm hauled back to the kitchen for more menial labor before it's time to set the table for dinner.

We've just sat down to eat when Dad starts with the bragging.

"Luke skipped two grades. Did he tell you?"

"He may have mentioned something about it." She shoots me a confused glance.

I give her a small shake of my head. This is how our conversations always go.

Mom scoops mashed potatoes onto her plate, then passes the dish to Lynn on her right. "His teachers always said he was the brightest student they ever had. Every single one, all through elementary and high school."

"Voted most likely to succeed in high school," Dad says. "Valedictorian and had a full scholarship to almost any college in this country. They were begging him to apply for admission."

"He graduated top of his class at Columbia." Mom reaches over and touches my hand with hers briefly. "You had such a bright future."

Mindy finishes chewing the food in her mouth and then speaks. "He still has a bright future. He's one of the most talented people I've worked with."

Mom's head bobs up and down. "Oh, yes. I'm sure he is. Our Luke has excelled at anything he puts his mind to. He's always wanted to be a doctor."

Vanessa, who's half turned in her seat, helping Cassie cut up her turkey, interjects. "Sorry, Mindy. They're still in denial."

"What do you mean?" Mom asks.

Vanessa hands Cassie a fork and turns around, scooting her chair closer to the table. "They haven't finished grieving the fact that they won't have a doctor in the family."

Dad blinks, a frown pressing the corners of his lips downward. "He's still a doctor. Just because he's taking a break doesn't mean the degree goes away."

Before anyone can follow up on that statement, Granny Bea interjects, tapping Mom on the shoulder. "Will you pass the gravy, Catherine? Who wants to get their butt kicked at Monopoly after dinner?"

Diana shouts, "Me, me!" Cassie following suit, likely because the four-year-old has no idea what she's agreeing to.

My eyes lock with Mindy's across the table, exchanging a sort of silent communication. I wink at her.

Her mouth twitches, then Lynn says something to her and she looks away, the moment broken.

After dinner, everyone ends up in the living room, either watching football or crowding one of the three game tables set up throughout the room.

I sit next to Granny Bea on the couch. "Thanks for the assist in there."

Her lips pinch. "Your parents need to let go of the past."

"They mean well."

"It's not fair to you. It's like they can't accept that it's your life and not theirs."

"It will all work out."

She sighs. "I know it, child. I like your girlfriend." She tilts her head over to where Mindy is sitting on the floor with Diana playing old maid.

Diana points at a card and says something, and Mindy laughs.

My heart clenches.

"She's not my girlfriend," I tell Granny Bea.

She pats my hand. "Don't worry. She will be."

Before I can correct her assumption, Adam bounds over and drags me off to play Trivial Pursuit with him and Daniel.

Daniel groans and waves a hand at me. "We don't want him to play. He remembers everything."

Adam laughs and hands me the die.

A few hours later, Cassie is cranky and whining, so Lynn and Daniel leave to get the kids home to bed. They don't live far, Lynn's house is three blocks away and Daniel's is a block beyond that.

As is our usual custom, we stand around saying goodbye for twenty minutes. When they finally depart, they take a big chunk of the noise with them.

"I'm heading up to bed, too." Granny Bea heaves herself up from the couch.

"I'll go with you," Vanessa says, taking her arm.

Vanessa is sleeping in the guest room. I'm sleeping on the pullout sofa bed in Mom's office, which is downstairs, off to the side of the entryway.

"Mindy, honey, I got you set up in the den down here. I'll show you where everything is."

Mindy disappears with my mom into the den before I can say goodnight.

Chapter Twenty

MINDY

"Thank you for dinner, Catherine," I tell Luke's mom after she shows me to my room.

"Oh, honey, it's no problem at all. It was lovely to have you here." She stands in the doorway, wringing her hands and watching me.

She spent the last ten minutes showing me the futon bed, the bathroom, and where the towels are located, a tour that should have taken thirty seconds.

"Do you think Luke is happy?" she blurts.

I blink, taken aback. I expected, I don't know, recrimination or blame for enabling Luke's departure from medicine.

After a second, I nod. "He loves music. And he's truly incredibly talented."

She worries her bottom lip. "When he was a teenager, he would lock himself in his room and play music all day, he and Kevin." Her lips tilt down. "It was just a hobby. Something they did for fun. I worry that he's wasting his abilities when he had so much potential."

"He was blessed with many gifts. One of those gifts is music. He's chasing the dream that will make him happiest."

She frowns, but after a second, she nods and her lips tilt up. "Sleep well."

"You, too."

After she leaves, I tiptoe across the hall to the bathroom to get ready for bed, throwing on a soft set of flannel pajamas, washing my face, and brushing my teeth while my mind turns over the events of the day.

Luke's parents are cute together despite the friction over Luke's career choices. The only examples of healthy relationships I've seen up close are Archer and Finley's, and Piper and Oliver's, but those are both recently begun. I can't imagine being married to someone for thirty years. That's like a lifetime. What would it be like to be that close to someone? To know all their faults and habits and for them to know yours? Would it be comfortable or suffocating? Would it be long-lasting, like Luke's parents' relationship, or a sham, like Blake and Jeanette's?

I exit the bathroom and run into a warm wall, releasing a short scream.

"Hey." Luke's hands cup my shoulders. "I'm so sorry."

"Holy shit, you scared me." My heart tries to beat its way out of my rib cage.

"I didn't mean to startle you. This is the only bathroom downstairs."

"Oh." I peer up at him. "Are you sleeping down here, too?"

He nods. "In the office. It has a pullout sofa."

"Ah."

His thumbs rub small circles on my shoulders. "Do you have everything you need?"

"Your mom made sure I had everything I needed and then some."

"That sounds about right." The dimple in his cheek makes an appearance.

My stomach clenches.

We stare at each other.

"Oh." He rips his hands away from my shoulders. "Sorry, I didn't realize."

"It's fine. I'll just get out of your way so you can—" I walk past him, gesturing to the bathroom behind me, "do whatever."

"Right. Wait, Mindy."

I stop at the door to the den and turn around.

He sizes me up. "Are you tired?"

I shrug. "Not really. I'm still a little wired from that cup of coffee after dinner."

After a moment of consideration, he asks, "When I'm done here, can I show you something?"

Tell him no. "Yeah. Sure."

Ten minutes later, he opens up the closet in the den, pushing aside the hanging coats to expose the back wall. He presses against a panel and the bottom slides away, uncovering a dark opening.

I gasp. "What is this?"

"It's a secret room."

I stare at him. "Are you serious?"

"Yep."

"Is this like one of those horror movies and I'm the young ingénue and this is where you keep the bodies?"

He chuckles. "You might be a young ingénue, but as far as I'm aware, it's body-free. Come on, I'll show you." Ducking down, he steps into the black hole. A second later, a faint pink light comes on.

I stoop down to enter the space. It's not huge, but it's wide enough to fit four or five full-grown adults comfortably if they were all sitting down.

"I think the kids were in here earlier," he says.

A cabinet rests in one corner with a pink lamp glowing on top of it. There are a variety of pillows and blankets strewn around along with a couple of seat cushions and a Barbie playhouse against the far wall. "Aha." He picks up one of the dolls. "There is a body down here. I knew Cassie was a psychopath."

I chuckle. "Four-year-olds usually are."

Posters are taped to the walls, The Temptations, The Doors, Weezer, and "Spice Girls?" I point.

He lifts his hands. "Lynn's contribution. Wait it gets better, lie down." He stretches out on one of the blankets, grabbing a couple of pillows.

I settle down next to him.

He clicks a button and then shuts off the pink lamp.

Little pinpricks of light scatter across the ceiling like stars.

Surprise and a little bit of wonder spark through me. "This is so cool."

"I used to love hiding in here when I was a kid."

I turn my head to look at his profile. "I would have, too. It's the perfect place to escape from your siblings."

"Unless they know about it."

"True."

We lie in silence for a few long minutes, gazing up at the fake stars and breathing in tandem.

"Thank you for sticking up for me with my parents."

"They love you."

He nods. "To be fair, I haven't done the best job explaining to them all the reasons I left medicine."

"Why not?"

He takes a deep breath. "I don't want them to feel bad for pushing me for so long toward something that made me miserable." His head turns and our gazes lock.

It's so like him to protect their feelings, even at his own expense. My vision has adjusted to the dimness, and there are just enough fake stars overhead that I can make out his features, his skin faintly glowing, his eyes dark and penetrating.

"When they realized how good I was at school, how easily science and math came to me, they really pressed me to excel. They latched on to my intelligence like it was the only thing that mattered. Mom was a teacher and Dad was a plumber, and to them, being a doctor was like this pinnacle of achievement."

"And to you, what was it?" I ask.

He shifts next to me, turning fully onto his side.

I mimic his movement, resting my head in my hand.

"It was what my parents wanted me to do. It wasn't what I wanted to do. It was never my dream, it was theirs. That was the main reason I left, but it was also more than that. Medical school and residency were like being in an abusive relationship. Especially since everyone involved and, you know, the world in general is convinced the entire profession is this great, noble cause, and you must be out of your mind if you don't want to be a part of it."

I tilt my head. "It's not noble?"

"Oh, it is, in a lot of ways. It's fulfilling, and helping people is never a bad thing, but it's more complicated than that."

"Most things are," I murmur.

He sighs. "It's hard to explain. Medical school was hard, residency was worse, but I thought it was all temporary. They told us from the beginning it would be grueling, but they also instilled this sense that it would all be worth the pain and sacrifice in the end, and you're just too sleep deprived to question anything."

"I've heard cults use similar tactics to assist in brainwashing."

He huffs out a short laugh. "I believe it. When I started working in the ER, I was sure that I had made it through the worst of it. That everything would turn around and then I would be happy."

"But that's not what happened."

His eyes lock with mine. "No. I mean, sure, I was helping people, sometimes, but I spent a lot of time and energy dealing with other doctors doing shitty things."

"What do you mean?"

A muscle in his jaw twitches. "Many doctors would refuse to help patients with Medicaid."

"Why?"

"It's harder to get reimbursed."

My jaw drops.

"Then, for those patients who had decent insurance, many of my fellow graduates would refer them for a barrage of tests they didn't need."

At my questioning look, he sighs. "Student loans are enormous. Money took priority over patient care." He waves a hand. "And that's just the tip of the iceberg. I won't get into the depression rates plaguing people in the medical profession."

"I had no idea. I'm so sorry you went through all that." And then some, from the sound of it. "How did the rest of your family take it?" They didn't seem too bothered to me.

"With Granny Bea and my sisters, I didn't even have to explain anything. I just told them I was done, and they accepted my decision."

I contemplate his words. "That's nice, that your sisters and Granny Bea are so supportive, at least. It helps to have people in your corner. When did Granny Bea move in with your parents?"

"After Kevin passed. She was alone, and we had to leave. I couldn't bear leaving her behind. We were close before Kevin died, but after he passed, we got much closer."

I nod slowly. "You mentioned before how you were angry with her."

"I was angry at myself for not seeing the signs. We both were. There were things we missed, like reckless behavior, drinking, weird sleep patterns." He rolls onto his back, his profile highlighted in the gleam of the starry ceiling. "He said something to me about death a week before he died. We had a whole conversation about what we thought would happen in the afterlife."

The urge to reach out and touch him is so strong my fingers twitch. "Luke, you couldn't have known. A lot of teenagers talk about those things and don't kill themselves."

He shrugs. "I know that now. It was hard to deal with when I was sixteen. Granny Bea had him in therapy when he was younger, for PTSD and some abandonment issues from when his mom left him. But he had gotten better under her care, for the most part. He was cranky and irritable sometimes but didn't seem clinically depressed. He was a teenager, we were both angsty sometimes. I mean who hasn't listened to Dashboard Confessional and cried?"

I can't help but smile at that. "That's just a teenage rite of passage."

His mouth tips up and we watch each other, a speck of buoyancy in the middle of a heavy topic.

I shift a little, giving in to the impulse to reach out, and rest my hand on the floor between us. "When people die, I don't know, it seems like they leave behind a cornucopia of guilt, no matter the cause."

"You feel guilty about your sister."

It's not a question.

"Yes. But it's more than that. It's not only about Aria. The truth is that Taylor saw Jake and Aria at a party the night she died. Taylor told them to go home, and they did, and they crashed. Neither of them had a license, but Taylor did. When Taylor told me, I completely lost it. I have been so angry at her, but the truth is that I'm not mad at Taylor for what happened. She was only sixteen. I'm angry with myself." I shut my eyes. "When Taylor told me about what she did, I was . . . resentful that she would share it with me. She had reached a point where she was ready to confide in someone about her guilt. But I hadn't. I didn't have the guts to face my own culpability. Every time I looked at Taylor after that, all I could see was my own guilt, my own fear, my own cowardice staring me in the face."

The warmth of his hand covers mine, a gentle pressure.

I lift my gaze to his.

His face is awash in compassion and concern. "Why do you feel guilty about Aria's death?"

I swallow and avert my gaze, focusing on his fingers. "Aria wanted to come stay with me that weekend. *The* weekend. We had talked before that, too, multiple times, about her coming to visit for a night or two so she could see the campus and hang out with me in the dorms. I kept blowing her off. She was feeling a little off, as teens do, and she just wanted to get away from home. But I was always too busy. I told her no. Maybe some other time. Every time, I said maybe some other time. Then she died." My heart pounds away even though sharing this past wound is like sawing it open and it should be incapable of beating.

When Luke speaks, his voice is low and even. "So when Taylor came to you and told you she saw them that night and told them to go home . . . ."

"It was easier to blame her than blame myself or acknowledge my own culpability. Because the truth is, it was *my* fault. *I* could have prevented it. I was too busy partying with friends and chasing boys I liked. I didn't want my little sister to ruin my weekend plans, and so after she died, I couldn't do it anymore. I stopped dating, I stopped having a life, and I focused completely on work." I sniff.

His hand squeezes mine.

I've never told anyone the full truth, and now that I have, it's like a dam bursting. "Then Dad got sick not long after Aria died. I threw myself into my work, like it was all that mattered, and I barely went home to see my family. Jake handled most of Dad's illness, he and Finley. Where was I? Working." I grind my teeth together, trying to suppress the desolation twisting through me. "I never got to say goodbye."

"Mindy. It's not your fault."

"I was twenty-one, Luke. I was an adult acting like a child. I made a choice that was like Taylor's, but she had the excuse of being a child, barely older than Aria and Jake."

"Hey." His hand moves up my arm, fingertips tracing up to my face to cup my jaw in his palm. He exerts the gentlest pressure until I meet his eyes, sympathy and understanding stamped all over his features. "It's not your fault, Mindy."

Water drips down my face. I blink and try to stop it, but I can't. It's as if a faucet behind my eyes is stuck in the on position.

His strong arms wrap around me, and I press my face into his chest.

The sobs are uncontainable, wracking my body, pressing me into Luke. He holds me and murmurs words

I can't make out over the roaring in my ears as a torrent of emotion surges through me.

He's so warm and solid and comforting that the quiet strength of him seeps through my skin and into my bones.

I don't know how much time passes while he holds me, but by the time I come up for air, the front of his shirt is soaked with my tears. It's like every feeling, every fight, everything I've been holding in from Aria's death, Dad's death, Blake's abandonment, losing my job, and the stress of the past six months, it's all coming out and being splattered all over Luke's T-shirt.

Eventually I run out of tears and pull back, wiping at my face with my hands.

"I think there's some tissue in here, hold on." He reaches overhead, pulling a tissue box out of a little cubby. "Here."

I take a few and wipe my face off. "I'm so sorry. I snotted all over you."

"Hey, it's fine." He's still holding onto me, one hand heavy on my waist. "What's a little mucus between friends."

A smile pokes at my lips. "Thank you for listening, and for being here, and letting me come with you for Thanksgiving, and for everything."

"Of course," he murmurs. "After everything you've done for me, it's the least I can do. You need a kidney, I'm your man."

I laugh.

Luke grins at me, his hand flexing on my waist.

Our eyes lock, his gaze as warm as a physical caress.

He licks his lips and I stare at his mouth.

Shifting, his hand leaves my waist, trailing up toward my face, his arm stretching over me.

I lean into him, wanting his mouth on mine more than I want to breathe.

Then my lips connect with his shoulder.

"Oh." His arm moves back down. "I was just, uh, reaching for the trash bag," he says, his expression sheepish.

Heat floods my face. I cover my cheeks with both hands. "Oh, shit."

I need a sinkhole to open up and swallow me and save me from this moment.

Chapter Twenty-One

Luke

"I'm sorry. I didn't mean, I mean, I know you don't want anything to happen between us because of your past and —" I wave an ineffectual hand "—all of that."

I should have kissed her.

I want to kiss her more than anything. With each passing minute, the rope of desire wrapped around me grows tighter and tighter.

"Right, I, um, I wasn't trying to *kiss* you kiss you, I was just, you know, I wanted to thank you for listening to me and, uh, is there any water in here?" Her face is flushed.

"Listen, Mindy. We should talk about this."

Her eyes are downcast. "Or not. We can pretend it never happened."

I shift closer. "We both know there's something between us."

"Right," she nods. "We should talk about it. Get it out in the open. We're both adults. We can behave like grown-ups."

I press my lips together. I don't want to behave professionally. I want Mindy. I want her over me, around me, underneath me. I want to hold her hand and have the right to touch her in public. I want to fall asleep with her in my arms and wake up with her in my bed. I want all of it, but I know if I push her too much too fast, she'll bolt.

I know she's been burned, and she's not wrong that if anything goes bad between us, or if it leaks to the press, it would be more harmful to her future than mine.

I would never want to put her in a position where she's uncomfortable.

"I would be lying if I said I never had thoughts of what it might be like if we—"

"But we can't." She cuts me off, her voice overly loud in the small space. She winces. "I'm sorry. We have to be able to set aside whatever this is," she motions between us with a hand, "and focus on work.

"Yeah. That's smart."

"We can do this. We can just not kiss each other, I mean how hard is that?" She chuckles, but the sound is forced. "I should go. We should go." She rolls over, crawling out of the hidden room, and I follow her out.

After an awkward goodnight, she practically shoves me out of the den. I lean against the wall, breathing in the darkness, trying to calm my raging . . . everything.

It's a long time before I can fall asleep.

~

The next morning, we eat breakfast with everyone before we leave.

Mom's hug is extra tight as we're saying goodbye. "I love you."

"I love you, too, Mom."

She searches my eyes. "You know I want you to be happy, right? I want what's best for you."

"I know."

She nods and releases me, reluctantly.

Granny Bea hugs me and then smacks me on the shoulder. "Don't be a stranger. You better get your ass up here before another year passes. No excuses. I don't care if you're a famous rock star, I will have your ass if I don't see you before next Thanksgiving."

"Yes, Granny."

Mindy walks over to give Granny Bea a hug. "I'll make sure he has time to visit in his touring schedule."

A gusting laugh trips out of her. "Touring schedule. That almost sounds like you're legit."

"I'm working on it."

"Drive safely." Mom peers up at the sky. "It looks like rain."

Once again, I get behind the wheel, this time so Mindy can get some work done.

The sky opens up a mile outside of Corning, so I focus on the road while she taps away on her laptop, dealing with press inquiries, emails, and the graphic designer she hired for the cover and press kit.

We've passed through Binghampton when her phone rings.

"Hey, Finley," she answers.

I turn down the music that had been playing softly in the background and switch lanes to pass a semi.

"Yeah, we're on our way back. Listen, I wanted to apologize for the other night. I was way out of line, and I intend to apologize to Taylor when I get back."

There's silence, just the tap of rain on the windshield while Finley replies.

"Oh, she did? Then maybe when she gets back . . ." she trails off.

I can't make out Finley's side of the conversation, only the general cadence of her voice.

"Okay. No, I didn't forget. Yes, I'll make sure I'm free." She glances over at me. "We can talk more when I get back. Yeah, love you, too. Bye."

They hang up, and she stares out the windshield for a minute, the silence interrupted only by the wipers sliding back and forth every ten seconds, her work forgotten in her lap.

"Is everything all right?"

"Taylor left early this morning to go stay with a friend. She's coming back, though, before next weekend, because Finley wants us all to go through our dad's stuff after your show. Piper is going to come back for that weekend, too. Finley thought it would be a good idea for us to clear out his room together."

I glance over at her. "What do you think?"

Her lips twist. "I'm not sure. I know it's time. It's past time. We've kept his room like a shrine. He's been dead for six years."

"What are you going to say to Taylor?"

"I don't know. I know I need to apologize. I need to admit the truth about where my anger came from, not just for her, but for myself. I think it's the only way I'll be able to move on, but at the same time, I'm terrified. Why is admitting fault so hard?"

"Our sense of self is tied to our actions. When we do something wrong, our idea of who we are is threatened."

"That and I'm just handing over ammo to her to make my life a living hell."

"You think she would use it against you?"

"I don't know. I held it against her for years. I would deserve anything she throws at me."

I want to reach out to her, but instead, I clench my hands around the steering wheel.

Her phone dings and she picks it up, thumbs moving across the screen.

"It's an email from Damon. He sent us one of the tracks he's finished." Her eyes brighten. "I can't believe he already has something done." She plugs her phone into the USB cord and pushes some buttons.

"One of my songs?"

"Yep. He says he couldn't sleep, so he started working on it last night."

The notes fill the car, bright and crisp, the acoustic tenor underscored by surprisingly nimble and fluid melodies.

I barely recognize my own voice. I click on the blinker and pull over to the side of the road, leaning my head back on the seat, amazement flooding through me as the song crests and then ends.

Mindy is vibrating in the seat next to me. She reaches

for me, clutching my arm. "This is incredible. You're incredible. I can't—I feel like I could burst."

She jumps out of the car into the rain, jumping up and down on the muddy shoulder, throwing up her hands like a lunatic and getting completely soaked.

I put the car in park and jump out to join her.

For a few minutes, we leap around grabbing onto each other and yelling nonsense to the wind, like a couple of wild children.

When we finally slow down to catch our breath, we're clutching each other's hands. Her hair is plastered against her head, water leaking down her neck, a drop disappearing beneath the collar of her sweater. I want to track its movement with my tongue.

She's beautiful, free, and happy.

I want her. Just like this. Glowing with joy, her face flushed, her eyes bright.

But I can't have her. So I pull her into my arms while the rain patters on our heads, holding onto each other for a long minute.

With supreme effort, I step away from her. "We should go."

"I hope Oliver doesn't mind water all over his seats."

We climb back in the car. "I can't wait for the show at Veronica's next weekend. People are going to freak when they hear you."

I nod but don't respond. Partly because there's no way in hell I can keep my feelings for Mindy at bay—I'm worried I'll open my mouth and admit how much I want her. And partly due to my nerves of singing in front of a group of strangers in a week.

Sensing my disquiet, Mindy pats my arm. "It will all be fine. You've got this."

Chapter Twenty-Two

MINDY

"Your terms are very generous. I'll have my attorney review them and get back to you with any issues. In the meantime, I have a few questions." Duncan's speaking voice is deeper than I expected for a lyric tenor, his gaze piercing and serious.

Duncan came to prominence when some short videos he posted online of himself singing pop covers went viral, and he quickly became one of the most followed artists on social media. He signed with C&C Records shortly after that. He already has a gold album and a sold-out tour under his belt.

He's blunt about what he wants and his goals for his music despite the fact that he's barely nineteen.

"Of course. I'm happy to answer any questions." I pick up the pen next to me, ready to take some notes.

I'm sitting at Finley's desk in her office, a room that

spans the front of the main house, using my laptop to conduct the video call with Duncan.

Finley's redone most of the room, the walls a fresh, pale blue, the oak desk new and shiny but also covered in paperwork and receipts from her work on the kids camp. Sunlight streams in through the front windows, casting squares of light across the gleaming hardwood floors.

His dark eyes are sharp for such a young person, but his expression is open and honest. "I know you've had some struggles finding people to work with in the industry."

I nod. No need to deny it.

"How will that impact the artists you intend to sign to your new label?"

Despite the fact Ursula warned me this would come up, thinking about all my mistakes still sends a pulse of shame vibrating through me. "I can't change my past. I can't control what other people think of me, either, or how they treat me, but I can promise you that I will be completely focused on the artists I sign and what's best for their careers and goals. I have forged a lot of important relationships throughout the industry over the past decade. Once I prove I know how to turn artists into stars," *for the second time in my life*, "things will die down. The industry has forgiven far worse."

Duncan's mouth twists into a wry smile. "Money is power."

A truth that can't be denied. "I don't think Rebel Records, or anyone in the industry, will be turning me away once Luke's album launches."

He nods. "I've seen the videos of Luke and Laila. They're doing great work."

"They are," I push out, swallowing back an instinctive denial. *Luke and Laila.* Ugh. As much as I hate hearing their names linked, the jealousy an irrational beast inside me, they aren't romantically involved.

"You think Blake will let things die down?"

I tap my pen against the notebook next to me. "Why wouldn't he?"

His brows lift in surprise. "Oh, you haven't seen it."

My stomach dips and twists. "Seen what?"

"He did an interview this morning since the album went platinum about the, uh, inspiration for some of the more passionate songs."

I stare at Duncan, his expression apologetic.

My mind buzzes like it's full of wasps ready to sting at any moment.

I knew Blake wrote about us on his album, that isn't a surprise, but I haven't been able to bring myself to listen to any of it. The thought makes me physically ill.

"Thank you for the heads up."

What the hell did he say in the interview? Did he mention me by name?

I shove the concerns to the side, stuffing them down in a box in my mind. I need to stay professional and focused on this call. It won't help my chances of signing Duncan if I fly off the handle or let anyone know how Blake's actions can still rattle me.

Not because I care what Blake thinks, but because if he continues to regurgitate our shared history, the industry will never move on. I've moved on. I need the rest of the world to join me.

Duncan asks a few more questions about Outfoxed Records, if I plan on incorporating various booking agents, managers, and PR to the team—which I do—and other aspects of the business. I answer his questions, the words gushing out on autopilot.

Thirty endless minutes later we end the video chat, and I immediately pull up a search bar.

I take a deep breath, but it does nothing to slow the pounding of my heart in my ears.

Blake Bonham interview, I key in and hit enter.

Search results fill the screen.

I scan the headlines.

Bonham Speaks Out on Cheating Scandal

Blake Bonham Salacious Interview on The Morning Show

Jeanette Adams Speaks Out on the Ultimate Betrayal

Jeanette is already commenting? I shouldn't read it. I have to read it.

My finger clicks the link.

Blake Bonham made headlines earlier this year for cheating on his wife of seven years, America's Sweetheart Jeanette Adams. Now, the musician and frontman for Vacation Mustache is speaking out on the affair.

"I made a mistake," Blake said this morning during an interview on the SX Morning News. *"I have been emotionally destroyed by the pain I have caused people I care about, and that's what this album is really about."*

The first single off the album, "Stone Cold Fox," is believed to be about his one-time A&R director Mindy Fox, the same person he was linked with romantically last summer. The song is full of passionate lyrics about unrequited love with a "stone cold fox." When asked about the song, Blake said, "Mindy will always hold a very special place in my heart." When pressed for comment on if they are still friends or on speaking terms, Blake would neither confirm nor deny any ongoing relationship with Mindy Fox.

Jeanette Adams immediately took to social media when the interview aired. In a post that has garnered over 600,000 likes and comments as of the time of publication of this article, she states: "Blake made a mistake. We all make mistakes. Obviously, I was humiliated and heartbroken, but I believe we are always learning and growing as humans. Our relationship has only gotten stronger over the past six months. More than anything, we are looking forward to being first-time parents and will be focusing on our growing family."

Immediately after the interview, the song "Stone Cold Fox" hit No. 1 on Rockify streaming service, and album sales have once again skyrocketed....

Irritation thrumming through me, I slap the cover of my laptop down with more force than necessary. Slumping down in the seat, my head drops into my trembling hands. Why would he be so vague about the current status of our relationship? There isn't anything to talk about. Why wouldn't he just say it's over and let it be? Let *me* be.

It's so *unfair*.

Blake's consequences for his poor decisions are nil. If anything, he's making money riding the tail of our scandal while I have to rebuild my career under the weight of it.

Shouldering that weight with me is the most captivating man I've ever met.

An image of Luke flashes through my mind, the way he grinned down at me while we danced around in the rain, his eyes going first warm and then heavy-lidded with heat.

I want him.

I know he wants me, too.

The tension building between us is as thick as smoke at a Grateful Dead concert. I'm nearly blinded by it.

I don't know how long I can keep from throwing myself at him.

If only I had stayed away from Blake, maybe I would have the option of pursuing a relationship with Luke without it impacting the rest of my life.

Although, if I *hadn't* slept with Blake and subsequently lost my job with Rebel Records, would Luke and I ever have connected?

The thought is troubling but no more than the fact that I have to sacrifice any potential happiness we could have had because of what people might think, because of my past, my bad decisions, not to mention this latest debacle with Blake.

"Are you okay?"

Finley's voice jerks me up in my seat.

"I'm fine," I croak.

She sits in the guest chair across the desk from me. "You're a liar."

I laugh, the sound feeble. Then I open my laptop and flip it around, gesturing for her to take a look.

She leans in, her eyes tracking over the words of the article, her lips turning down further and further the more she reads. "What the actual hell?"

"Yeah."

Her gaze lifts to mine, her brow wrinkled with worry. "Is this going to impact your work?"

I shrug. "No clue. It depends on how people react to it, including Duncan Santos."

Her gaze sharpens. "How did the call go?"

"It was fine. He's going to follow up with me in a week or two. He's the one who told me about all this." I wave a hand at the computer.

Her lips purse. "This won't affect him signing with you, will it?"

I shake my head. "I have no idea."

"Have you thought about—?"

"Hey." Archer's broad frame fills the open doorway connecting the office and the main part of the house. "There you are." He takes in my slumped posture and Finley's troubled face. "Is everything okay?" He moves to her side, bending over to brush a kiss over the top of her head.

The motion is brief but effective.

When he pulls back, Finley smiles up at him, her face fairly glowing, as if the simple movement is enough to assuage any worries, relieve the heaviest burdens. His responding look is just as warm and blazing with tenderness.

Rough waters are easier to navigate when you aren't the only one handling the oars.

What would it be like to have a partner to shoulder my troubles?

What would it be like to have Luke gaze at me the way Archer looks at Finley, like she's the sole reason the sun shines every morning?

The problem is I think Luke *does* look at me that way, or at least something similar, but I can't acknowledge it, let alone accept it.

Can I?

"Everything is fine," I say.

Their gazes break away from where they are locked on each other.

Finley's face tightens in concern. "I was just going to say, have you thought about talking to Taylor about some of her connections in the music industry? She's met so many people over the years."

I swallow. "I need to talk to her about other things first."

She nods in understanding.

Finley agreed to help me get Taylor alone when she comes back home. We've tentatively planned for the day after Luke's show, when all of the siblings will be here, to go through Dad's room. I need to find a way to speak with her privately before she takes off again.

I stand up, grabbing my laptop from the desk and shoving it into my briefcase. "If she forgives me, I'll ask her if she wants to help me with Outfoxed Records. I'll even offer to pay her. But I have a feeling she isn't going to forgive me, so it's a moot point."

I don't deserve forgiveness, but I will do my best to at least try and repair our relationship, even if it's irrevocably broken.

Finley reaches over the table, grabbing my hand. "You can only do the best you can. I just want you to be happy."

"That's what I want, too."

I want my career. I love working in music. I want my label to be successful, and I want Luke, too. Imagining what it might be like, to truly have it all, sets off an explosion of nerves in my belly, a mixture of fear and excitement.

I examine the emotions. Am I afraid of what people think, of my career being affected, or am I afraid of being hurt again?

Losing Blake was brutal. He broke my heart.

Losing Luke would be worse.

But if there's even the slightest possibility that I can keep him, if I could have love and my career?

Hope blossoms inside me, a burst of light as dazzling as the brightest of stars.

There's really only one way to find out.

Chapter Twenty-Three

Luke

I can't breathe. My ribs ache like an elephant stepped on them. I don't have this. I don't have anything. What I have is a stomach full of nerves and hands full of sweat that couldn't lift a pen, let alone pluck some complicated notes.

"Luke, five minutes." The roadie that came with Laila and her crew calls out at the office door before shutting us back in the little room.

I might throw up. My heart is pounding. My chest is tight. This is what a heart attack feels like. Exactly like a panic attack.

"Hey, look at me." Mindy's face swims into focus.

I blink. "I'm okay." My voice emerges on a croak.

"We've practiced a thousand times. This is just like that. Pretend it's only us out there."

She's completely right and yet completely wrong all at the same time. We *have* practiced a thousand times, on the very stage outside this room. Mindy has been a stalwart, an extremely sexy, untouchable champion of my progress, pushing me to practice at Veronica's every night this week so that I had a chance to get comfortable at least with the space, if not the fact that hundreds of people are listening. There are usually no more than a handful of people in the crowd.

Tonight, there is more than a handful. It's packed. And not just with some random spectators. Oh no, there are press, influencers, musicians, publicists . . . and it's not only me performing.

Laila is on the stage—which is really more like a raised platform, her voice strong and clear, sounding like an angel even through the walls between us. The crowd has been loving Laila's acoustic performance so far, the cheering in between songs has been shaking the building.

Everyone we invited showed up, and then some. Mindy and Ursula sold it as an exclusive event, which made people clamor to be invited.

The plan is for Laila to finish her solo set, then I'll join her for a duet. After, she'll exit and I'll take over, going into my solo act. Solo. Alone. On stage, in front of hundreds of strangers, singing my own songs.

My heart thumps hard enough to leap out of my throat while my stomach churns.

I might not make it.

"Let's take some deep breaths. Are you warmed up?" She bites her bottom lip, her eyes worried as they scan me.

Shit. If she's nervous, I'm really screwed.

"If I get any warmer, I might combust." I could jump in a tub of snow and still be slick with sweat right now.

She cocks her head, listening to the music seeping through the thick walls of the building behind her. "This song is nearly over."

I jump up out of the sagging couch in Veronica's office, pacing back and forth in front of the desk. "I can't do this. I should leave. Can I leave?"

"Luke, stop." She steps in front of me, halting my progression. Her eyes search mine. "You just need a distraction. I have an idea."

"Are you going to punch me? Knock me out?"

Her mouth twists. "I hadn't planned on it."

"You have some fast-acting Valium on you?"

The corner of her mouth twitches. "No. No violence, no drugs. Just this." Without further warning, her hands slide up my body, curling around my neck.

Every nerve ending in my body shivers to life, and all of my attention is laser-focused on the woman in front of me, touching me. We've taken care over the past week to avoid any accidental physical contact.

Her hair is down, curling around her face in soft waves, her lips shiny. A deep pink sweater dress hugs her figure. She moves into me, her chest brushing against mine, the faint scent of something floral and sweet tickling my nose.

And then she kisses me. Her mouth presses against mine, her lips softer than rose petals but the pressure of them insistent and sure.

Mindy is kissing me.

Shock roots me in place.

Kiss her back, you fool.

The thought jolts the rest of me to life, pulling her flush against me. My hands take on a life of their own, running down her back to her hips, gripping her ass in two handfuls. Her mouth opens with a gasp and then my tongue brushes against hers and the world disappears. All that matters is this moment, this kiss, this woman.

Laila's song ends, the roar of the crowd inside loud enough to break the spell her mouth has cast over me.

I pull back but I don't go too far, resting my forehead against hers. "Mindy."

"How do you feel?" she asks, the words brushing against my lips.

I swallow. "Horny."

She chokes back a laugh. "Yeah, same."

The door opens. "Luke, it's time," the roadie calls out.

We break apart.

Out on stage, Laila is giving the crowd the segue we practiced.

"Mindy, I—" I can't go out there *now*. I search her eyes for regret but find none.

She smiles, grabs me by the lapels of my suit coat, and presses another kiss to my lips, a quick, hard movement, uncaring of the roadie watching us from the open doorway.

"Go."

I gape at her flushed face.

It's like the world has exploded and reassembled differently.

"Luke, you have about ten seconds to get your ass out there. Go." She gives me a little smack on the rear.

I toss her a surprised grin over my shoulder while hustling out to the main room.

In a daze, I climb up onto the stage and take my spot on the stool next to Laila.

The tightness in my limbs has been replaced with an incredible sense of . . . hope.

What does this mean? Did she change her mind about us?

Maybe my nerves plunged me into some kind of fever dream and none of this is real.

Laila plucks at the strings of her guitar with quick, light movements, playing the chorus notes to one of our duets. "I am so pleased to welcome my friend to the stage with me tonight. We wrote this song together, and I know you will love it as much as I do." Laila nudges me with an elbow. "Why don't you introduce yourself, friend?"

I glance out at the audience. The spotlight above us is bright enough to block out the crowd, rendering them a bunch of black smudges in the dark.

"Hi everyone. I'm Luke Fletcher." The microphone emits a high-pitched whine of feedback. My anxiety rumbles underneath me, a monster ready to pounce. I shift on the stool, trying to get comfortable.

Mindy kissed me. Then she smacked my ass.

A few people clap. Someone whistles a catcall. Probably Jake.

The thought makes me smile.

"Come on now, we can do better than that." Laila lifts her hands over her guitar and claps, the crowd joining in.

She lifts her brows at me. "Ready?"

"As I'll ever be."

Her fingers fly over the strings with more force, and after a second, I join in.

Chapter Twenty-Four

Mindy

When Luke opens his mouth and sings, the crowd releases a collective breath of relief. Or maybe it's just me. The relief quickly turns into awe and wonder at the magic of Laila and Luke playing together, the inherent chemistry between them filling the entire venue.

I can't take my eyes off him. Neither can the people around me.

A minute ago, that gorgeous mouth was pressed against mine, and heaven help me, despite my best intentions, all my mistakes and past history, and the fact that I know better, I still can't wait to kiss him again.

Shutting my eyes doesn't halt the impulse. His voice brushes down my spine like the sound itself has velvet palms, sweeping against my every nerve ending.

I spin around and walk toward the wall, circling the periphery of the crowd. This is work. Focus on work. I need to get a sense of the reactions from our curated guest list.

I amble up behind a group of twenty-somethings wearing designer clothes and clutching trendy handbags.

"He is *hot*. Like hot hot."

"He's so hot. Hotter than hot."

I'm both elated and irritated, a confusing mix. I mean, who doesn't love a charming man playing guitar? But he's *my* charming man.

And now he won't be. He'll become famous.

That's when everything will change. He'll dump you for an actress, or another musical star, or twelve groupies.

I shove the thoughts away. Luke isn't like that.

The duet comes to its gradual conclusion and the crowd goes absolutely wild, yelling and cheering.

Laila exits the stage, moving to the backroom to rest. The plan is to give them both a break after their set lists to recover before mingling with the crowd for a meet-and-greet.

I move around the edges of the space, eavesdropping as more people *ooh* and *ah* over Luke's performance.

Over the past week, since Thanksgiving, I've had to suppress the urge to just rip off all my clothes and throw myself on top of him.

Now, after our first kiss . . .

That kiss.

Letting him walk away was almost unbearable. It's like there's some invisible rope tying us together, the strands becoming more and more taut with tension the farther away I moved, like it's a rubber band and eventually I will either snap back or break completely. Even now, it's pulling me toward him like a tractor beam.

The rest of his set is thirty minutes, and he moves through the set list like a champion, like he's done this a thousand times before. He takes a minute between each song to thank Laila, to thank the crowd for being there, to tell the audience about his upcoming album and tour—and sure we rehearsed all of it, but if I was a simple spectator, I would never guess it. The audience eats it up.

Pride rushes through me. I'm so proud of him for overcoming his fears. He's absolutely crushing it.

When he finishes and the final chord is ringing in the air, the responding roar of the crowd is deafening. It fills the room. His grin is blinding. He flushes a little, bows, and then attempts to exit toward the backroom, but his progress is halted by multiple people. Thankfully, we have some roadies and security that help him wade through the throng.

I should meet him and Laila in the back office, check in with them, but now that the hardest part is over, and it was fantastic, I'm spent. It's like a balloon has been slowly filling my chest for the past six months, and it's now popped, leaving me ripped to shreds.

I take a few minutes to greet some reporters and direct them to the open bar, and then I escape out the backdoor and into the night.

The bracing chill is sharp against my heated skin. The light is on over the door, a glaring white spotlight pointed at the dumpster. I take a deep breath, inhaling the stench of old food and stale beer.

Gross.

I move around the side of the building, where it's dark and the air is fresh.

My mind keeps going back to the moment I kissed Luke. The feel of his hands on me. The taste of his tongue in my mouth, like mint and heat and man. He kissed me like he was ravenous and I was his last meal. I want to do it again, but . . . what if I'm making a mistake?

I can't ruin my career again over a man.

Maybe I won't. Maybe I can have Luke and eat him, too. Or whatever.

There is no record label breathing down my neck. Would it adversely impact his career? No. But it could impact mine if I develop a pattern of sleeping with musicians. Ugh. The world already thinks I'm some kind of homewrecking tramp.

The backdoor opens, the drone of conversation getting louder for a couple of seconds and then cutting off as the door shuts, muting the roar down to a dull hum.

I hold my breath, muscles locking with tension, waiting intently for any sign of motion. Footsteps head my way.

A figure appears around the corner, peering in my direction, illuminated by the back light.

Is it Luke, or am I imagining things?

"Mindy? Is that you?"

"I'm here."

"Are you okay?" He approaches slowly.

Of course. He's worried about *me* after having this amazing night, knocking it out of the park, really, on top of overcoming his huge fear of singing in front of strangers.

"I'm sorry," I say.

He stops a few feet away, a dark shape a few feet in front of me. "For what?"

I take a step toward him. "I lied to you."

"About what?"

I move another foot closer. "I know I said I could never mix business with . . . not business, but I've basically been a giant asshole idiot up until now, and so I just think maybe we could try to—"

He cuts off my words with his mouth.

Yes.

My entire body exalts. I melt into him.

His arms envelop me, his fingers sliding into my hair.

More.

The kiss deepens, his mouth opening over mine. This is no meek declaration of intent; it's a brutal force of nature, a frantic discovery, like this might be the last chance we get to learn each other's taste. I clutch at his shirt, needing to get closer.

He pulls back a fraction to speak, his lips brushing against mine as he talks. "I've wanted you for so long."

He dips his head to suck the skin on my neck between his lips, setting my nerve endings on fire and sending chills racing down my back.

A moan flows out of me.

On a gasp, he pulls back, his breathing labored. "Are you sure this is okay?"

I tug him closer. "Shut up and keep doing that thing with your tongue."

"Yes." The word is accompanied with a rumbling groan.

His mouth captures mine again, and hunger ricochets through me. I need more. I want him so badly I'm ready to jump out of my own skin with pure, unadulterated want. It's as natural as breathing, lifting my legs to circle his waist. He presses me against the wall, the brick against my back a cool contrast to the raging heat flowing in my veins and setting my entire body on fire.

Then he angles his hips and his hardness nudges at me *just right* and I almost lose it right there, outside Veronica's bar.

If I don't get him inside me, I might actually die from unsatisfied lust.

I've never felt this way. Not with Blake, not with anyone. Because it's more than lust. Luke is one of the best, most decent humans I've ever met.

"Luke! You out here, man?"

My libido comes to a screeching halt when the voice of one of my siblings belts into the air.

Chapter Twenty-Five

Luke

I drop Mindy's legs, making sure she's steady before taking a giant step back.

Jake rounds the corner, illuminated by the cone of light shining from the back of the building.

"People are waiting. Laila is out there alone mingling." He pauses. "Why are you chilling in the pitch dark? Mindy, is that you?"

"We were just getting some air," I say, surprised when my voice emerges without sounding like I'm about to expire from the sheer amount of desire coursing through my body.

Jake takes another step closer. "Right. Well, Luke, people are waiting to talk to you, and Mindy, you might need to answer some of these marketing questions, and isn't this why we're here, you weirdos?"

"We'll be right there," Mindy says.

Jake disappears. After a couple seconds, the backdoor shuts with a slam.

Mindy runs her hands through her hair, trying to flatten the wayward strands, then smooths down her dress over her hips.

We have to go back inside, but my body is on fire, and I can't stop staring at Mindy and thinking about the softness of her lips, the curve of her hip under my fingers, the taste of her skin, the responsive little sounds she made that shot straight to my groin.

I cannot go in there with this raging erection. I need more than fresh air to cool down—I need a giant ice bath.

Sensing my . . . difficulties, Mindy squeezes my hand. "I'll go in and let them know you'll be right there. You have five minutes. Think about Granny Bea naked."

Definitely a good boner killer.

I choke back a laugh, but damn if that doesn't work.

A few minutes later, I'm back inside Veronica's schmoozing with the crowd. I answer questions about my songs and my process and take photos with influencers and industry peeps. Throughout it all, my gaze keeps straying to Mindy. When she's laughing with a group of businessmen in suits, when she's taking a sip of water, or when she's just walking across the room and existing, my gut tightens and I can barely focus through the haze of lust crowding my vision.

I go through the motions, making conversation and bantering to the best of my abilities. A lot of the questions revolve around Laila and any "relationship" between us. Both Mindy and Ursula advised us to play coy and basically respond with "no comment," but it's so misleading.

Wrong even, especially after Mindy and I . . . my gaze locks with hers from across the room and I can't look away.

"Later," she mouths, and my skin grows tight with anticipation.

Is she trying to kill me?

Someone taps her on the shoulder, and she turns away, the spell broken.

Eventually the crowd thins, and security helps Laila and I make our escape out the back and into a waiting sedan.

I slide into the passenger seat, nodding to Jake behind the wheel. Laila gets in the back.

"Where's everyone else?" I ask, but really, I only care about one person.

"Archer and Finley are waiting with Mindy. She and Ursula have some work to finish up before they can leave. I'll come back after dropping off you lot to pick them up and head home."

Less than five minutes later, I'm opening the door to my cabin after waving goodnight to Laila while she made her way into the bungalow next door.

Once I'm alone, I pull my phone out of my back pocket and stare at the blank screen.

My veins are still buzzing from the evening, from the performance but also because of Mindy and what happened between us and what I want to happen between us. That can't be it. There has to be more. I haven't spent nearly enough time with her mouth.

I leave my phone on the counter in the kitchen, then head upstairs to take a cold shower, rinse off the gel in my hair, and change into something more comfortable.

When I'm finished, I make my way back downstairs and pick up the phone. Nothing. My thumbs have a will of their own and click on the text icon, pulling up Mindy's name.

But doubt trickles in.

What if she was caught up in the excitement of the moment and now that it's over, she's regretting it?

Maybe I'm just convenient. Maybe she was right all along and it's a bad idea to do this since we're working together and if everything goes bad then that could negatively affect her career and shouldn't I be thinking about—

A rapid knocking jars me from the spiraling thoughts.

My heart thumps a staccato beat as I race to open the door. Mindy immediately throws herself into my arms, her mouth pressing against mine, her hands in my hair, and all my fears and doubts crumble under her eager hands.

She's still wearing the dress from earlier, but she's traded the heels for boots and thrown on a coat.

I kick the door shut and press her back against it, fine tremors rushing through my body, unable to contain the thrilling fact that's she's here, in my arms.

Her hands slip under my shirt, running up my back, gripping and tugging me toward her.

I cup her face in my hands, warring with competing impulses, wanting more than anything to be inside of her as soon as humanly possible and simultaneously wanting to slow us down so I can take my time and enjoy every luscious second.

Before I can choose between the devil or the angel on

my shoulders, someone bangs on the door, the vibration echoing through me, and we both jump, our eyes locking in mutual confusion.

"Who?" she mouths.

I lean over and she shifts her head to the side so I can peer through the peephole.

"Jake," I whisper.

She rolls her eyes, ducking out from between me and the door. She gives me a saucy wink before disappearing into the coat closet in the entry. I lean my head against the door, taking a few deep breaths and once again trying to calm my raging erection.

After a few seconds, I let him in.

"Dude." He stalks past me, heading for the kitchen. "Can I talk to you about how freaking hard it is to be in a bar where I used to get wasted and not have a single drop?"

I follow him, resting an arm against one of the stools while he opens the fridge and grabs a soda.

"It is hard. One of the hardest things in the world, and yet you did it. You should be proud of yourself."

He stares down at the can in his hand, frowning for a few seconds before lifting his gaze to mine. "Remember the other day, you said something about how life is always going to have shitty times, and it doesn't last forever, and you need some kind of tools to get through it to the happy bits, or whatever?"

I move farther into the kitchen, leaning back against the counter. "Yeah."

"What tools do you use?"

"Songwriting, mostly."

"Oh." He pops open the soda and takes a long chug. "That makes sense."

"That's what worked best for me. There are a lot of different approaches, though. Writing is only one of them. It doesn't have to be a song or anything creative, either, sometimes just freewriting your feelings is a way to sort of release them. You can also try things like exercise, meditation, or finding a grief support group."

"Right."

I'm not sure he's ready, but I throw another option at him. Jake already uses humor to deal with stress. "A lot of times, laughter can be the best medicine. Sharing funny stories or happy memories of Aria with your friends and family is a powerful way to heal." And it would just be an extension of a tool he already has. He needs to talk about Aria. He won't heal until he can.

His jaw tightens, and he takes another swig of soda before giving me a stiff nod. That's the only acknowledgment I get before he changes the subject.

"So, how long will you be here before Mindy forces you out into the real world?"

"We're heading back to the city sometime next week."

We chat about the upcoming tour, how long it is and where I'll be performing. I do my best to give Jake my full attention, knowing he's trying to distract himself from thoughts of drinking and I can't just kick him out.

But Mindy is still hiding in the hall closet, and my eyes keep drifting to the clock over the oven.

Finally, Jake crushes the soda can while letting out a burp and chucks it in the trash. Then he slaps me on the shoulder. "Thanks, man. You're easy to talk to. I love Archer, but he's like a really annoying uncle."

"Anytime. Truly. Call me if you ever need to talk, even if it's late or early or . . . whatever."

He nods. "Thanks."

As soon as I shut the front door, the closet pops open and Mindy steps out.

"I'm sorry. That took longer than I thought. He needed to talk and I—"

She halts the rush of words by stepping into me and wrapping her arms around my waist, hugging me tightly. "Thank you."

"For what?"

"For talking to Jake." She pulls back and regards me, her eyes glossy. "For trying to help him." She kisses my jaw. "For being here for him." She kisses my cheek. "For being so incredible." She stretches up, feathering a light kiss over my mouth before her lips trace the edge of my jaw. She sucks lightly on my neck, just under my ear, then her hot breath puffs against the column of my throat.

I swallow.

How is it the simplest of her touches affect me so viscerally?

"Luke," she whispers, her hand sliding down my stomach, over my pants and then grasping my once again raging erection through my clothes.

"Yes?"

"I want you."

Our bodies align like two puzzle pieces snapping into place, and then we're kissing again. I could kiss her forever and never tire of the sensation. Heat surges through my veins, melting me from the inside out.

I pull away to tug her dress off, sliding it easily up and over her head, hesitating a second to take in the black lace bra cupping what must be the most perfect breasts in all of existence.

"Too many clothes." I kneel in front of her, taking off one boot at a time before peeling off her nylons. Once those are flung to the side and she's wearing only her bra and underwear, she pulls on me, attempting to tug me back to standing, but I don't acquiesce.

Instead, I lean forward and press my mouth between her legs, rubbing my lips against her over her panties.

She gasps. Her hips tilt toward me, a soundless plea for more, and my erection jerks in my pants.

Fuck.

I look up at the passion etched over her features, her head thrown back, eyes drowsy with lust, and a wave of heat seizes me by the balls. The image of her in the throes of desire will be scorched into my memory forever.

This is not going to last long.

"Luke," she groans out my name, tugging on my head. "Let's go upstairs. Do you have condoms?"

I move my mouth away from her body with effort.

"Yes," I say, the automatic agreement rising to my lips before I've quite registered all of her words—wait. Condoms? "No."

"No? What do you mean, no?" She's panting, staring down at me, her chest moving up and down rapidly.

My eyes trace the perfectly formed globes.

So beautiful.

I pull my two functioning brain cells together and stand up so I can kiss her again. “Yes to upstairs, but no to condoms.” I run my lips down her neck to the sensitive spot where it meets her shoulder.

“No condoms?” she squeaks.

I lick her neck. She tastes like lust and sugar. “It’s okay.”

She groans, the sound more frustration than arousal. “Is it?”

I pull back from tasting her skin to nip at her bottom lip, which is sticking out in a pout. *God*, I love her mouth, especially that little piece of pink, kiss-swollen skin.

My entire being expands with anticipation and delight. “It’s fine. It’s great, actually.”

She frowns at me. “What are you talking about? What are we going to do?”

Pulling her against my erection, I thrust against her, making her breath catch in her throat. “I have quite a few ideas.”

Chapter Twenty-Six

MINDY

I can't believe he's so unconcerned about the fact that we have no condoms. What does he mean he has other ideas? What can be better than—*oh*.

Once again, he kneels in front of me in the entryway, warm hands nudging my feet apart. Then he pulls my panties to one side and moves closer.

"Oh, God." I hold onto his head, my legs trembling.

His movements are careful at first, his tongue and lips exerting only the slightest of pressure against my core.

Slowly, oh so slowly, and incrementally, the force increases until I'm panting and squirming and he's driving me absolutely mad with need.

"Luke," his name is a groan of frustration. I pull his head closer, needing so much more, and he complies, finally, opening his mouth over me and using the flat of his tongue right where I need it most. Then he groans, and the vibration nearly lifts me off my toes.

When his finger pushes into me, my body, wound as tight as a bowstring from his careful ministrations, releases with a snap, shoving me over the edge, the orgasm rushing up and over me with the intensity of a tsunami.

My knees give out, but he's already shifted upward to support me.

"I'm not done with you yet," he says, lifting me into his arms in a bridal carry and hauling my boneless body up the stairs.

I still haven't fully recovered from the strength of my orgasm when he lays me down on the bed. My eyes are half closed and yet my attention is completely focused on Luke while he tugs his shirt over his head, tossing it to the side. Next his sweats are shoved off, down over his strong thighs, lightly sprinkled with dark hair.

I bite my lip to hold back the groan of appreciation for his lean, muscular form, the definition in his chest and abs, not to mention the bulge apparent even through his navy-blue boxer briefs.

He leans over me, grasping my underwear on either side of my hips and yanking them down and off, tossing them over his shoulder.

Arousal rushes through me, heat filling my center once more.

Leaving his briefs on, he slides over me and captures my mouth in his.

I wrap my arms around him, reveling in the feel of his skin under my fingers, tracing the muscles in his back.

He settles between my thighs and thrusts gently, rubbing his covered erection against my still sensitive, heated flesh.

He licks into my mouth, and I arch my hips up against his prodding length.

Our bodies move together in perfect symphony.

It feels sooo good.

"Mindy," he whispers my name against my neck, his breath hot against my skin. Then he pulls his upper body away, slightly, his hardness still prodding at the apex of my thighs, and curves toward me, drawing the cup of my bra down so he can take my nipple into the heat of his mouth and suck at it, the pull of his lips working in time with the thrusts of his solid length against me.

"I can't." I pant. I can't handle the pleasure, it's too much and yet not enough. "Luke."

He stops moving, immediately searching my eyes. "Is this okay?"

I nod. "I want more. I want to feel you. Take off yours." I motion to his underwear.

His brows dip. "Are you sure?"

"Yes. We don't have to do, you know . . . I want your skin against mine."

He swallows once, hard, and then nods. Within seconds, his briefs are gone along with my bra, and his thick, rigid flesh slides easily through wet folds. We both groan, gasping with the sheer pleasure of it. His bare chest brushes against my breasts, the spattering of hair an erotic graze against my overly sensitive nipples.

Seconds later, another forceful orgasm crashes over me, throwing me into a bright swirl of bliss and ecstasy.

When I finally return to my body, Luke is still over me, his hips moving faster, his eyes intensely concentrated on my face, and then he's crying out, his face contorting with the strength of his own release. He shudders, jerking, shouting out my name before collapsing his full weight on top of me.

He rolls away from me but doesn't go far, grabbing his briefs to wipe his release off of both of us before pulling me into him.

We don't speak for long minutes. We lay together, holding each other and catching our breath.

Finally, I brush a kiss across his collarbone. "That was the best non-sex I've ever had."

He chuckles. "I came on you like a horny teenager."

"I feel like a horny teenager."

"I feel about as hungry as one."

I prop myself up on an elbow, looking down at him. "You didn't eat before the show." He was too nervous. "Do you have any food downstairs?"

"I think a frozen pizza?" His brows waggle at me. "You rest, I'm on it." He slides away, sitting on the edge of the bed.

The muscles in his back flex as he moves and drags up his sweats. I take a minute to appreciate the broadness of his back, his narrow hips, and taut rear before they're covered up with fabric.

"This view is spectacular."

He twists around to grin at me. "I aim to please."

For a few seconds we stare at each other, smiling. An unfamiliar sensation, a sort of soothing pressure, expands through me, making my heart nearly ache with it.

Then he stretches over me, capturing my mouth with his, nipping at my bottom lip before pulling back again. "I'll be right back."

He makes his way down the stairs and I stare after him, long after he's disappeared from view.

He could really hurt me.

The unwelcome thought makes my eyes sting. I thought I loved Blake. But with Blake, the sensations were never so expansive, never this all-consuming.

I flop back on the bed and stare up at the ceiling. Is this a mistake? What if it ends badly?

This can't last forever.

He hums, tinkering around in the kitchen. I don't want to waste a second of our time together since I don't know how much time we'll have. Once we leave Whitby, that might spell the end.

Pushing myself out of bed, I head downstairs without bothering to get dressed.

"Do you need any help?"

He spins around, and when he takes in my complete nudity, his eyes go hot and a muscle in his jaw ticks.

My eyes dip to the bulge in his sweats, brows rising in surprise. "Again? So soon?"

"Around you? Permanently."

I can't stop the grin spreading across my face. It starts with a glow in my chest, unfurling and swelling outward, encompassing my entire being.

The way he watches me . . . I want to purr and arch my back like a satisfied cat.

He stalks toward me, a tiger, except this prey is more than willing to be devoured.

His arms surround me, both hands dipping down my back to cup my ass.

He groans, kissing my neck. "You need to put something on or I'm going to give up on food completely. And sleep. Needs essential for basic functioning will all become a distant memory."

"We can't have you starving."

"I might be okay with it, actually." He bites my neck gently. "Who needs food?"

I reach down and cup the hardness prodding my hip. "You need to keep up your energy."

"Good point." He pulls back, his hands moving up to grip my waist, his eyes devouring every inch of me.

The oven beeps.

He doesn't move, his hands clenching against my skin.

"Are you going to get that?"

His head shakes slightly. "I don't think I can let go of you."

I chuckle, kissing him and then stepping away with a sigh. "I suppose I'll put on a shirt or something, for now."

When I return, wearing the T-shirt he discarded earlier because it smells divine and I couldn't resist, he's sitting in the living room. The fireplace is on, casting an ambient glow over the two plates of pizza and two glasses of water set out on the coffee table in front of him.

"Romantic," I say, sitting next to him and tucking my legs underneath me.

We eat in silence for a moment before he turns to me.

"Will you stay the night?"

The murmured inquiry shifts my focus from our cozy haven to the outside world. What will happen tomorrow?

How will I explain this to my family? What are we even doing?

Doubts and panic nibble through the post-orgasm haze of pleasure I've been wrapped in.

His hand reaches out, covering my bare knee. "It wasn't a trick question."

I look up at him. This is Luke. I know Luke. It will be fine, if temporary. It can just be a little, fling or whatever. Getting it out of our system. He hasn't said he wants anything more, and I'm not going to bring it up. The world can't intrude on this, at least not right now. I'll save my worries for tomorrow. Maybe the next day. Or next week. "I want to stay."

His smile is relieved. "Good. I want you to stay. Does anyone else know you're here?"

"No. I went up to my room and then snuck out the window."

He chuckles. "You did? Did you do that a lot as a teenager, sneak out to meet boys?"

I reach over for the cup and take a sip of water before replying. "No. Well, not always. Sometimes I just needed to get away. I dated a little in high school and college, but then after Aria passed—" I stop the words. He already knows I gave up having a life.

"And then Blake," he says.

I nod. "We all know how that turned out."

He sets his plate down and then scoots closer to me on the couch, holding out his arm.

That's all the incentive I need to snuggle into him, his arm wrapping around me.

"What about you?" I ask. "Have your past relationships been as exciting and dramatic as mine?"

He rests his chin on top of my head. "Nope. I'm incredibly boring. I had a couple of short-lived relationships in high school, a slightly longer one when I was getting my undergrad, but during med school and in the ER, I didn't have the time or energy for anything serious."

I gasp. "You mean it's not like *Grey's Anatomy*? Everyone dating everyone else and getting it on in the on-call room?"

He chuckles. "Maybe for some people. Not me, though."

We watch the flames in silence for a few long minutes, enjoying the quiet, enjoying the feel of each other.

We cuddle on the couch and talk late into the night about anything and everything, stories from our pasts, our likes and dislikes, whatever comes into our heads without reservation.

As we chat and laugh and touch, a sort of awareness falls over me, as soft and sure as being covered by a thick, downy blanket.

He makes me happy. Happier than I've ever been. Even when I thought I was on top of the world, when I had a kickass job, I wasn't this content. I still felt . . . like something was missing. Like I needed more and more, like my life only had meaning if I was chasing something that was just out of reach. Working constantly was the single path forward. Now I can see that there might be more routes, more directions I can choose. Maybe there is one where I don't need to have it all, where I only need what I already have.

Where I'm at is just right.
It's enough.
Maybe I'm enough.

Chapter Twenty-Seven

MINDY

When Finley has an objective with a time limit, she turns into a wild, rabid, organized tyrant.

"Okay, people, we need to separate everything in three piles: donate, trash, and keep." She paces in front of us in the hall outside of Dad's room.

We're all lined up, like the good little soldiers we are, dressed in comfortable clothing and ready to work.

Jake straightens from where he's been leaning back against the wood-paneled wall. "Sir, yes sir!" He salutes her.

She rolls her eyes. "Any photos you find can go in here," she points at the empty box at her feet, "but place them carefully. No chucking things in here like we're playing in the NBA." She narrows her eyes on Jake.

"Don't look at me. Piper's the sloppy one." He nudges her with an elbow.

"I am not sloppy." She shoves back at him with both hands, making him stumble into me.

I push him back to rights. "Yes, you are."

She sticks out her tongue. "You're a neat freak. You can't chime in here."

"Children, pay attention," Finley says. "Clothes that are in good shape can be donated unless it's something anyone wants to keep. Otherwise, we can throw any items for the trash in the bags out here." She gestures to the roll of trash bags on the floor outside the door.

"Are we ready?"

"As we'll ever be," Taylor grumbles.

I still haven't had a chance to talk to Taylor in private. She just came back to town the day before Luke's show.

A shiver ripples through me as memories of the night before replay through my mind.

I really hope Luke can get his hands on some condoms today.

But what if that's all this is? What if it ends?

An ache twists through me at the inevitable questions. It *has* to end. This can't continue. There is too much at stake.

Shaking off the thoughts—not what I want to have in mind when I'm surrounded by my siblings—I focus on the task at hand.

Finley opens the door to Dad's room. "Let's do this."

We file in after her, Taylor, Piper, Jake, and finally me.

For a few seconds we're all frozen like statues. Stuck in the past, staring at Dad's room, which hasn't changed in the six years he's been gone. The bed is neatly made, a paperback resting on the nightstand. The digital clock glows with pale-green numbers: 1:32. If it wasn't for the inch of dust covering every surface, I might be able to convince myself that no time had passed.

Finley blows out a gusty breath. "I'll start on the closet." She squares her shoulders and then slides open the closet door, grabbing as many hangered items as she can and setting them on the bottom of the bed.

Taylor moves next, stopping at the dresser.

Jake kneels by the bed, reaching underneath and sliding out a brown cardboard box.

Piper stoops next to him, tugging out a large plastic storage container.

I head over to the other side of the closet. We're mostly quiet, only speaking to discuss whether to toss or keep various items, our voices hushed like we're in a library or a church or something.

We never talk to each other about our shared tragedies, the loss, the pain. We never speak about the things that are hard, but that doesn't make them go away. If anything, it makes the subject even bigger, turning stones into boulders and boulders into mountains. It shouldn't be this way. We need to change. I can't change them, though, or force them down the right path, but I can show the way.

A few minutes later, an opportunity comes. I set aside a stack of old empty picture frames, and a crack of laughter pops out of me as I pick up an old, raggedy porcelain doll.

"Oh, my God. Finley. Do you remember this?" I hold it up.

Her mouth pops open and she takes a few steps

toward me, staring at the doll in my hands. "He still had that thing?"

"What is it?" Piper walks over to us and makes a face. "That thing is creepy."

"It really is." The doll is pale white, her dark hair set back in two braids, her eyes coal black, and she has a painted smile that brings horror movies to mind. She's stuffed in a shabby blue dress.

"Why did he have this?" Jake asks.

Finley chuckles. "You were too young to remember. I was, what, nine?"

I nod. "Yep. I was eight. I won this monstrosity when he took me and Finley to the fair that one time." I look over at Jake. "You were all being watched by Veronica."

Finley's eyes brighten. "That's right. He wanted to spend time with just the two of us. We were both a little needier than usual because . . . ." She shrugs, not saying the rest. We missed our mom, and we were the only siblings old enough to recognize the loss.

I swallow, shoving that thought aside, and tell the rest of the story. "Anyway, I was so proud when I got this prize at one of the game booths. I showed it to Dad, and he, well, he looked at it in abject horror, declared that I could not bring her home because she would curse our family, and chucked it in the garbage."

Piper releases a startled gasp. "Did you cry?"

I shake my head. "No. I believed everything Dad said at that age. I truly believed that he had rescued us from a terrible curse."

Jake, listening nearby, scrunches his nose at the doll in my hands. "Then how did it get back here?"

"A couple of months later," I gesture toward Finley, "we walked into our room, and there she was. On my bed, covered in trash and leaves."

Piper sucks in a breath. "No way."

Finley props a hand on her hip. "Yes way. We both screamed our heads off until Dad stalked in, grabbed the doll, and said—"

"I told you not to bring this thing home. Now we're cursed," I finish, imitating his gruff tone.

Finley touches the doll's porcelain hand with a finger. "And then he ran out of the house with it, at a full sprint."

Laughter bubbles out of me, making my eyes water.

Finley sniffs. "He told me later that he threw it in a bonfire."

"And then," I continue, "About six years later, I think I was about fourteen or fifteen—"

Jake barks out a laugh. "No. He didn't."

My fingers clench around the awful toy. "Oh, he did. I went to cabin six to listen to that old record player we had in there, and imagine my shock when I flicked on the lights and there she was. On the sofa, staring straight at me."

Everyone laughs, even Taylor.

"What did you do?" Piper asks between giggles.

"I brought it to him. He was in the shed working on something with Piper, and I said, 'What is this? I thought you got rid of it.' He groaned in terror and said, 'Oh no, not again,' grabbed it out of my hands, and ran off with it."

I can barely finish at this point, the laughter bursting out of me. My siblings are in equal bouts of hysterics.

"It's so him," Finley manages to get out.

"He really went the distance with that one," Jake says, wiping at his eyes.

Finley tugs the doll from my grasp, her other hand squeezing my shoulder. "We're putting this in the keep pile."

We continue working through the room, but the mood is lighter. The silences, when they happen, are more comfortable, and we share some more of our finds, more of our memories.

Inevitably, my thoughts return to Luke. I left his bed early this morning, sneaking back to my room before anyone was the wiser.

It's not like I'm trying to hide anything from my family, it's just that I don't want to complicate things. Not yet. I still have some lingering shame over what happened with Blake. Something else I need to work on.

"What are those? Letters? Who are they from?" Piper's voice pulls me back into the moment.

Jake is sitting on the edge of the bed, and Piper is cross-legged on the floor next to him. The top drawer of the nightstand is open, and Jake is holding a large stack of envelopes, ragged around the edges and all bundled together with multiple rubber bands.

Taylor perches next to Jake, peering over his shoulder. "If they're from Mom, I say we burn them."

Finley snorts. "Mom writing us letters? She wouldn't bother herself, trust me."

"No return address." Jake pries off the rubber bands, unfolding a letter written out on lined notebook paper.

His eyes scan down the page and then flip it over. "It's from someone named . . . Ryan? No last name."

"Ryan?" Piper scrunches her nose. "He never talked about anyone with that name."

Taylor gasps. "Was he having an affair?"

Finley rolls her eyes. "With someone named Ryan?"

Taylor waves a hand. "You never know."

Piper frowns. "Why wouldn't he use email if it was something he wanted to hide?"

Taylor shrugs. "He was old-school."

"Let me see it." I crawl across the bed to look over Jake's shoulder.

Within seconds we're all crowding around Jake to try and get a better look.

He shoos us. "I can't read this when you're all in my dance space. Here, take this." He hands a letter to me and then passes out one to each of us.

Paper rustles while we all read and try to make sense of it.

Piper frowns, flipping through some pages. "These are mostly about someone named Mia?"

Taylor's mouth twists. "Ryan *and* Mia? Like a thrupple?"

Finley smacks her on the shoulder. "Ew, no. Would you stop with that? Dad didn't have a second family. He had no time for another family or even a simple relationship, let alone a liaison involving multiple people."

What if he did, though? How could he keep a secret like this, whatever this is, from us?

Jake holds up a hand. "Wait. This one has a picture."

He passes it to Finley and then she hands it to me.

It's a girl, no more than fourteen, holding a baton up in the air, wearing a shimmery, sequin-bedecked costume, and grinning at the camera. She's standing in some kind of park, the background a little faded. We all take turns studying it.

"She's young," I say.

"Just a teenager," Finley agrees.

I skim down the letter in my hand. It's an update on this Mia person. The girl in the photo, maybe? How she loves to dance, how she's doing in school, how . . . she used to hate dogs and had a deep fear of them but suddenly wants one and stops to pet every animal they see.

Why would someone be writing this to my dad? What does that even mean?

"Did he have another child?" I ask.

We glance uneasily at each other.

"Are any of them dated?" Jake asks.

I flip my page around, searching for a date. "Not mine."

"Not mine either," Piper says.

"They are postmarked, though," Finley points out.

Piper is frowning at the photo. Her eyes lift to Jake. "What's the postmark on the letter with this picture?"

He shuffles through the envelopes. "Nine years ago. But no return address." With a frown, he holds his hand out. "Here, give them back."

"Why?" Finley asks.

"We need to read through them, but I want to put them in date order."

Taylor hands hers over, then stands and takes a few steps away, her arms crossing in front of her. "I don't know if I can handle this right now. I don't want to read them."

Jake puts the letters back in their envelopes, then wraps one of the rubber bands around the pile. "I can do it."

Finley watches him, concern puckering her brow. "Are you sure?"

He stares down at the stack in his hands. "Yes." His head lifts to meet her gaze. "This is good. I need this. It gives me something to focus on. I'll see what I can find, and I'll tell you all as soon as anything becomes clear."

She squeezes his shoulder. "Okay, Jakey."

Piper blows out a breath and stands, stretching her arms out in front of her. "I think I've had enough for one day."

Finley nods. "We made good progress. I'll text Archer to come up and help with hauling some of this stuff out. Taylor, will you run to the office and grab my iPad? I need to take some photos and make a list of the donations for the accountant. It's in the drawer in my desk."

"Sure." Taylor stalks out of the room, probably grateful to get away from me after being in such a confined space for so long and not literally exploding.

Finley winks at me, and after a few seconds I follow Taylor.

Downstairs, I take a deep breath before stepping into the office.

Taylor is standing at the desk off to the right, digging through the drawers.

I clear my throat. "Can we talk for a minute?"

She freezes, her movements coming to a screeching

halt, gaze flicking up to me. Then she stands up straight, crossing her arms over her chest, her eyes frosty. "About what?"

I move closer, holding on to the back of one of the cushioned guest chairs facing the desk. "I want to apologize."

She stares at me and then bursts out laughing. "Is this a joke? This is a joke, right, some kind of weird thing where you act like you're sorry for treating me like garbage for eight years and then take it all back to make me feel even crappier?"

I wince. "No, I'm being serious. I've had some realizations recently, and I know I have issues I need to work through regarding Aria's death. I have my own guilt, you see, and I've been projecting that anger onto you when really, I've been angry at myself, but I couldn't . . . I just didn't see it. Until now."

Man, that was lame.

Her lips thin, her head shaking back and forth slowly. "No. No, you don't get to do this."

I blink rapidly. "Do what?"

She raises her hands. "Act like you're the good guy here."

"I know I'm not. That's what I'm trying to say. I'm the bad guy. It was easier to blame you than it was to accept my own culpability. I know that now, and I want to make it right."

"What the—?" She cuts off, shutting her eyes for a second and taking a deep breath before opening them again. "You're trying to tell me that you put me through hell for years and it wasn't even about me?"

"It wasn't. And I wasn't fair to you, and I am truly sorry. I'm going to be better, I promise. I won't make snide comments anymore about . . . anything."

She presses her lips together. "Well, that's great for you, but I don't forgive you."

I swallow. I knew it would go this way, but even anticipating her reaction doesn't stop the throb of hurt and dismay. "I understand."

I'm not going to give up. I can't control Taylor's lingering feelings of resentment and anger, but I can work on myself and be better.

I leave the office, knowing I've done all I could for now and hoping that maybe someday, maybe even someday soon, Taylor will find it in her heart to forgive me and things will get better between us.

Even though nothing has been resolved, it's still like a heavy weight that's been pressing on my chest is suddenly thrust away, like my animosity toward Taylor was a boulder tethered to my body.

It's not perfect, but at least it's progress.

Chapter Twenty-Eight

Luke

I'm sitting on the couch with my notebook, playing with lyrics for a new song that started poking at me this morning, when the front door opens and slams shut.

"Luke?"

As if it's controlled by a motor directly attached to her voice, my heart thumps harder.

"In here."

She's already in the living room, shrugging out of her coat and tossing it on the chair. "Did you get condoms?"

I fight a smile. "Yeah, I put them in—"

"Good." She jumps on me.

My notebook and pencil clatter to the floor and I grip her waist as she straddles my hips.

"Sorry," she says, in between kisses, not sounding sorry in the slightest.

"I'm not sorry."

"I need you," she says, her mouth moving down to my neck.

I groan, already hard and straining for her. Need isn't a strong enough word for what I feel for her. I'm not sure one exists that could encompass it.

She leans back, resting on my knees, grabs the bottom of her shirt, and draws it over her head. I help her toss it to the side and then I reach for her bra, undoing the clasp in the back. She tugs the straps off and it joins the rest of her clothes on the floor.

I take in the view of her bare breasts, her flushed face, her eyes drowsy with desire, and I swallow hard, trying to calm the swell of arousal hurtling through my body.

She tips forward and I cup one of her breasts, barely brushing it with my lips, rubbing my mouth over it with delicate movements.

She groans, the sound better than the strains of my favorite song. "Luke." Her hips swivel against me, seeking release. "Please tell me you have a condom in your pocket or something."

I remove my mouth from her body reluctantly. "You're in luck." I shift my hips and she lifts up slightly. I reach into my pocket and pull it out.

"You really are a genius." She grabs it out of my hand. "Now take off your pants."

A startled laugh huffs out of me. "Whatever you say." With a little bit of fumbling, we manage to shove my pants down, and she yanks my T-shirt up and off.

Her leggings hit the floor next to my clothes along with her panties.

Then she's sliding the condom on me, her gentle hands inciting a fresh riot of lust pounding through me.

She straddles me again, positioning herself over my covered length, and I watch her movements, fascinated, enthralled, and so turned on I think I've died and gone straight to heaven. "Luke."

My eyes fly to hers as she sinks down on me, sheathing me inside her in one smooth movement.

Shit.

For a minute neither of us moves, gazes locked. My breath catches in my lungs, complex sensations wrenching their way through my heart. I'm inside her, and yet it's not close enough.

Air hisses out of my mouth at the blissful sensation. I grab her head and pull her in to kiss her beautiful mouth before biting gently at the curve of her jaw and then pulling on the tender, sensitive skin of her neck with lips and teeth.

Her hips move, riding me, chasing her pleasure, and I move back to her mouth, our tongues brushing, seeking, and tasting.

When she pulls back for air, arching her back, her breasts are right in front of my face.

Perfection.

I return my attention to her nipples, offering gentle sucks and nips.

She throws her head back on a moan. "Luke, it's too much. I need more."

"If it's too much, wouldn't you need less?" I ask against her hot skin.

She grips my head. "Semantics."

I pull my head back to look up at her. "If you can spout words like semantics, I am clearly doing something wrong."

She smiles down at me, her dark hair loose and curling around her shoulders.

So beautiful.

I rub my swollen lips, so softly, against her nipple while she watches. Then I suck it into my mouth.

Her mouth drops open, eyes falling shut, hips moving faster and faster, getting lost in the pleasure.

"That's much better." I resume my attention to her breasts, sucking a little harder now, my mouth more demanding.

She rides me, pressing down after each lift, tilting her hips so my body hits her *right there.*

As soon as she quivers and shakes with release, the orgasm that's been hovering and waiting in my core rushes through me like thunder, shaking me from the inside out for long seconds.

She collapses on top of me, and I hold her, rubbing her bare back with long, smooth strokes of my palm while we catch our breath.

After a minute, she climbs off me. I get up to dispose of the condom and then return quickly to stretch out with her on the couch, grabbing a blanket off the back of it to cover our cooling bodies.

She ducks her head to me, her hand stroking my chest.

One arm is stretched underneath her head, supporting her neck, my other hand resting on her waist.

For long minutes we lay together, holding each other, basking in the sensation of skin-on-skin contact.

After a while she tilts her head back slightly to meet my eyes. "That was . . ." she trails off.

"Yeah," I agree.

She bites her bottom lip, and I bend over to kiss her before biting it myself.

That lip will be the death of me.

She smirks.

"I don't want this to end." The words pop out, a thought that's been bubbling in the back of my throat for weeks. We don't have much more time together, not like this. It's already December. The album is set to be released next month, and then my tour begins right after. What will happen to us then? Will there still be an us?

Her eyes search mine. "I don't want this to end either."

"Good." My voice is low and graveled. I want to tell her more, explain to her how it feels, this sprawling, intense emotion spreading inside me like wildfire, but I can't find the words.

Despite the assurance of her words, a dark fear lingers in her eyes.

But then she kisses me, the press of her lips is soft at first, quickly escalating to frantic and frenzied, her movements a reflection of the very sensations pulsing through me.

All thought flies out the window, and I lose myself in her body.

~

"Are you hungry?" Mindy tosses the question over her shoulder at me as I enter the kitchen.

She's standing at the stove, spatula in hand while something simmers in a pan in front of her.

I step up behind her, wrapping my arms around her midsection and peering over her shoulder.

"That looks good."

"Veggie omelet. It's the one meal I'm good at. You want one?"

I move one hand back to cup her ass. "This looks good, too."

She's wearing one of my shirts over her underwear and nothing else.

"Does it?" She arches back pushing her rear further into my palm.

The arousal is immediate, my cock waking up and poking against my briefs, trying to get to her.

I groan, my forehead dropping to her shoulder. "Are you trying to kill me?"

We spent most of last night working halfway through the box of condoms. I didn't think I had any more lust to spare, but apparently Mindy can draw it out of me.

"Aw, poor baby." She reaches over and shuts the burner off. Then she spins around and grabs my hand, pulling me over to the counter. She jumps up on it, pulling me between her hips. "This is a nice height, but you have too many clothes on."

I glance down. "I'm only wearing underwear."

She waves her hand. "As I said, too much. Take it off."

"Yes, ma'am."

I capture her mouth in mine, my hands drifting to

my waistband, but before I can pull them down far enough, the front door opens and someone stomps inside.

"Hey, Luke, you awake, man? Have you seen Min—holy shit!" A second later, the front door slams shut.

Mindy's hands clench on my shoulders. "Oops." She chuckles. "He finally caught us."

I huff out a laugh. "Third time's a charm, I guess." Since he interrupted us at Veronica's, then again when he came over after the show, this time we didn't stand a chance.

"We should check on him."

She waves her hand. "He's probably halfway to Canada right now."

Nonetheless, I put on some pants and open the front door, peeking outside.

Jake is on the front porch, flat on his stomach, banging his head against the wood, muttering something.

I tiptoe closer. "Jake? You all right?"

His mumbling gets clearer as I approach.

"Why, why, why?"

I crouch down next to him. "Hey, you okay?"

He stops muttering and lifts his head. "No. I am not okay. I came over to find Mindy and see if you wanted to help me kick Oliver's ass at fishing, but now I can't stop picturing. . . ." He grimaces and waves his hand.

"I'm sorry."

He gives me a sardonic look. "No, you aren't."

"You're right." I grin. "I'm not. Well, I *am* sorry we were interrupted."

His eyes narrow. "If you keep looking all blissed out

like that while talking about my sister, I might actually punch you."

Mindy pads out onto the porch.

I turn around to watch as she walks over to us. She's pulled on a sweater and her leggings from yesterday. "Sorry, Jake."

He rolls to a sitting position, scowling but not meeting her eyes. "Whatever."

"Is everything okay?" she asks.

He shrugs. "Yeah, everyone just wondered where you got off to since you didn't come home last night, and I wanted to invite Luke out with the guys." He shakes his head. "I should have known," he mutters. Then he squints at her. "Taylor took off this morning."

Mindy frowns. "She did?"

"Yeah. Did something happen with you two?" Jake asks.

Mindy and I exchange a glance. She shared the details of her conversation with Taylor last night in between rounds of lovemaking.

She shrugs at Jake. "Why do you ask?"

"She was acting weird." He rubs his chin. "Weirder than normal."

"What do you mean?"

He rolls to his feet, brushing dust off his jeans. "Normally she gets sarcastic or angry when anyone talks about you, but last night at dinner it was more like she was depressed or something." He lifts a shoulder and drops it. "I don't know. Maybe I imagined it. Anyway, Luke, you want to go fishing?"

Mindy rests a hand on my shoulder. "You should go. I

have some work to do anyway. I got a couple inquiries from musicians seeking representation, and I want to check them out."

I cover her hand with mine. "Really? You didn't tell me. That's great, Mindy. I'm so proud of you."

She shrugs, her cheeks flushing. "They might suck."

"They might not."

We beam at each other.

Jake clears his throat.

"Okay, weirdos, you about done? Can we go now, Luke?"

I keep my eyes on Mindy when I answer. "Yeah, you go ahead. I'll be right there. Just give me 15 minutes."

Jake sighs, his footsteps passing us as he stomps down the patio. "God save me if Taylor ever finds a boyfriend," he grumbles.

Chapter Twenty-Nine

Mindy

"Thank you for helping with all this."

I chuckle. "You've thanked me at least thirty-seven times, Finley. Stop it already."

Her lips purse. "Have you been keeping count?"

We're standing in the center of the cobblestone drive, near the cabins, waiting for the first busload of kids to arrive.

"Are you excited?" I ask Finley.

She hasn't stopped fidgeting since we came down here to wait, and I'm pretty sure we still have at least fifteen minutes until they'll arrive, but she was crawling up the walls in the house.

She taps on the clipboard in her hand. "I'm so excited and nervous I don't even know what to do with myself."

I put a hand on her shoulder. "It's going to be great."

She shifts on her feet. "I just don't want anything to go wrong."

"Are you kidding me? Between me and you, Jake, Archer, Oliver, Luke, the four counselors you hired, and the three chefs, I think it will be okay. Maybe."

"You're right. I know you're right. I wish Taylor was here."

I pat her shoulder but don't say anything. It's my fault Taylor left early for her music festival, which is typical although it's for a different reason than usual. Normally she bails because I'm being a psycho bitch. This time she bailed because I apologized and shifted her world on its axis.

The guilt pokes at me, and I let it. Now at least I can recognize it for what it is: shame at my own behavior and poor choices. I can't change the past, but I can do my best to be better now. I accept the guilt and then push it to the side.

"She'll come back," I tell Finley.

She nods, distracted, and peers down at the list of students on her clipboard.

Luke and I plan on heading back to the city next week. We're going to stay at Oliver's until Christmas while Luke does some interviews and a few small performances I've set up. He needs to practice before the tour. His stage fright, while better, isn't completely gone. It probably won't ever be.

Then next month, we'll be on the road for a bit and things will change.

My stomach twists.

Change is inevitable. He'll go on tour, and I'll accompany him for as much of it as I can, but I also need to grow the roster for Outfoxed Records, and that will take up much of my time. If Luke's album and tour do well, I may get enough capital to hire someone to help me, but that's a big if.

Our little bubble of . . . whatever we are is about to be exposed to the rest of the world, and I am already anticipating the pop.

Duncan hasn't committed to signing with Outfoxed Records, but he hasn't turned me down yet, either. He has another label he wants to talk to, and he's been very honest at least. I can't imagine he'll sign with me since I'm sure the competition will offer more than I can currently. I can only wait and see.

It helps that there haven't been any more articles, social media posts, or comments from Blake and Jeanette since that last interview. I can only hope he forgets my name and everything related to me forever and ever, but those are weak hopes.

Over the past week, I've talked to a few other artists on the phone, none as well known or as established as Duncan but definite up-and-comers with a lot of talent. So far there is one I definitely want to sign—a young lady from Tennessee. The others are question marks, but since word of Luke's talent has been bubbling, I've received more and more inquiries through the basic website I set up.

Luke has been busy working on some secret song he's refused to share in spite of my numerous attempts to wheedle it out of him. I smile, remembering the way I tortured him last night, first with my fingers and then with my mouth and tongue and—

"They're here!" Finley grips my arm, squeezing so tight she nearly cuts off my circulation.

The bus ambles up the driveway, brakes hissing as it comes to a stop.

Finley jogs over to the doors at the front, and I follow her at a slower pace.

Figures inside the bus are on the move, shrugging on backpacks, jumping around, little faces peering out the windows creased in curiosity and excitement.

The door whooshes open and noisy children tumble out along with one of the counselors, who is attempting to talk over the bustle and telling the kids to line up outside.

Finley steps into action, greeting each person as they come off the bus and facilitating the lineup in order to do a head count.

I can't help but grin as I watch her. She absolutely does not need me here. I'm more of an emotional support sibling.

Behind the bus, a black sedan pulls up, the windows so darkly tinted it's impossible to make out the driver.

I point it out. "Who is that?" I ask Finley. "One of the instructors?"

She glances over at it, shaking her head. "No. They're all on the bus with the kids."

She motions to one of the instructors, a tall, bearded man in his twenties. "Do you know who that is?"

He frowns at the car and then shrugs. "No one I know."

"I'll go check it out," I reassure her. I'm halfway to the vehicle when the driver's door opens and Blake steps out.

Oh, shit.

I glance behind me. The bus is nearly empty, about thirty tweens lined up alongside it. The few nearest me gasp, nudging the person next to them. The motion is like a wave down the line as they all come to the jarring realization that one of the biggest rock stars on the planet has just arrived.

Damn it, Blake.

What the hell is he thinking? He isn't. He's lost his damn mind.

My heart pounds harder, and I increase my pace. I have to get him out of here before—well, maybe it's a nonissue. These are kids from disadvantaged homes, they probably don't have—

Snap, snap, snap.

Too late.

Where there are tweens, there are cellphones and, therefore, cameras.

"Finley," I yell over my shoulder. "Confiscate the cellphones!"

Without question, she jumps into action, calling out to the other counselors to help her—hopefully, before anyone has a chance to text or snap or whatever the kids are doing these days.

"Get back in the car," I hiss at Blake.

He lifts his hands. "Only if you agree to talk to me."

"Do I have a choice?" Anger and frustration boil through my veins. I want to scream. "Get in the car, Blake."

He motions to the passenger door, brows raised, waiting.

With a growl I get in.

He finally complies after I do, sliding back into the car and shutting the door.

I really hope Finley is able to confiscate the photos before any hit the Internet. That's all we need, a story all over social media about Blake showing up at my childhood home, complete with images of me getting into his car with him.

"Go up the drive," I bark at him.

"I'm really digging the warm greeting, Mindy. It's pretty sexy."

"Just drive."

He finally cooperates, guiding the car around the bus. I direct him to park in front of the house and then I hop out like the seat is on fire.

I can't talk to him in his car, the space is too confined, and I might punch him in his stupid face. I wait for him to get out.

After a second, the door pops open and he faces me.

He gestures to the house. "Can we go inside to talk?"

I shake my head. "No. What are you doing here?"

He ducks his head, shoving his hands in his pockets. "It's cold out here. Can we please go inside?"

Is it cold? A blaze of fury is heating me from the inside out.

"No. You should have brought a coat. What are you doing here, Blake?" I repeat.

He sighs. "You weren't replying to any of my texts or calls."

Is he deluded? Dumb question. Of course he is. "Why would I?"

His chin dips, and he kicks at a rock in the drive with the tip of his Air Jordans. "I heard you're doing well. I listened to some of the work you've done with this"–his nose wrinkles—"Luke person. The buzz is that you're making a comeback and that your new label will be a real contender."

It just might be. Of course, it would help if he would stop talking about me in interviews and writing songs about me and showing up where he's not wanted, but I don't want to tell him that. I can't tell him that. I know Blake. Trying to tell him what to do is like trying to tell the world not to turn. He's going to do what he wants, and any demands will likely just make him dig in his heels.

I need him to leave, so I remain silent.

"I wanted to congratulate you. And see you." He takes a step closer.

I hold up a hand. "Stop. I know you didn't come all the way out here just to congratulate me."

"I miss you, okay? I started missing you the minute you walked away from me."

I shake my head in disbelief. "Blake. We've had this conversation." Months ago. And once was more than enough. "Your wife is pregnant."

"She's not."

I stare at him, the words failing to register even when I play them over in my head three times.

"What?"

He takes another step toward me. "Jeanette's not pregnant."

I lift a hand, pressing my fingers to my temple. "How is that possible?"

He squints up at the sky, a sad smile on his face. "She lied, Mindy. She lied because we were going to divorce and she found out about you. She got jealous and lied so I wouldn't leave her. She does things like this a lot. She's a little erratic."

I can't understand what is happening right now. My brain cannot process the information; it's like he's speaking a foreign language.

He moves closer, close enough to reach out and touch my arm. "We were really great together. Didn't you think so?"

"I did." Before I met Luke and realized what it's like to be with someone who accepts me without question, without limits or judgment. Exactly as I am. I haven't quite learned how to accept myself, but I'm working on it.

Not to mention the fact that Blake truly believed she was pregnant with his child, which means they were intimate around the same time we were together. He's not exactly innocent here. He lied about their relationship at the very least. He could be lying now for all I know. How can I trust any of it?

"We can be together. In truth." He grabs my hand, drawing me closer.

I tug back. "No. No, we can't."

He grips my fingers tighter.

"You came to talk, and now we have, and now you can leave."

His eyes implore me, face creased in confusion. "But Mindy, doesn't this change anything?"

"No. Let go of me. Now." I add force and volume to the words, needing to get through to him.

He blinks, shock covering his features. He's not used to hearing no.

I twist my fingers harder, attempting to wrench my hand from his grasp, but he won't release me.

"Blake—"

"Mindy." He yanks me forward.

I stumble into him. "If you don't let go of me right now, I will hurt you."

He laughs.

Red haze covers my vision. I jerk my knee upward, right into his groin.

With an oomph, he releases me, hunching forward.

"Mindy? Are you okay?" Luke jogs up the drive toward us, eyes tracing over Blake, bent over in front of me. A smile quirks at his lips.

Blake is recovering quickly, almost standing at full height now.

I didn't hit him too hard; I didn't have the best angle, and I just wanted him to let me go. Of course, testes are rather delicate organs.

Luke stops next to me, close enough that his arm presses against mine. He frowns at Blake.

Blake glares at him. "I see you're fucking a new musician now. Do I have to be on your roster to get a spot in your bed?"

Luke takes a menacing step toward him.

I stop him with a hand on his arm, the limb tense under my fingers. "It's time for you to leave, Blake."

Blake glares at Luke and the moment stretches, coated in hostility.

"Please leave."

Blake turns, gets back in his car, and a relieved gust of air whooshes out of me.

He takes his sweet time, but once his car has disappeared down the drive, I turn toward Luke.

His arms are open and waiting.

I step into him, snuggling my face into his neck so I can breathe in his bright, clean scent. Relief sweeps through me. He's like a heavy blanket on a cold, blustery day. He brushes a kiss across my head, resting his cheek on my hair. The tension from the encounter with Blake crumbles in the face of Luke's easy affection.

"Are you okay?" he asks after a minute has passed.

I nod and squeeze him tighter.

He blows out an exasperated breath. "Was he ever aggressive with you like that before?"

"No. He's never been like that. Even when I rejected his advances before he would only increase the charm, he would never . . . but I guess once I said yes, he thought that acceptance was open forever."

"That's not an excuse."

"No, it's not. He wasn't wrong, though."

"About what?"

"About me." I swallow past a lump that's suddenly formed in my throat. "Sleeping with musicians."

He leans back to meet my eyes. "It's not the same between us."

I can't hold his searching stare. I can't handle the vulnerability stamped across his face.

Whatever he reads in my expression makes him blanch. "It's not the same, Mindy, right?"

"No, I mean, yes, you're right." He is right. But how will this ever work out between us? Misery engulfs me, threatening to drag me under. How can we be together without it affecting the rest of our lives? Our work is now tied up together, our mutual dreams and goals, and if people find out—"Oh, no, the kids!"

He blinks. "What kids?"

I cover my face with my hands. "Blake showed up right after the bus got here. All the kids took photos of Blake . . . and of me getting into his car." I groan. "Finley took their phones, but it's a matter of time before it leaks to the press and then who knows what they'll say now."

His hands cover mine, gently removing them from my face. He tips my right hand over and kisses my palm. "We'll get through this."

Despair clogs my throat. "None of this is fair to you."

"I'm not worried about me."

I set my jaw. "I am."

"Well, don't be." He kisses my other palm.

I clench my hands into fists, staring down at our joined hands. "It's literally my job to worry about you."

His thumbs rub at my wrists. "No. It's your job to help me launch my album and schedule my tour dates."

"PR is a part of it," I insist.

He doesn't immediately reply, and I glance up at him, my jaw clenching. Maybe it would be best if we ended things now, before we get even closer and it's even harder to step away. But the thought of no longer being *with* Luke, of not being able to touch him or kiss him whenever I want, sends a shaft of sharp pain through my gut. I can't handle it.

His normally bright gaze darkens in hurt. "Please don't do this."

I swallow. I've never seen him like this, his voice tortured, his face stark with impending grief. I don't want to hurt him. I don't want to hurt myself. But I definitely can't be the one to put those shadows in his eyes.

"Don't build up walls between us." He releases my wrists and cups my face in both of his warm hands. "Please. You mean more to me than any fallout from the press. I will stand with you, no matter what. Whatever happens, we can get through it together. Don't push me out. Let me walk beside you."

I should say no. I should walk away and save him from the potential damage to both of us. Save myself from future pain. But it's already too late. I've fallen for Luke, harder than I ever thought possible. Worry that it won't work out clashes with the hope that it will.

I don't want to deny Luke's request, especially when it's what I want, too, more than anything. He won't cut and run on me, not like Blake. If Duncan won't sign with my label because of my relationship with Luke . . . I'm not sure I want an artist like that on my roster.

The thought of going back, of returning to a purely platonic professional relationship, is like an ax in the chest.

And with that, the decision settles over me, clicking into place with the *rightness* of it. Something inside me releases, relaxing the tension in my limbs.

"Okay."

Relief blankets his face, the tension in his expression draining away. "Really?"

"Really. We're in this together. No matter what happens. But you're going to regret it. Maybe I should put it in the contract: You're officially stuck with my bullshit, and I cannot be held liable for any impact it has on your career."

He laughs. "Good. I love your bullshit."

My heart dips and dives, and I don't have a chance to evaluate his verb choice because his lips press against mine. And then my mouth opens, and the world goes fuzzy.

Wrapped in Luke's arms, secure and warm, it's easy to believe that everything will work out just fine.

But as I've learned, anything that can go wrong probably will.

Chapter Thirty

Luke

"If I'm your date, does that mean we can make out up in the loft?" Mindy inclines her head toward the stairs, keeping her voice low in the crowded room.

We're at an art gallery in SoHo to support the unveiling of Piper's latest piece.

I lean into her, whispering into her ear. "We can make out wherever you want. Right here is just as good."

We returned to the city last week, and we've been staying in Oliver's building—for now. Christmas is in a couple of weeks, and then my tour starts next month, after New Year's.

She fights a smile. "I wouldn't want to take the attention away from Piper's moment."

"Her work is truly incredible."

We both turn toward the sculpture in the center of the room. It's swarmed with people and only partially visible from where we're standing, but we already got an up-close view of it before the show started.

It's a sculpture within a sculpture. The outer piece is made of some kind of metal grating forming the shape of a person sitting down with their head in their hands. Inside is a bronze statue of a child holding a kite, the string in their outstretched hand arching toward the sky, their legs stretched out mid-run. The figure gazes up at the kite with a wide grin.

It's called The Inner Child.

"I don't know how she does it," Mindy says. "I like how they all have the same theme." She gestures to the painting hanging on the wall in front of us, a black-and-white sketch of a child playing jacks, the bright knucklebones being tossed onto the ground are the only splash of color.

I rest my fingers on her lower back, craving the touch even if it's through the fabric of her slinky black dress and despite the fact that a lot of the past week has been spent in bed in between work.

Her phone dings multiple times in quick succession.

Almost immediately after, my phone buzzes in my pocket.

She frowns and slides the cell from her clutch. Her eyes fly to mine. "Let's go up to the loft."

I grimace. "I'm guessing this isn't to make out."

She shakes her head, takes my hand, and then we're on the move, weaving through the throng over to the stairs in the back that will take us up. It's an artist's space, open and empty with stark white walls and bench seating that runs along the bank of windows facing the street.

Since it's nine o'clock, the windows are dark except for lights coming in from the street and a few dim sconces on the walls.

We sit side by side on one of the benches. "One of the videos of Blake showing up at Camp Aria just hit the web. I got news alerts and a message from Ally, my old assistant." She turns the screen so we can watch together, our bodies touching from thigh to shoulder.

She presses play, and the video starts with Blake standing by his car. Mindy approaches the vehicle, her back to the camera. Her head turns to the side and a blurry profile is visible for a split second before she stops. She and Blake have a short conversation, not audible in the video. The sounds of children laughing and talking are the only audio. After a moment, Mindy climbs into the passenger seat.

The video stops.

"What does the article say? Does it mention where he is?"

She closes the video window and we read over the article together. It's short, stating that Blake Bonham was spotted at a camp for kids in New York and was in the company of an unidentified woman.

Requests for comment from Blake Bonham and Jeanette Adams have not yet been answered.

"The quality is low. I don't think anyone would be able to tell it's you." I rub the back of my head. "Could be worse."

"It could be. Unless someone figures out the camp is tied to my family and puts two and two together." She bites her lip.

I press a quick kiss to her mouth, unable to help myself. Before I can pull too far away, she reaches out and grabs me, kissing me more fully.

We break apart but stay close, our foreheads still touching.

She sighs, and the air gusts over my lips. "I need to find out how Blake is going to respond to this."

"Do you think he would tell the media he went to see you?"

She shrugs. "To sell more albums? Maybe. I don't want this to affect the label, and you by extension."

She's been working so hard to sign new artists, including Duncan Santos. Getting him would be a huge boon to her label, but the negative publicity surrounding Mindy and Blake has made him hesitant. "Don't worry about me—" My phone buzzes in my pocket again, and I lean away to slide it out. I had nearly forgotten it had gone off before. "It's Laila. She wants me to call her. She says it's important." I raise my phone to show her the text.

Her brows dip. "Maybe it's related?"

"Only one way to find out."

I hit the call button and put it on speaker.

"Hey, thanks for getting back to me so fast," Laila answers.

"Yeah of course. Mindy's with me. We have you on speaker. What's going on?"

"Oh, good, I'm glad she's there with you because this involves you both. Someone sent me a video of you and Mindy together."

Mindy and I exchange a shocked look.

"What? What kind of video?" I ask.

"You're standing outside of the main house at the camp, hugging and then kissing, and then it cuts off. The camera angle is coming from the driveway, like someone was standing in the trees, filming you. Hella creepy."

I scan through my memories. The only time I kissed Mindy outside of the main house was right after Blake left. It's possible he didn't leave and instead stuck around to try and harass Mindy more and ended up with this footage of us.

Laila continues, "They sent a message with it that reads 'I think you'll be interested in this.' Maybe someone who's a little too invested in our musical chemistry?" She sounds perturbed. "I knew we should have just told those reporters there's nothing going on between us."

"They may not have believed you anyway," Mindy says.

Laila sighs. "This is true. But still, why send this video to me?"

Mindy shifts on the bench next to me. "To stir up drama, hoping you'll take to social media and put me and Luke on blast."

She humphs. "They don't know me at all then."

"Will you text the video to me?" I ask.

"Absolutely. I was going to forward it to you right away, but then I thought I should call first for context."

"Thank you for letting us know," Mindy says.

"I'll send you a screenshot of the number it came from, too."

"Will you read it out to us?" Mindy asks.

After a second, Laila rattles it off.

Mindy's eyes go wide. Her thumbs tap over her

phone. "It's from Blake." She holds it up to show me his contact info.

"Blake? That's Blake Bonham's number?" Laila squeaks. "Why is he texting me a video of you two kissing?"

Our eyes lock over the phone, sharing our confusion.

Mindy shakes her head. "I have no idea, but we're going to do what we can to find out."

~

"Do you think Blake will release the video of you and Luke to the press?" Piper asks Mindy.

We're all sitting around in Oliver's living room after sharing the details of the news and the subsequent conversation with Laila with Piper and Oliver.

Mindy and I are on the plush leather sofa. She's tucked into my side, her laptop set to the side because she was driving herself to distraction searching for any additional news.

Piper is on the loveseat, her legs tucked up underneath her. Oliver is in the kitchen making tea.

"I really don't know what he's going to do."

"Why would he send that to Laila at all?" Piper asks.

Mindy taps at something on the computer before replying. "It can be hard to think like a narcissist, but if I had to guess, I would say he wants Laila to release it to the press or to her fans or somehow put it out there to cause problems for Luke and me that won't be traced back to him."

Piper frowns. "Why would he want that?"

Oliver walks into the living room with a tea tray in hand and sets it on the glass table. "People have been assuming Luke and Laila are an item. Upon receipt of this video, in his mind, Laila would believe Luke was being duplicitous and therefore use the video to enact some kind of revenge that would have negative implications for Luke and for Mindy."

Piper wrinkles her nose. "But why? What does he want? What's the endgame here?"

I lean forward to grab a mug of hot tea from the tray, dropping a cube of sugar in it and holding it out to Mindy. "My guess is he wants to get back at Mindy for rejecting him. The real question is how do we stop him? What's to prevent him from going to the press with all of this and making up whatever he wants about you?"

Mindy takes the cup from me and blows on it before taking a sip. "I don't know."

Oliver takes a seat next to Piper, resting a hand on her knee. "We should get out in front of it now."

Mindy nods slowly. "Yes. That would be ideal. Find a media outlet to run a story that we can spin however we want, so we control the narrative before Blake does. But Blake is a superstar. When he speaks, half the world listens. The press doesn't care about me or Luke. I'm only peripherally famous, mostly because of my former association with Blake. Luke's star is just now rising. How do we find a way to get the truth out to a lot of people, enough to take power away from anything Blake might put out there?"

I rub my jaw, thinking. "I bet Laila would help."

"That's a good idea." Mindy gives me a half smile.

"We know she's got decent pull. It's not Blake Bonham pull, but it's significant."

Her phone rings. She reaches over to pluck it off the coffee table, her expression baffled. "I don't know this number."

And it's eleven o'clock at night.

She answers. "Hello?" Her brows lift to her hairline, her gaze immediately locking with mine. "Blake?"

Chapter Thirty-One

MINDY

"Slow down, I can't understand you." As soon as I picked up the phone, Blake started whining. "What did you say about Jeanette?"

I pull the phone from my ear and put him on speaker. Without missing a beat, Luke slips his phone out of his pocket and hits a button to record the conversation.

So smart. I want to kiss him, but Blake is talking, and I suppose we have more pressing issues to attend to.

"She stole my phone and disappeared. Have you seen her?"

"Why would I have seen her?" I've never met Jeanette Adams.

He doesn't answer for a few long seconds.

"Blake. What is going on?"

He speaks in a rush. "It's possible that she believes

that you and I are back together and that I'm leaving her for you. Again."

Luke and I exchange a baffled glance. "What? Why would she think that?"

"Because I told her?"

I lift my hand to my temple, where a headache has started to throb. "Is that a question?"

He sighs. "No. I was just angry about her lying about the pregnancy, and I wanted to make her angry."

That's probably the most self-aware sentence Blake has ever uttered.

I look over at the phone Luke is holding, still recording, and my mind sorts through various ideas and possibilities.

"How long ago did Jeanette leave?"

"This morning, around ten."

Does this mean Jeanette is the one who texted Laila the video?

"And you said she has your phone?"

"Yep."

"What do you think she's going to do?"

He blows out a breath, the sound gusting over the phone line. "Maybe she'll go to the press to try and make me look bad, maybe she'll try to find you and blackmail you, I really don't know. All I know is she's got my phone and she wants to hurt me, and she definitely has the ammo right now."

What the heck else is on Blake's phone?

Also, what if Blake is lying? I don't know why he would unless this is all some convoluted scheme to . . . what? Get me back? Not likely.

"If there are things on your phone that you're worried about leaking to the public, then you should come clean first. Release the story yourself so you can control the narrative."

It's the same thing we planned on doing, but if Blake is the one to come forward, it would have a lot more sway.

"I don't know, Mindy. She's got everyone on the planet completely snowed. Who would believe me?"

"You tell me, Blake: What would be worse? Coming forward with your story and your side of things first or letting Jeanette do whatever she wants and ruin your life and mine?"

"I don't know."

I shake my head, irritated. I swear he loves all this drama as much as Jeanette does. They're probably perfect for each other. If he won't man up, a little nudge won't hurt. "I'm recording this conversation. If you don't come forward and make this right before Jeanette starts spreading stories about us, I will share this conversation with the media myself."

He doesn't speak. Maybe I've shocked him into silence.

Luke's hand squeezes my knee in quiet support.

"Talk to your PR team," I say, when Blake still hasn't responded. "I'll let you think about it for twenty-four hours, but if you haven't made a statement by then, I'm coming forward."

I hang up and glance around.

Luke's grinning.

Piper's hands are covering her mouth, her eyes wide.

Oliver is eying me with a glint of respect. "Well done."

I toss my phone on the table. "That should do it."

~

"Remember when I said you wouldn't be playing for thousands of people? That may have been a lie." I twist around in my chair to look at Luke.

He's sitting on the bed, shirtless, back against the headboard, legs stretched out in front of him, crossed at the ankle. His guitar is in his lap, fingers strumming a familiar tune.

So freaking hot.

I've been finishing up last-minute work. Christmas is less than a week away, and I don't want to worry about work while spending time with my family and with Luke. We've divvyed up the holiday so we won't have to spend any time apart. We're spending Christmas Eve with his family and then Christmas Day with mine.

His mouth quirks in a smile. "You lied to me, huh?"

"May have." My eyes track down his form, taking in the broadness of his bare shoulders, the flex of his forearms, and his fingers picking at the strings.

"Like what you see?"

"Maybe."

It's a good thing we're in the north wing of Oliver's building and they're too far away to hear anything. It's also good that Oliver invests in sturdy beds.

Blake made a wise decision and released an official statement the morning after our little chat, spilling the truth about Jeanette's pregnancy and publicly announcing their separation.

Included in the statement was a brief note: *Any rumors about Mindy Fox and myself are completely unfounded. We worked together for many years, and while we remain on friendly terms, there is nothing more between us.*

Not long after that, Jeanette appeared on Blake's social media accounts, posting videos blasting him, blasting me and quite a few other women—ostensibly based on the DMs and texts and who knows whatever else he had on his phone.

Unfortunately for Jeanette, her eyes were red and hazy, her words slurred and chaotic. If anything, all she accomplished was adding credence to Blake's statement.

A day later, reports came out that she checked into a posh treatment center in California.

Two days later I got a call from Duncan Santos. He's the fourth artist to join my label, after a few other unknown acts I had found. Just like I anticipated, once I hooked such a large fish, the calls and messages started pouring in. Not just from other artists interested in submitting to Outfoxed Records, but from producers, booking agents, and managers.

"I want to play you something new. You want to hear it?"

Work forgotten, I leap up from the desk and race to the bed, crawling over it to get closer to him and sitting back on my legs. "You'll finally let me hear the song you've been working on?" He's been so secretive about it, and it's been killing me. I've heard the tune, a bit of the melody, but he won't let me see his notebook, and he hasn't sung any of the words in my presence.

"Yep. You ready?"

I bounce up and down. "Yes, yes, yes."

"Oh, you'll be saying that word just like that again later."

I burst out laughing and then clap my hands. "I'm sure, now sing for me."

He ducks his head. "It's probably too long, and there's, uh, no chorus, so it's probably not marketable."

I smack him on the leg. "I don't care, quit stalling."

He watches me, the dimple in his cheek making an appearance, his eyes glossy. "This is for you, Mindy."

Then he opens his mouth and sings, his eyes trained on mine, never once faltering.

Every day I would wake up and feel
Like I was missing something, something real
But then I see your face and I know
All I need is you to make me whole

'Cause you are my heart, my life, my light
You keep me going through the bleakest of nights
I couldn't live without you by my side
You are my heart, my heart, my life.

Your heart is the beat that keeps me alive
A flame that burns and never dies
You carry my heart, my soul, my everything
With every breath I take, you're inside of me

I can't imagine life without you by my side
You are the reason why I feel alive

This love, this love
It's fire in my bones
This love, this love
It's the beat to my soul
With you, with you
I'm never alone
This love, this love
Has made my heart a home

He finishes, setting his guitar to the side, then swallows. "Well?"

I'm struck speechless, unable to move, let alone form words. I can't think straight. He wrote this song for me. A love song.

An adorable crease forms in his brow. "What did you think?"

I pounce on him, not the most graceful of movements since I spring from a sitting position and it's a soft bed.

I'm immediately enveloped in the refuge of his arms. Holding his face in both hands, I kiss him, his mouth, his chin, all while squirming on top of him, trying to get closer, but it's not close enough.

I pull back far enough to meet his eyes. "I love you, too."

Then we're kissing, and it's not soft or delicate—it's

fierce and desperate. His mouth opens, his hands running down my back, gripping my hips and pulling me closer.

When we finally have to breathe, pulling apart only slightly, he speaks against my lips. "I think I loved you before I met you."

Laughing and breathless, I kiss his neck, nipping at his skin just to make him groan. "The first time I listened to your song, I was so turned on by the sound of your voice I burned my omelet."

He swings a leg, rolling us over so he's lying on top of me, his hardness prodding between my legs.

He beams down at me. "Did you?"

I nod, face heating. Then I wiggle my hips, sucking in an aroused breath through my teeth when we're perfectly aligned.

His head tips to one side. "Do you remember the interview you did where you said 'music is potent enough to remove you from time, strong enough to carry you through storms, and gentle enough to touch our emotions. It can heal thousands of souls, all at the same time and without a scalpel'?"

My mouth drops open. "How do you remember that?" That interview took place years ago.

"I remember everything, especially about you. That interview was the reason I sought you out. It was like I knew you, even then, as creepy as that might sound." He chuckles, color staining his cheeks with the admission.

My heart squeezes in my chest.

"I love you," he says. "I love your strength, how smart you are, how brave you are. Brave enough to love me and let me love you back even though you're scared. Brave enough to forgive Taylor and to forgive yourself."

His lips are hot, passionate, his hunger mirroring my own.

I tug him down to press my mouth against his, yearning for him to be closer, wanting everything, craving the feel of him more than I need my next breath. "I love you, too. So much. I learned about courage from watching you."

He rubs his nose against mine. "Let's be brave together, every day."

I grin. "I'll put it in your contract."

Epilogue

One month later

Mindy

"Luke will be so happy you made it," I tell Walter as I guide him inside the building and then through the scattered crowd.

"Thank you for inviting me and for sending the car." The skin around his eyes crinkles underneath his thick framed glasses when he smiles down at me.

"Of course. We reserved you a seat with Luke's family, over this way." I link my arm in his to lead him over to one of the couches lining the wall where Luke's family is sitting and waiting for the show to begin.

Once I've settled Walter in between Granny Bea and Catherine, Luke's mom, I head back through the audience toward the stage. Luke is waiting for me in the greenroom. My way back is slow since I get stopped every few feet.

I plaster on a smile, not wanting to let my impatience leak out.

We rented out The Mercury Lounge, a small but vibrant indie venue on the Lower East Side, to kick off Luke's tour. The crowd is comprised mostly of our friends and family.

He has multiple shows in New York through February and then he'll head south through Pennsylvania and Virginia, into Tennessee, and then west to Texas. We sold out shows in Dallas and Austin already, and those shows aren't until April. I've been able to coordinate some of my schedule with his so we won't have to spend more than a week or two away from each other at a time. I have interviews in D.C. and Nashville next month with potential clients and meetings set up with producers as well—some in person and some through video calls.

Finally I make it through the throng and turn by the stage, picking up the pace once I'm out of the crowd. I want to have more than a few minutes alone with Luke before the show starts.

Rounding the corner, I run into someone coming in the opposite direction. "Sorry. Oh."

Taylor glares at me, like I collided with her on purpose. She's dressed in a flowing long-sleeve bohemian dress with a chunky silver necklace and high, fringed boots.

Cue major awkwardness.

Before she can step around me, continuing her ongoing crusade of subjecting me to the silent treatment, I say, "Thank you for coming."

She crosses her arms over her chest, not meeting my eyes. "I came for Luke."

"Right. I know he appreciates it."

Jaw tight, she turns to leave again.

"Wait, Taylor."

She sighs before rounding the corner, her stony gaze meeting mine. "What?"

"I just wanted to thank you for everything you did with Ursula and Laila, and if you ever want to . . . I don't know, work in the music industry in any capacity, I would be happy to introduce you to people or return the favor in any way I can."

Her eyes darken. "If that was something I wanted to do, I wouldn't need your help."

I wince. I'm making things worse. "I'm sorry. Forget I said anything."

She lets out an irritated huff. "You don't have to keep doing this."

"Doing what?"

She flicks a hand. "Being all, nice or whatever. It's weird."

"Taylor, I don't want it to be weird. I want to be nice to you."

Not that it's helping our relationship heal at all. Yet.

She rolls her eyes. "It's great you've made your peace with all the crap you put me through, but I haven't. Can't we just ignore each other?"

I take a breath and release it. "I get it. I was terrible. I can respect your wishes and leave you alone if that's what you want. I won't talk to you unless strictly necessary."

"Perfect." She steps around the corner to join the crowd, but a second later, before I've even had a chance to move from my current position, she returns, slipping back behind the wall with a curse.

"What are you doing?" I ask.

She peeks around the wall toward the crowd. "Nothing." She pulls back again, her face tinted pink, her breath coming out faster. "It's nothing. I'm fine."

"It's obviously not nothing." I walk past her and scan the scattered clumps of onlookers beyond the stage. "Who are you scared of?"

"I'm not scared of anyone."

"Then go out there." I gesture to the audience.

She sticks her head out from behind the wall, and I make an attempt to track her gaze before she ducks back again. Her eyes darted to the far left.

I lift up on my toes, checking out that corner of the venue.

"Are you avoiding Finley?" Maybe they're fighting.

She glares at me. "No."

"Is it one of her employees?"

Finley brought some of the new camp hires—a couple of chefs, a counselor, and some kind of scientist helping with the wilderness-themed camps coming up this summer. She thought a trip to the city, including Luke's show, would be a good team-building event. Plus Oliver wanted to meet them. Hopefully he won't scare them away.

I eyeball the new recruits, trying to decipher why Taylor would want to avoid any of them. My gaze comes to a halt on a vaguely familiar face in the group standing right next to Finley.

"Hey. Who's the big guy?" I point. He's even bigger than Archer, his broad shoulders taking up more space than two Finleys, and he's at least a head taller than the rest of the room.

She grabs my arm and jerks me back behind the wall and out of view. "Could you be any more obvious?"

I bite my lip to keep from laughing. She will definitely murder me if I laugh in her face. "Is he an ex-boyfriend?"

"No," she snaps.

"Do you wish he was?"

She groans and covers her face.

I rub my hands together. "It must be something juicy if you're willing to spend extra minutes with me just to avoid him."

She almost laughs, the sound bubbling up in her throat, but then she cuts off the sound with a cough. "Ugh. You are the literal worst." Straightening, she stalks past me down the side of the stage.

I chuckle as Taylor disappears into a crowd of people on the opposite side of the room from where Finley is standing with her crew.

As curious as I am to know the answer to this little mystery, I have something more important to take care of right now.

I find Luke in the greenroom, sitting on a wooden bench, his legs propped up on a chair while he plays his guitar and hums, warming up his voice.

"Hey, you." I lean against the door frame.

He grins, his whole face lighting up when our eyes meet.

I love his smile. I love watching him play his guitar. I love watching him, period.

He sets his guitar to the side and opens his arms.

That's all the invitation I need. I sit on his lap, perching on his leg and wrapping my hands around his neck.

Our mouths meet in a move that's become second nature over the past month. His warm palm rubs up my leg while his tongue strokes against mine. The world disappears. I'm no longer worried about Taylor or the upcoming tour. It's just me and Luke and our shared breaths.

After a long minute, we break apart and his nose brushes mine. "You made it."

"Of course I made it." I promised I would give him a kiss before his show, before every show I can, to commemorate our first kiss.

If I have the choice, I'll kiss him every day for the rest of our lives.

"Are you ready for this?" I ask.

He blows out a breath and winces. "As ready as I'm ever going to be."

"I'll be in the front row."

His hands move up to cup my face, his eyes searching mine. "Mindy, I love you. With you in my corner, I could face a coliseum full of people."

I relax in his grip, knowing he will always catch me, safe in his easy acceptance. We've only begun piecing together the notes to our song, and while I don't know what the final chord will be, these first key melodies, ones of love and understanding, will get us through even the shakiest of verses. "I love you, too, so much."

The End

About the Author

Go here to sign up for the newsletter!
www.authormaryframe.com
Mary Frame is a full time mother and wife with a full time job. She has no idea how she manages to write novels, but it probably helps that she's a dedicated introvert. She doesn't enjoy writing about herself in third person, but she does enjoy reading, writing, dancing, and damaging the ear drums of her co-workers when she randomly decides to sing to them.

She lives in Reno, Nevada with her husband, two children, and a border collie named Stella.

She LOVES hearing from readers and will not only respond but likely begin stalking them while tossing out hearts and flowers and rainbows! If that doesn't creep you out, e-mail her at: maryframeauthor@gmail.com

Also by Mary Frame

Imperfect Series:

Book One: Imperfect Chemistry

Book Two: Imperfectly Criminal

Book Three: Practically Imperfect

Book Four: Picture Imperfect

Book Five: Imperfect Strangers

Book Six: Imperfectly Delicious

The Dorky Duet (Plus a companion novel!)

Ridorkulous

Geektastic

Nerdelicious

Time after Time Series:

Time of My Life

If I Could Turn Back Time

Castle Cove Mystery Series

Fake It to the Limit

Too Much Crime on My Hands

You're the Con That I Want

Fox Family Series

Between a Fox and a Hard Place

The Fox and the Rebound

Another Fox Bites the Dust

Some Like It Fox

www.ingramcontent.com/pod-product-compliance
Lightning Source LLC
La Vergne TN
LVHW041114080826
845145LV00007B/1816

9781954372207